FATAL AS A FALLEN WOMAN

Other books by Kathy Lynn Emerson

The Diana Spaulding Mystery Series:
Deadlier than the Pen

The Face Down Mystery Series:
Face Down in the Marrow-Bone Pie
Face Down Upon an Herbal
Face Down Among the Winchester Geese
Face Down Beneath the Eleanor Cross
Face Down Under the Wych Elm
Face Down Before Rebel Hooves
Face Down Across the Western Sea
Murders & Other Confusions (short stories)
Face Down Below the Banqueting House

Nonfiction:
Wives and Daughters: The Women of Sixteenth-Century
England
Making Headlines: A Biography of Nellie Bly
The Writer's Guide to Everyday Life in Renaissance England

Novels for Ages 8-12:
The Mystery of Hilliard's Castle
Julia's Mending
The Mystery of the Missing Bagpipes

FATAL AS A FALLEN WOMAN

A Diana Spaulding Mystery

KATHY LYNN EMERSON

PEMBERLEY PRESS
CORONA DEL MAR

Published by
P E M B E R L E Y P R E S S
P O Box 1027
Corona del Mar, CA 92625
www.pemberleypress.com

A member of The Authors Studio
www.theauthorsstudio.org

Second volume in the Diana Spaulding Mystery Series
Cover art by Linda Weatherly
Cover design by Kat & Dog Studios

Library of Congress Cataloging-in-Publication Data

Emerson, Kathy Lynn.
  Fatal as a fallen woman : a Diana Spaulding mystery / Kathy
Lynn Emerson.
      p. cm.
  ISBN 0-9702727-9-0 (alk. paper)
  1. Women journalists--Fiction. 2. Denver (Colo.)--Fiction. 3.
Mothers and daughters--Fiction. 4. Fathers--Death--Fiction. 5.
Missing persons--Fiction. I. Title.
  PS3555.M414F38 2005
  813'.54--dc22
                                        2005047654

To the rest of the team:
Pat Ricks and Linda Weatherly S.

CHAPTER ONE

ဢᏇᏪ

April, 1888

The contents of the lodgers' rooms at Mrs. Curran's boarding house on Tenth Street in Manhattan were simple—a narrow brass bedstead, a washstand with all the standard furnishings, and a small, comfortable chair flanked by a pie-shaped table surmounted by an oil lamp. Diana Spaulding had filled the remaining space with a Saratoga trunk, a large Gladstone bag, a crocodile-skin gripsack, the capacious tweed bag she sometimes slung over her shoulder for ease in carrying, and assorted boxes.

"Cart ahead of the horse," she muttered as she surveyed the chaos. She should not begin to pack her belongings until *after* she mailed the letter accepting Ben Northcote's proposal of marriage.

Diana could feel a smile blossom on her face at the thought of Ben. They'd had such a whirlwind courtship, filled with so many extraordinary events, that at first she'd been afraid to trust the strength of her feelings for him. She'd made the mistake of marrying in haste once before and had lived to regret it. Life with Evan Spaulding had consisted of soaring highs and dizzying descents into misery and had quite literally brought her to the brink of ruin.

This time would be different, Diana thought as she reread the brief missive one last time, then folded the single sheet of paper and tucked it into an envelope on which she'd already written "Dr. Benjamin Northcote, Bangor, Maine." Like Evan, Ben was charismatic. Like Evan, he was handsome. Six feet tall, dark of hair and eyes, and superbly well coordinated and fit, Ben had a deep, resonant voice and a face sculpted by a master. But it had been his gentleness that had won Diana—his kindness. Ben was a man to whom hearth and home mattered more than fame or fortune. He loved his family above everything, and a fortnight earlier he had asked her to become a permanent part of that intimate circle.

She had not given him an answer at the time. She'd felt she needed to take a step back, to think. And so she'd left him in Bangor and returned to New York City. Since then she'd examined both her mind and her heart and realized that her love for Ben was no passing fancy, no enchantment, no foolish young woman's misguided romantic daydream. What she felt was real and lasting.

He'd never shared her doubts. She smiled again as she remembered how he'd looked on that most memorable of days. Weary but confident, his eyes full of love for her, he'd made her a promise: *If you haven't returned by the end of April, I'll come to you.*

Each day's mail had brought a new declaration of devotion until finally, yesterday, she'd made her decision and resigned her position as a journalist at the *Independent Intelligencer.* Last night she'd composed the most important piece of writing of her life. This morning she had only to take that letter to the post office and send it on its way north. She'd spend a day or two saying goodbye to a few old friends and shopping for a gown in which to be married. If all went well, she'd be ready to depart by the end of the week.

Humming softly, Diana tucked the letter into her skirt pocket. The latest spring fashions were on sale at Redfern Ladies' Tailor on Fifth Avenue and in the shops on West Twenty-third Street—Best and Company and nearby Stern Brothers, who'd advertised newly arrived imported walking dresses. She did not have a great deal of money to spend on clothing, but she wanted something special for her wedding to Ben. When she'd eloped with Evan, she'd been wearing a white dotted-Swiss dress, the most bland of schoolgirl frocks.

She grimaced at her reflection in the mirror above the washstand as she released and recoiled thick, mahogany-colored hair. With a few deft movements, she shaped it into a neat bun at the nape of her neck. She'd just added a small green hat with feathers when someone rapped at her door.

"That man is here again," Mrs. Curran called.

In an involuntary movement, Diana's hand clutched the cameo broach she wore at her throat, a gift from Ben. The scalloped edges of the gold setting bit into her palm. "That man," to Mrs. Curran, meant only one person—Horatio Foxe, editor and publisher of the *Independent Intelligencer* and Diana's former employer.

"I've put him in the small parlor," Mrs. Curran added, making Diana chuckle in spite of her sudden anxiety. Her landlady would have shown a valued guest into the more formal drawing room. She hadn't forgiven Foxe for all the trouble he'd caused Diana with unauthorized additions to her column. In a quest to boost the newspaper's sagging circulation he'd gone after scandal, heedless of the harm he might cause to those whose foibles he revealed in print.

"I'll be along directly." Diana removed the hat and hung it on a peg alongside the dark green, fur-trimmed coat she'd been about to collect. It might be mid-April, but there was still a chill in the air.

As she left the room and walked briskly along the corridor, where a hint of lavender lingered to mark Mrs. Curran's recent passage towards the stairwell, Diana told herself it was foolish to feel nervous just because Foxe had come to call. She could guess what he wanted. He planned to make one last attempt to convince her to stay.

Her column, "Today's Tidbits," was popular with readers, even without the scathing reviews and theatrical gossip Foxe had tried to persuade her to add. More significant, the news stories she'd written during the past two weeks, reporting on criminal activity in New York from a woman's point of view, had drawn new readers to the paper.

Foxe would try flattery first. Then he'd attempt bribery—he'd already offered her a generous raise and a permanent spot on the police beat. Finally, he'd work on her sense of guilt, demanding to know how she could think of leaving him in the lurch after all he'd done for her.

It was true she had reason to be grateful to him, but Diana knew she'd more than repaid his many kindnesses. In fact, he was the one who should feel guilty. He could be unscrupulous when intent on getting a story, and just recently his pursuit of headlines had ended by putting her life at risk. She owed him nothing more than the courtesy of hearing what he had to say.

The small parlor doubled as Mrs. Curran's sewing room, where she displayed her collection of thimbles in a special glass-fronted cabinet. Copies of the latest *Godey's Ladies' Book* and the E. Butterick & Co pattern catalogue for summer 1888 were scattered here and there, even on the looped carpet. An adjustable dress form wearing a pale blue silk afternoon dress stood in one corner. Next to it was a sewing machine with a nightgown draped across it. It appeared that Mrs. Curran had been interrupted while making repairs. The fabric, although still held in place by the needle, trailed down over the treadle as if it had been abandoned in haste.

Horatio Foxe sat perched on the edge of a plush-covered settee, plainly ill at ease in these surroundings. He'd taken off his hat and run ink-stained fingers through his sand-colored hair, a nervous habit that meant he was either irritated or upset.

"What's wrong?" Diana demanded.

Foxe bounced to his feet, both hands outstretched. In the depths of his hazel eyes, Diana encountered an emotion she'd never seen there before. It was pity. "Bad news, m'dear. I'm so sorry."

Please, God—not Ben!

A suffocating anguish engulfed Diana at the possibility that something terrible had happened to Ben Northcote. She knew too well how easily, how suddenly, a vital life force could be snuffed out. As she fought for breath, her limbs turned to ice and frozen muscles refused to carry her farther into the room. Only with great effort did she manage to speak.

"Tell me quickly," she begged. Whatever news Foxe had brought, it could not be more dreadful than the appalling scenes crowding into her head. She had a very good imagination and more than a passing acquaintance with the stuff of horror stories.

He reached into the inner pocket of his four-button cutaway suit coat and drew out a sheet of paper. She recognized it at once as the typescript of a news dispatch sent by way of the special telegraph wires the Press Association leased from Western Union. Foxe regularly reviewed everything that came in "over the wire" to decide which items would most interest his readers. "I recognized the name," he said as he handed it over. "William 'Timberline' Torrence."

Not Ben! Relief broke over her like an incoming wave before the undertow caught at her ankles and sent her staggering again. No, not Ben, but someone who had once been as dear to her . . . her father.

As she took the paper, Diana's fingers trembled. The headline read, "Silver Baron Murdered in Denver Hotel."

"Dead?" she whispered in a shaky voice. "Murdered?"

It did not seem possible. Her father was a monolith, as unyielding and immutable as a rocky cliff. Nothing short of an explosion should have been capable of bringing him down.

"I'm sorry, Diana," Foxe said. "And it gets worse. You'd best read the entire dispatch for yourself."

The page rustled in her hands. She knew there were words written on it, but they swam in front of her eyes. The tears surprised her. In the past she'd shed so many because of her father that she hadn't thought she'd have any left to mourn him. With icy fingertips, she dashed the moisture from her cheeks.

William Torrence hadn't been one to grieve, or to forgive. When events moved beyond his control, he reacted with cold anger.

"You are dead to us now," he'd said to her the last time she'd seen him. *"Your name will never be spoken in this house again."*

On that fateful day six years ago, when Diana had brought her new husband home to meet her parents, her father had seized the family Bible, taken up a pen, and blacked out her name. While she stood still stunned in appalled silence, he informed her that she was no longer his daughter. He'd never *had* a daughter. She was not just dead to him from that moment on. She had never even existed.

And now he was the one who was dead. Diana had expected to feel nothing when this day came. Hadn't she already mourned his loss? But she had to swipe one hand across her eyes before she could bring the text of the dispatch into focus.

The facts were brutally clear, even if the details were sketchy. William "Timberline" Torrence had been stabbed to death. The person believed to have killed him was his former wife.

Former wife?

With each word Diana read, her chest constricted. Her heart was hammering so loudly in her ears that she scarcely noticed when Foxe grasped her arm and steered her towards the settee.

"Sit before you fall," he ordered.

Since her knees were about to give out, she obeyed. She shook her head in an attempt to clear it, then wished she hadn't. The room spun wildly.

"Thunderation, Diana! Are you going to faint on me?" Foxe

sounded equal parts alarmed and annoyed.

"Not if I can help it." She swallowed convulsively, then took several deep breaths. She flattened the dispatch on her lap and held the edges in a white-knuckled grip.

Regrets assaulted her, along with a sense of guilt. She had made no effort to see either of her parents again after that hideous confrontation in the parlor of the Torrence mansion, not even during the month she and Evan had spent in Denver before moving on to Leadville. She could have attempted a reconciliation. Why hadn't she? Even if her father had refused to acknowledge her, she might have talked to her mother. She might have . . . what? Ended the estrangement?

More likely she'd have created greater dissension among people who were already bitterly unhappy. She stared at the lines of print. The words were a blur again, but it hardly mattered. They'd been imprinted in her memory. According to the dispatch, the "former wife" who had killed Diana's father was her mother. Sometime during the six years since they'd disowned their only child, her parents had also rejected each other. An agonized sob escaped Diana in spite of her best efforts to hold it in.

"Mrs. Curran!"

Foxe's shout made Diana jump. Her thoughts fragmented, leaving her light-headed.

"Fetch smelling salts!" Foxe bellowed. "Confound it, woman! Get a move on!"

His fingers bit into Diana's shoulders as he shoved her head into her lap. The pounding at her temples had begun to diminish by the time the swish of bombazine and a whiff of lavender heralded Mrs. Curran's arrival.

"And what is it you've done to her now?" Diana's landlady demanded, the lilt of Ireland stronger than usual in her speech. It got that way when she was agitated.

"Did you bring smelling salts?" Foxe demanded. "She's had a shock."

"I did, yes."

"No," Diana protested. "No smelling salts." The mere thought of being forced to inhale Mrs. Curran's powerful homemade blend of liquid ammonia, rosemary, lavender, bermagotte, and cloves was sufficient to bring her bolt upright. She blinked away the last of the dizziness and straightened her spine. "I am quite recovered now."

Horatio Foxe and Francesca Curran turned on her with identical beady-eyed stares and suddenly Diana felt an overwhelming desire to laugh. The two of them had the look of a pair of buzzards, contemplating some poor soul lost in the desert and dying of thirst. Her lips quirked but she managed to fight off the bubble of hysterical laughter.

"Oh, dear," she murmured when she'd recovered a little. "I must be more overwrought than I realized."

The thin and wiry Foxe strutted closer. She'd always thought he resembled a bantam rooster.

"You're white as a sheet," he informed her.

Diana glanced at Mrs. Curran. With her bright curious eyes and tendency to collect shiny objects like those thimbles, what else could she be but a magpie?

"You look," said the magpie, "as if a goose just walked over your grave."

The words put an end to Diana's strange flight of fancy and vanquished every trace of humor. She sobered instantly. "So it has, Mrs. Curran. My past has come back to haunt me."

And the past, she realized, must be dealt with before she could go forward into the future. One finger at a time, she released her grip on the dispatch until her right hand was free to search out the letter in her pocket. Slowly and deliberately, she ripped it in half. She would not be mailing her acceptance of Ben Northcote's proposal of marriage. Not today. Perhaps not ever.

∞⌘

Horatio Foxe insisted on accompanying Diana as far as Weehawken Terminal, where a combination of five ferry slips and sixteen passenger tracks linked New Jersey to every conceivable destination. She meant to catch the first train headed west.

Ordinarily, she'd have spent the ten-minute crossing watching the variety of water craft on this stretch of the Hudson River—everything from oyster sloops to transatlantic liners. But on this trip, she scarcely glanced up from the point on the rough wooden railing in front of her where silk-gloved fingers occupied themselves worrying loose a splinter. For the most part, this activity also allowed her to ignore Foxe's fulminating glare.

"You're a fool to rush off half-cocked like this." He stood close beside her, one hand on her elbow and the other clamped to the rim of his bowler to keep it from being blown away. Diana's brown straw hat was securely anchored with pins, but her thin gray illusion veil filled and deflated with every gust of salt-tinged air.

"What else would you have me do? My mother is suspected of killing my father. I can scarcely ignore her plight." Diana risked a sideways glance and saw that irritation had scrunched Foxe's features into a formidable scowl.

"Send a telegram to Denver."

"To say what? And if she's in jail, she may not be able to receive or send messages." *Arrest imminent,* the dispatch had said. Denver's police chief had been quoted, vowing to have Elmira Torrence in custody by nightfall. That had been two days ago.

Diana's grasp of the legal system was shaky. She didn't cover trials, had never visited a prison, and didn't want to. She'd stuck to writing about the commission of crimes and the capture of the criminals. Though she supposed it was short-sighted of her, her interest had always stopped with the villain's arrest.

"If she's already in jail, you may arrive too late to be of any use," Foxe said.

Diana's hands tightened on the rail, causing the splinter to imbed itself in her thumb. "There will have to be a coroner's inquest, and a grand jury indictment." She knew that much about the law. "And a trial."

Stories of "frontier justice" swirled through her mind as she extracted the shard of wood, removed her glove, and gingerly sucked at a small bead of blood. The breeze seemed suddenly colder, raising goose bumps on the newly exposed flesh of hand and wrist.

The Denver Diana had known as a child had been a wild and unsettled place, full of gamblers, saloons, and the occasional lynch mob. A well-brought-up female wasn't supposed to know about such things, but servants talked and girls just approaching womanhood were curious.

Diana remembered all the details of the most scandalous event of the year she'd turned thirteen. Two fallen women had fought a duel over a man. It had taken place on the outskirts of Denver and when it was over it had been the man who lay bleeding from a gunshot wound. That victim had lived, though. There'd been no arrest or trial, let alone a lynching.

Diana wanted to believe that Denver was more civilized these days, but she had her doubts. If Elmira Torrence had sufficiently outraged the local citizens by brutally murdering her former husband . . . or if they believed she had killed him . . . anything could happen.

Foxe gave Diana's arm an awkward pat. "Have you considered that your mother might be guilty? Accusations of murder are not made lightly. What if she did kill him?"

Diana did not want to think about that possibility, let alone talk about it, but Foxe's question deserved an answer. "My mother is not a demonstrative woman, but she's always had strong views on duty and loyalty. She supported my father in anything he wanted to do, even disowning me, because she was brought up to believe it is a wife's duty to defer to her husband in all things. She'd never strike out at him, no matter what the provocation."

Foxe gave her a sideways glance and a sardonic smile that showed far too many tobacco-stained teeth. "People change, Diana. You haven't seen her in years. You didn't even know about the divorce. What if the sheer disgrace of it pushed your mother into an uncharacteristic act of revenge?"

Diana frowned. Foxe's words reminded her that she and her mother had never been close. Diana's impetuous marriage was all it had taken to shatter the tenuous familial bond that had survived her years away at school. Did she really know her mother, or what Elmira Torrence might be capable of doing?

An incident from Diana's childhood surfaced, unwanted, to taunt her. She'd been five or six. The Torrences had not been wealthy then and Diana's mother had been obliged to take in laundry to make ends meet. One of the miners had made a suggestion—the adult Diana understood what it must have been even if the child Diana had not—and her mother's reaction had been to clout him on the ear with one of the heavy iron tongs she used to fish clothes out of boiling water. He'd bled profusely. There had been talk of an arrest for assault—and a great deal of cussing—but most of the men in the mining camp had felt Elmira's action was justified, and nothing further had come of the incident.

The memory made Diana shiver. It was proof her mother's prodigious self-control could crack, releasing pent-up frustration. But kill William Torrence? Murder the man she'd have continued to regard as her husband, divorce or no? Never. Diana wouldn't believe such a thing unless she heard it from Elmira Torrence's own lips.

A sudden shift in the wind carried smoke into Diana's eyes. Foxe had lit one of his noxious cigars. "She won't look for your help," he mumbled around the obstruction in his mouth. "She may not even want it. You don't have to go."

"She'd contact me if she knew how. That she doesn't is my fault. I could have written to them at any time. Besides, it hardly matters if Mother expects me to come to her or not. She's all the kin I have in the world. What else can I do but offer her support in her hour of need?"

"So you're rushing across the country out of a sense of duty?" Foxe sounded skeptical.

"That's as good a reason as any." Diana hoped there might be more left between them, even after a six-year estrangement, but no matter what happened when she saw her mother again, she knew she would not be able to live with herself if she didn't go to Denver.

"Balderdash!" Foxe turned away from her to stare in the direction of the rapidly approaching New Jersey shore. "You don't owe your mother a thing."

"I owe her life," Diana snapped. "She gave birth to me, raised me, loved me in her own fashion. And if she was obliged to divorce Father, she has suffered enough. You know how divorced women are reviled by society, and the good opinion of Denver's upper crust—the people they call the 'sacred thirty-six'—was important to her."

"So you're hell-bent on haring off to Denver when you'd planned, in a day or two, to board a train for New England. Does this mean the engagement is off?"

"It wasn't on. Not yet." She smoothed a hand down the skirt of her gray flannel traveling suit. The feel of the soft fabric soothed her.

"Did you send for him?"

"Of course not. There's no time to waste waiting for him to get here. Besides, I can't ask Ben to leave his brother when Aaron was near to death such a short time ago."

"He'd come if he thought you needed him."

"That's precisely why I can't let on that I do. And I don't. Not really." She put temptation behind her, along with Manhattan's shoreline. She could handle this crisis herself. "I'll deal with my family's problems on my own. Ben and I aren't married yet, so the Torrences shouldn't be his concern."

"He'll see things differently," Foxe warned.

"That can't be helped."

"At least send him a telegram before you leave." The ferry had docked but neither of them left the rail.

"I already have."

"You told him what happened?"

"Only that I have to go away for a little while." His brows lifted in an expression of mockery that exasperated her. "Do you intend to help me with my bags or not?"

"Why else am I here?" Foxe reached for the heaviest pieces in the pile by her feet and followed her towards the gangplank. "If he's expecting a letter agreeing to his proposal of marriage, he won't be put off by a telegram."

"He'll have no choice. I didn't tell him where I'm going."

"So you're running away without an explanation? Northcote's not going to like that." Foxe tsked.

"I won't involve Ben in this! It's not his problem."

She'd considered dispatching a detailed explanation to Maine, but there was very little to report until she discovered what had really happened in Denver. Worse, if she told Ben what she did know, he'd want to rush to her rescue. She couldn't allow him to make that sacrifice. He was a physician with patients who needed him.

More importantly, his family needed him. Diana refused to deprive Aaron Northcote of either his brother or his doctor. Aaron had suffered grievous injuries because of her. The least she could do was make certain he had the best of care until he was fully recovered.

Foxe escorted Diana to the platform where her train waited before he spoke again. He made a valiant attempt to inject a teasing tone into his voice. "I think you're just looking for a reason to get out of marrying into the Northcote family. A few minutes in that old woman's company would give anyone second thoughts."

By "that old woman" he meant Maggie Northcote, matriarch of the clan. Diana's smile was genuine if rueful. "She'll turn you into a newt if she thinks you've insulted her. She was doing research into magic spells when I left."

Foxe gave a theatrical shudder. "Woman's mad. Ever think Northcote might like an excuse to visit Denver?"

"Maggie's merely eccentric," Diana informed him, echoing the opinion she'd heard over and over again during her time with Ben. "And such comments won't make me change my mind. I don't want any of the Northcotes involved in this. You're not to interfere." She jabbed him in the chest with one finger for emphasis. "No letters or telegrams sent to Maine on my behalf. Understood?"

Foxe threw his hands in the air and cast his eyes towards Heaven. "I won't write a word to him, not even if he tries to contact me."

"Good. See that you keep that promise." She had to shout to be heard now above the noise on the platform, and fight not to cough as they were engulfed by a shower of gritty cinders and billowing black smoke from the engine.

Foxe cleared his throat. "Might help if you kept your position with the *Independent Intelligencer.* Make it easier to get information if you go in with a reporter's credentials." He could not quite hide the cunning look on his narrow face or the speculative glitter in his eyes.

"Are you by chance suggesting I send you a firsthand account of my mother's trial?"

Foxe feigned surprise at the suggestion, but Diana was not deceived. This was what he must have had in mind all along. Annoyed, she gripped her tweed bag more firmly in one hand and seized the hatbox with the other, prepared to stalk away the moment she located a porter to collect her Gladstone bag and gripsack. She'd packed her books, additional clothing, and assorted memorabilia in the Saratoga trunk and left it in Mrs. Curran's basement.

"You'll need money," Foxe reminded her.

"I have what I've saved for my wedding gown." Mentally she bade farewell to the confection of white corded silk and point lace that had featured in recent daydreams.

"Cost of a wedding gown, eh? Well, that might last a day or two."

Diana whirled around to glare at him and found herself staring at the train ticket in his hand. "I am perfectly capable of paying my own way!"

"Part of the deal if you're still in my employ." He talked right over her sputtered protests. "Diana, listen to me. As far as I'm concerned, you never left your job at the *Independent Intelligencer.* File whatever reports from Denver you wish and I will pay you for them. Return to New York when you can. Anytime you want to reclaim it, your desk will still be there in the city room."

"You just want a juicy story."

"Scandal sells newspapers," he reminded her, but with a sheepish look on his face.

In spite of herself, Diana was touched. In his own way, he was trying to look out for her. "You are a terrible man, Horatio Foxe."

She kissed his cheek, tacitly accepting the arrangement. What choice did she have? She had almost no money of her own. That was why she'd been working for him in the first place.

Foxe mumbled an excuse about needing to get back to the office and retreated, setting off at a brisk pace along the platform. He hadn't gone ten yards before he abruptly reversed direction. By the time he reached Diana's side once more, he'd produced two magazines from a bulging pocket.

"Something to read on the journey," he said, shoving them into the open outer compartment of her tweed bag. She caught a glimpse of the masthead of one and saw that it was the latest edition of *The Journalist,* a professional periodical for those in the newspaper business.

The second offering was also unmistakable, thanks to the eye-catching color of its pages. *The National Police Gazette* was wholly inappropriate reading material for a lady. Even gentlemen claimed they only read it while they waited at the barbershop for a shave or haircut. Torn between annoyance and amusement, Diana thanked him and boarded the train.

Like it or not, it seemed she was still writing about crime and scandal for Horatio Foxe. And if her father's killer turned out to be anyone other than her own mother, she *would* file that story. In fact, it would be the best piece of reporting she'd ever done. She owed Foxe that much.

"Here you go, miss," the conductor said, indicating a private compartment.

"This can't be right."

But it was. Foxe had booked first class passage for her all the way to Denver. Although notoriously tight with money, he had spent a hundred and twenty dollars when he could have gotten her a standard-fare ticket for only eighty-five.

As she stowed her possessions and took her seat, she sniffled audibly. She would need all her wits about her when she reached her destination, and she might not get much rest en route, even with one of Mr. Pullman's beds to sleep in each night, but Horatio Foxe's generous gesture would make a difference. Instead of arriving in a state of total exhaustion, she might just get to Colorado with a modicum of her ability to function still intact.

Diana fought against weeping, but it was no use. Now that she was alone, the emotions she'd been holding at bay forced their way to the surface. As the train pulled out of the station, she succumbed to tears, indulging in a good long cry. Memories of her childhood came thick and fast as she sobbed. So did worries and doubts.

When the bout of despair and self-pity was over, Diana mopped her face and straightened her shoulders. Oddly, she felt better, but the improvement did not last. Before long, her vexation returned. What would she find in Denver?

She closed her eyes, attempting to put worry about her mother aside long enough to think calmly about the practicalities of a journey that would occupy the next few days. Ben's face swam into the darkness behind her eyelids, his expression conveying both hurt and reproach.

She sought diversion in the passing scenery next, but the view from her compartment was not sufficient distraction to keep her from worrying about Ben's reaction to her telegram. Finally Diana resorted to giving herself a pithy lecture comprised of trite but true sayings.

"No sense crying over spilt milk," she muttered. It would be best if she tried not to think about Ben at all.

She retrieved *The Journalist* from her tweed bag and forced herself to concentrate on reading an article chosen at random.

Diana's train was halfway to its first stop, at Rochester, before she turned in desperation to her only other choice of reading matter and discovered that her cantankerous, treacherous, sneaky editor had been even more generous than she'd realized.

Tucked between the pale pink pages of *The National Police Gazette,* next to a story about a young woman's disconcerting experience in a dining car on the New York to Baltimore line, was an envelope with her name on it. It contained a bank draft for a hundred dollars and a letter of introduction to the editor of the *Rocky Mountain News.*

CHAPTER TWO

⚜

Ben Northcote felt the pulse in his neck throb, a sure sign he was about to lose his temper. "Mother," he warned, "you are treading on thin ice."

"I only want what's best for you, dear heart." Maggie Northcote regarded him with annoying calmness from the far side of the front parlor of their Bangor, Maine home.

Although she was past fifty, she looked at least a dozen years younger and had a heart and mind so unique, Ben despaired of ever predicting what she would do or say next. He'd expected her to be as concerned as he was about Diana. Instead she seemed bent on turning him against the woman he loved.

Posed like a queen on her favorite rococo sofa, the elaborate scroll work on the back framing her like a throne, she stroked the long-haired black cat on her lap. An enormous jade ring reflected light from the chandelier overhead with each sweep of her hand.

"Any woman who'd send you a telegram like that one doesn't deserve to marry you. Look at you, all worried and upset."

His hand clenched on the crumpled ball in his pocket. He didn't need to look at it again to remember how the message read. Typical of the frugal woman to whom he'd given his heart, the missive contained only ten words, the maximum number she could send without paying extra: "MUST MISS DEADLINE. FAMILY MATTER. WILL EXPLAIN UPON RETURN. DIANA."

He'd responded at once with a cable of his own, demanding details, but the reply had come from Diana's landlady, Mrs. Curran. Diana had gone away for a few days. Mrs. Curran did not know where, only that she'd left in the company of Horatio Foxe.

"It's plain to me she doesn't care enough about your feelings to take the time to write a proper letter, even if it's only to cry off. I say good riddance. Fussing about her whereabouts is just a waste of your valuable time."

"I thought you liked Diana."

"I found her most entertaining as a houseguest. And she was gracious about forgiving me for that little incident in the family crypt. But I'm not certain she'd have suited as a daughter-in-law. She's an intelligent young woman, I grant you, but flighty."

"That's rich, coming from you."

Ignoring Ben's rudeness, she chucked Cedric under the chin, then looked deep into the big cat's eyes, which were identical in color to her own. "I believe we have established a harmony of thought."

"You and Cedric, I presume," Ben muttered. *He* certainly had no idea how Maggie Northcote's mind worked. "If Diana doesn't contact me again within a day or two, I'm going to New York."

"What?" She jerked bolt upright, dislodging Cedric, who sent a baleful copper-eyed glare in Ben's direction before stalking off in a huff. "How can you even think of abandoning your brother? Aaron needs you close by. What if infection sets in? What if he has a . . . a relapse?"

There would be little he could do, Ben thought, but he could hardly say so aloud to Aaron's mother. His brother had been close to death, in spite of all Ben's skill as a physician. He would be convalescent for some time yet. He needed constant care and supervision, but Ben wasn't certain, now that the first medical crisis was past, that Aaron needed his older brother hovering over him every moment.

"I won't make any decision yet," Ben promised.

"She eloped when she married before, didn't she? That tells you something right there."

"It tells me Diana learned from experience not to rush when making important decisions. She didn't want to make the same mistake twice. That's why she went back to New York. To think things through."

"Well, there you are. She did her thinking and decided marrying you was unwise."

"No." The telegram hadn't said that, and it would have, he believed, if Diana had decided she didn't really love him. "Whatever is going on, nothing has changed the way she feels about me. I know her."

"Well, then, Ben, tell me this—what do you *know* about her background besides the fact that she went to work as a newspaper columnist after her husband died?"

"Not a great deal." He gave her a hard stare. "Don't tell me you're worried about Diana's family connections?"

"Her ancestry doesn't matter to me in the least. How could it, when I am myself descended from a long line of witches, Gypsies, and vampires? But there must be something disreputable in her past. Why else refuse to talk about it?" Easing to her feet, she crossed the room to his side. Unblinking eyes regarded him with just a hint of reproach. "Ben, dear, you know I'm not one to criticize, but it seems to me that you might have thought to ask a few questions about her family."

"Why didn't you conduct an inquisition, if you were so curious about her?"

"Well, I didn't know then that you meant to marry her, did I? And I had a few concerns of my own at the time."

Ben scraped his fingers through his hair, knowing she was right. Besides, on her best day Maggie Northcote was self-absorbed. She'd only have "interviewed" Diana if she'd suspected there was a sufficiently dramatic story to be tweaked out of her.

What *did* he know? During their time together they'd had other matters to occupy them. Ben hadn't thought to ask about her parents. It came as a shock to him to realize he didn't even know Diana's maiden name.

"Her father disowned her for marrying Evan Spaulding," he said slowly. "She met Spaulding when she was at boarding school."

"Which one? Where?"

"I don't know, but she had a friend there. Rowena. Horatio Foxe's younger sister." That meant Foxe must know Diana's family background. So would Diana's actor friends from Spaulding's old company, but Todd's Touring Thespians were at present playing a series of one- and two-night stands all over the country. Ben had no idea how to contact them.

"What do you know about the husband?"

"He was a second-rate actor and failed entrepreneur who deceived her from the beginning."

Her brows shot up and she fingered the ring. "Indeed? She didn't murder him, did she?"

"No, she didn't murder him."

But Ben didn't know precisely how he had died, only that it had been after he'd left Nathan Todd's troupe of players to start his own company. Diana had told him about their horrendous journey from Denver into the Colorado mountains to . . . where had it been?

He couldn't recall the name of the town and doubted it mattered. Spaulding had died there a few months after their arrival, leaving Diana destitute. In dire need of employment to keep body and soul together, she'd turned to her old school friend, and Rowena Foxe's brother had come to the rescue, hiring Diana as a regular contributor to his New York newspaper.

He'd have to contact Foxe, Ben decided. The editor undoubtedly knew where Diana had gone and why. Ben didn't much like the man, and he knew Foxe wanted Diana to stay on at the *Independent Intelligencer,* but surely he'd respond to an urgent telegram.

"A husband has a right to know."

"What?" Lost in thought, Ben hadn't been listening.

"How could you ask her to marry you when you knew so little about her? And after all the trouble she caused us, too!"

"She didn't know I was going to ask her to marry me until just before she left. She had no reason to confide in me." A short bark of rueful laughter escaped him. "It isn't as if I spent much time talking about the Northcotes." Diana knew as little of his childhood and youth as he did of hers. "She learned more about our family history from reading brasses in the crypt than she heard direct from me. I've got to go."

She caught his arm. "What do you intend to do? You can't follow her. You don't know where she's gone. And you have responsibilities here. Your brother—"

"Don't lecture me about responsibilities! You're the one who persuaded me to abandon my practice for months on end when it suited *your* needs." Shaking her off, he strode towards the door. "Don't worry, Mother. I'm only going as far as the Western Union office. Horatio Foxe must have some idea where Diana is. It won't take me away from my *responsibilities* to make a few inquiries."

෨෬

Diana changed trains for the last time at Cheyenne, a hundred and seven miles short of her goal. Her route had taken her from Weehawken to Rochester to Buffalo, then through Cleveland and Toledo to Chicago, at which point she'd had a choice of routes to Denver, one through Omaha and the other through St. Louis and Kansas City. Exhaustion had already set in when she made her choice. Another three days of constant worry and little rest had stretched her physical and mental abilities to their limits.

She'd hoped to find a telegram from Horatio Foxe waiting for her at one or more of the stops, but either he'd learned nothing new about her father's murder or the messages had missed her. When she arrived at Denver's Union Depot late in the afternoon of April 19, eight days after William Torrence's death, she knew nothing more than she had when she'd started out.

Rumpled, short of sleep, and riddled with self-doubt, she stepped off the train and was immediately accosted by a touter from the Tremont Hotel. When he tried to snatch the Gladstone bag that contained a change of clothing and other essentials for long-distance travel, she kicked him—hard—with one booted foot. He danced away with a howl of outrage.

His colorful curses went unnoticed in the cacophony that surrounded the handsome stone train station. Runners from dozens of rival hotels competed to attract potential customers to their establishments. Ringing bells and beating gongs, they yelled out their pitches and hurled abuse at the competition. Those who had already corralled their marks, herded their hapless patrons outside, where a line of brightly painted hotel buses waited, each drawn by two horses. Larger hotels, like Charpiots, the St. James, the Windsor, and the American, owned their own conveyances, their names emblazoned on the sides. Smaller establishments sent rented wagons with removable signs attached. Hacks were at a premium, given the number of newcomers arriving in Denver on any given day.

The porter who had collected the rest of Diana's baggage cleared his throat. "If you'll tell me where it is you want to go, ma'am, I'll find you a reputable driver."

Diana produced a gracious if tired smile. One of the things she'd thought about during the endless journey west had been where she would stay in Denver. Her parents' house, she assumed, now belonged to her mother.

Difficult as it was for her to accept the fact of a divorce, she had no doubt that her mother had been the one to sue for it. She'd not have stood for unfaithfulness in a husband. If he'd committed adultery, as Diana supposed he must have, she'd have divorced him, though reluctantly. In such cases the wronged wife was the one who kept possession of the family home. In some rare instances, she even managed to retain her social standing. There was certainly a precedent for that here in Denver. Even on tour with a theatrical troupe halfway across the country, Diana had heard news of Senator Tabor's scandalous divorce and remarriage.

"Broadway," she told the porter. The Torrence mansion was only a few doors away from the house Augusta Tabor had kept after divorcing her cheating spouse for carrying on with a woman with the unlikely name of "Baby" Doe.

The porter led Diana past the remaining touters and a line of surreys, wagons, and gleaming black six-passenger hackneys to a gig hitched to a sturdy, broad-backed bay mare. Accustomed to the Hansoms and Gurneys that plied their trade on New York City streets, Diana hesitated.

"Irish Harry at your service, ma'am," the driver said. He didn't sound at all Irish, though he did look a bit like a leprechaun.

A woman traveling alone had to be careful whom she trusted. Diana eyed Harry. He grinned at her around a toothpick and squinted to see how much she tipped the porter.

"Where to?" he asked when she was settled in the gig along with her luggage.

Diana gave him the address. His brows lifted, and a speculative look came into his eyes. "The Torrence house? I suppose you've heard about the murder."

"I suppose everyone has," she retorted, and resisted an urge to ask what her driver knew about Elmira Torrence's current status. She did not want to hear bad news from a complete stranger. She'd find out soon enough. Even if her mother was under arrest, there would be servants in residence.

Diana expected Dorcas was still the Torrence cook. She'd been too much of a "treasure" for Diana's mother to let her go under any circumstances. And perhaps old Morris would be there, too.

He'd done odd jobs for the family for as long as Diana could remember, even before her father had struck it rich. She was sure she could persuade Dorcas or Morris to let her stay at the house. She wasn't so certain what her mother's reaction would be.

"I'll have you there in a jiffy," Irish Harry said. He clucked to the horse, and they were off, splashing an unfortunate pedestrian as the gig's wheels went through a puddle. "Sprinkling tankers leave those," he commented. "City uses water to keep the dust down." The paving was the same hard gravel and clay Diana remembered.

On Seventeenth Street, one of Denver's busiest thoroughfares, they were swallowed up by heavy traffic. Landaus, traps, and dogcarts vied for space with dray wagons and men on horseback, all competing with the horse-drawn cars of the Denver Tramway Company.

Irish Harry spat in the general direction of the tracks and muttered, "electric street railway," in a tone of disgust.

He glanced at Diana. "Be glad they're back to four-legged power," he told her. "Up till last year the tracks had underground power conduits. Trouble was, folks trying to cross the street got shocks if they stepped on the mid-track slotway and one of the rails at the same time. So did horses. Caused a lot of rearing and bolting before they abandoned the system. I hear they're putting in new underground cable traction now. Supposed to work this time. Hah!"

Tired as she was, Diana could not fail to notice how much Denver had grown since her last visit. There had been a spate of new building along the fourteen blocks that separated Union Station from Broadway, still mostly of orange-red brick, but here and there a structure of gray limestone rose above the rest.

The smell had not improved, she thought. The stench from the South Platte was faint but pervasive. People living here got used to it after a while.

Diana sincerely hoped she wouldn't be staying in Denver that long.

When the gig turned onto Broadway, businesses quickly gave way to expensive private homes. Here there were more trees, mostly cottonwoods, planted in rows along sidewalks laid with large flagging stones. The trees were well irrigated. A steadily flowing stream bubbled along the gutters.

Diana's tension increased as they neared her old home. Her shoulders felt stiff, her chest tight. What had happened to her mother? Had she been arrested? Was she even now sitting in a jail cell awaiting trial? Or had the real killer been caught?

She prayed the crisis was past, that her trip here had been unnecessary, but by the time the big bay came to a halt, her hands were clenched tightly in her lap and she'd gnawed her lips until they were raw. She dabbed absently at her mouth with one hand, barely noticing the tiny bloodstain she left on her glove. Leaning forward, she fixed her eyes on the house that had once been her home. At first glance, it appeared unchanged.

With the narrow frontage typical of Denver houses, the Torrence mansion stretched back on its lot. The gate opened on wide, high steps leading to a front porch, which her father had called a piazza and her mother the veranda.

For an instant, Diana was catapulted back to the time she'd first seen the rugged rhyolite façade with its contrasting sections of smooth red sandstone. She'd been awed by the sheer size of the place, even before she'd discovered there were twenty rooms inside, each one decorated with fancy imported wallpaper. She recalled being particularly impressed by the steam heat and indoor plumbing.

She'd been nine. After years of poverty, her miner father had struck silver in the mountains west of Denver. The first thing he'd done was commission an architect and build himself a house. The second was to hire tutors for his daughter. She was going to be a lady, he'd told her, whether she wanted to be or not.

"Will you be staying here, ma'am?" asked Irish Harry.

"Yes," she said with more confidence than she felt. "Please bring my bags to the porch." Mother would not turn her away. Nor, if Elmira Torrence was in jail, would her servants.

She tipped the hackman as generously as she could—she had not yet had an opportunity to cash Horatio Foxe's bank draft—and alighted from the gig, leaving her driver to transport her belongings. Chin thrust out and shoulders thrown back, she marched towards the ornate front door with its glittering glass knob.

Out of the corner of one eye, Diana caught sight of a lawn decoration that had not been there six years earlier. Surprised, she stumbled, then stopped to take a closer look. The bronze statue represented a deer, and it was not the only one. Several more, together with a half dozen bronze staghounds, stood scattered among the flower beds. Diana frowned, unable to imagine the mother she remembered choosing such rustic ornaments.

Then again, she didn't suppose she'd ever really known either of her parents. At fourteen, she'd been sent away to finishing school. At eighteen, she'd married Evan. For all Diana knew, her mother had redecorated the entire house with a deer-and-dogs motif.

Turning her attention back to the door, she rang the bell. The black ribbon fastened to it forcibly reminded her of why she'd come. Her father was dead. He'd been murdered.

Diana had to fist her hands to stop them from shaking. A long moment passed during which she feared she was about to lose whatever thin veneer of composure she had left. It was the sound of the latch being lifted that brought her back from the brink.

A young maidservant with coffee-colored skin answered the door.

"Yes, mum?" Her black cloth dress was very plain, but over it she wore a froth of an apron ruffled with lace.

"I am Mrs. Spaulding," Diana said. "William Torrence was my father."

The girl, who had not been in the family's employ when Diana had last visited this house, looked confused. "I expect you'll be wanting to see Mrs. Torrence, then," she said after a moment. "You'd best come in."

"Mrs. Torrence is at home?" Diana's heart leapt. She had scarcely dared hope her mother would be able to avoid arrest. In the dispatch, the chief of police had sounded so certain he had the right suspect.

"Yes, mum," the maid said, stepping back to allow Diana to enter.

Relief, and the trepidation that followed hard on its heels, left her feeling a trifle lightheaded. The reunion she both dreaded and longed for was upon her and she had no idea if she would be welcomed with open arms or sent away. When she turned too swiftly to pass through a door to her left, her vision blurred. She tripped over the edge of the carpet, clumsy as a newborn foal.

"If you'll wait here, mum?" Regarding her warily, the maidservant backed out of the room.

"Er, yes. Yes, of course," Diana murmured.

Left alone in the sitting room, her first thought was that she was glad the girl hadn't shown her into the more formal parlor, the scene of her final confrontation with her father. She did not want to revisit that memory just yet.

She drew in a deep, steadying breath. This was no time to behave like a weak and helpless female. She was a strong, independent woman, self-sufficient, well-traveled, and intelligent. Diana smiled a little at the egotism of that assessment, but it would not do to show a lack of self-confidence before her formidable mother.

Calmer now, she idly studied her surroundings while she waited for the coming confrontation. The fine oriental rug on the floor of the sitting room was the same one she remembered, but the golden oak woodwork had dulled with time and lack of attention. Diana frowned, finding that strange. Her mother had always been a great one for dusting and polishing.

The heavy brocade drapes and the pressed *papier mâché*

wallpaper were new. So was the rubber plant given place of honor in the bay window. Its shiny green leaves also needed dusting.

The unfamiliar furniture—chairs, footstools, and occasional tables—was much more ornate than the pieces that had previously been in place, and there was a great deal more of it crammed into the room. The pedestal that had once held a small marble statue, a tasteful nude, now displayed a plaster cast replica of the Venus de Milo with an eight-day clock in her midsection.

Diana was not surprised to see that electricity had been installed. Her father had always liked to be up-to-date. He'd insisted upon having a telephone as soon as service had become available, even though there'd been few others here in Denver with whom he could converse.

She turned in a slow circle, seeking other changes, and froze when she noticed the painting above the mantel. Her hard-won self-control faltered, and a knot of anxiety settled in the pit of her stomach. That spot should have been filled with a rather stern-looking likeness of Elmira Torrence. Now it contained the portrait of a young, attractive blonde with amber eyes, delicate facial features, and a figure remarkably similar to that of the plaster statue.

The soft sound of wood brushing against wood made Diana turn towards the pocket doors that led from the dining room. The woman in the portrait stepped through.

"Mrs. Spaulding?" she inquired in a soft, pleasantly-modulated voice. Barely five feet tall, she was what gentlemen called a "pocket Venus." Her small, shapely form was clad all in black, her skirt and waist trimmed with folds of English crepe, but a cluster of yellow ringlets tumbled around her face, brushing against pink-tinged cheeks.

"I am Diana Spaulding," Diana agreed, "but I'm afraid you have the advantage of me."

"I am Miranda Torrence," the young woman said. Silk swished as she approached. She was, at most, a year or two older than Diana. "Mrs. William Torrence."

"M-m-mrs. Torrence?" Diana felt the color drain out of her face. The possibility that her father had remarried had never occurred to her—in spite of Senator Tabor and his "Baby" Doe— let alone that he'd have brought his new bride to live in Elmira Torrence's house.

"I didn't know," she stammered. "I expected . . . someone else."

"Elmira, I suppose?" Even with an expression of extreme vexation on her face, Miranda Torrence managed to look attractive.

"Er, yes."

"Elmira Torrence left this house four years ago when William divorced her and married me."

Diana heard what Miranda said, but it made no sense to her. Her *father* had sued for divorce? But that meant he must have charged her *mother* with adultery. Impossible!

Miranda's eyes narrowed. "Just who are you, Mrs. Spaulding?"

Diana had to swallow several times before she could speak. "I told your maid. William Torrence was my father."

"That girl!" Exasperated, Miranda planted her hands on her hips and glared at Diana. "One cannot find well-trained servants these days. She should have known not to let you in."

"Were you expecting me?"

"Why should I be?"

"Because my father died?"

Miranda waved a dismissive hand. "He'd cut you off. Years ago. The lawyers told me so."

"The *lawyers* did?"

Tiny frown lines formed around her mouth. "William never spoke of you, except to warn me once that strangers tend to come out of the woodwork any time there's an inheritance to be claimed. It doesn't matter. You don't get a thing. He may once have intended to leave you something, but he didn't. I get it all. Every penny. I've seen the will."

"He kept his promises," Diana murmured. He'd even, it appeared, kept his vow never to speak her name again. She suppressed a sigh. "I have no claim on his fortune, nor do I want one. As you say, Father disowned me years ago. I only came to this house because I thought my mother still lived here. Since she plainly does not, perhaps you would be so kind as to tell me where to find her?"

"If I knew that I'd be a happy woman! She killed William. Murdered him in cold blood."

"No. That's not possible." Diana took a step closer, desperate to convince the other woman that she must be wrong.

Miranda's eyes filled with sudden fear. "Stay away from me," she warned, and reached up to yank on the bell-pull used to summon servants.

Surprised by Miranda's reaction, Diana wasn't sure whether to apologize or pursue the advantage it gave her and try to appear even more threatening. With an exasperated sigh, she backed off. "Just tell me where to find my mother and I'll leave."

"I'll tell you where she ought to be. She *belongs* in jail, but she got away from that fool of a police chief."

"She's . . . she's a fugitive?"

"The U.S. Marshals are looking for her." Miranda jerked on the bell pull a second time, putting so much force into it that she almost tore the braided rope loose from the wall.

"My mother is a fugitive?" Diana repeated, stunned. Without thinking, she took another step in Miranda's direction, only to stop short when the other woman gave a shriek of alarm.

"Stay back!"

"Murderous tendencies are rarely inherited," Diana said in a dry voice. She held both hands out in front of her in a placating gesture. "Why do you believe my mother killed him? What evidence is there that she stabbed my father?"

"She ran away when the police tried to question her! What more proof do you need!"

"A great deal, I assure you."

The arrival of a scrawny boy and a crookbacked older man

with mean little eyes put an end to any hope Diana had of getting more information out of her father's widow. She didn't recognize either of them, and the man did not look like the sort of person she could reason with.

"Show this woman the door," ordered the second Mrs. Torrence.

Diana didn't wait to be evicted. Spinning on her heel, she stalked out of the sitting room and left the house before either of Miranda's lackeys could make a move.

Irish Harry was long gone. He'd left her luggage in a neat pile on the front porch. Gathering up as much as she could carry by herself, Diana descended the steps. She'd reached the street before she realized she had no idea where to go.

CHAPTER THREE

ℰᴑᴄᴙ

As Diana stood dithering before the gate, she heard a hail from beyond the hedges that sheltered the house next door.

"Diana? Miss Torrence? Is that you?"

Diana recalled that, when she was a girl, the neighbors were a Mrs. Hastings and her son. Mrs. Hastings and Diana's mother had been friendly, after a fashion, since they'd moved in the same social circles. The son—Mike? No, Matt—had been several years older than Diana. They'd had little to do with each other, but she remembered him without difficulty when his tall, gangly frame and homely face appeared.

Matt Hastings had always made her think of a clean-shaven Abraham Lincoln. His resemblance to portraits of the assassinated President was less marked now that he'd allowed side-whiskers to grow, but the dull brown hair and watery blue eyes were unchanged. He blinked at her, the eager, hopeful look on his face overshadowed by uncertainty when he got a good look at her. Doubt crept into a voice so deep it reverberated with each word. "Diana?"

This unexpected encounter, coming so soon after the emotional scene with Miranda, unsettled Diana further. She had to shake off a sense of trepidation before she could manage any semblance of normal conversation. Feeling unaccountably flustered as he continued to stare at her, she forced herself to speak.

"I am flattered that you know me. I was still a schoolgirl when we last met."

A smile of welcome flashed her way before he recalled why she must have returned to Denver. "You've heard about your father."

"And my mother. But with scarcely any details."

"You'd best come in." He nodded towards the residence on the opposite side of the street. Diana looked the way he indicated just in time to see a curtain twitch. Matt apparently wasn't the only neighbor interested in what went on at the Torrence house.

"You're right. We shouldn't talk in the street." This was her opportunity, Diana realized, to get answers to at least a few of her questions. Matt was bound to know something about the new Mrs. Torrence. They were neighbors, after all.

Besides, she had nowhere better to go.

A short time later, she found herself ensconced on a pillow-strewn couch in the sitting room, a steaming cup of tea in her hand. The last of the day's sunlight streamed in through tall windows, picking out dust motes and illuminating the plethora of family photographs, small figurines, and assorted bric-a-brac set out on the richly embroidered cream color scarf atop an ebony piano. More pictures dotted the walls.

As yet, Diana knew nothing more of her own mother's fate, but she had learned that Mrs. Hastings had died two years earlier. Matt, a lawyer, now lived in this large red-brick house alone, save for a cook, who had her own quarters near the kitchen, and a single manservant.

"The remainder of your luggage has been safely rescued and deposited in the entry hall," he reported, rejoining her. He'd sent his man to retrieve her belongings from the veranda of the Torrence house.

"Thank you. I'm sorry to be such a bother."

"I only wish I could do more to help." He poured himself a cup of tea and settled into the chair opposite her. His knees stuck up at an odd angle. All the furniture in the sitting room was low, with broad seats, better suited to women and children than to a tall man.

"If you really mean that, then you can answer a few questions for me. My father's . . . widow was not very forthcoming." To her dismay, her hands began to tremble. Bone china rattled ominously.

Diana despised herself for this show of weakness. Anger would have been far better, but she didn't seem to have the strength to summon any.

The hard contact of Matt's big hand, patting her forearm in an awkward gesture of sympathy, very nearly sent the cup and saucer tumbling to the carpet. To avert catastrophe, she hastily placed the as yet untouched tea on the nearest table. It was still too hot to drink, and, in truth, she'd lost interest in politely sipping a beverage better suited to society's poses and pretenses than to the harsh reality that had brought her to Denver.

"I didn't know about the divorce, let alone that Father had remarried. I've been estranged from my parents since my marriage six years ago."

"Your husband is . . . ?"

"I am a widow. I reside in New York and earn my living as a journalist. That's how I heard about Father's murder. Through a dispatch. But it was lamentably lacking in detail."

Matt took a moment to sip his tea and absorb the information she'd just given him. She supposed most of it came as a surprise to him.

"Perhaps I should have waited in New York for more information to come in, but I felt I needed to be here."

Matt looked ill at ease but determined. "I will try to answer your questions. I'm afraid I know very little myself."

"Father was murdered. Stabbed to death. Where?"

"In a suite at the Windsor Hotel."

"The Windsor?" Diana could not keep the surprise out of her voice.

She remembered the hotel, not from her childhood, but from the month she'd spent in Denver in the autumn of 1885. The hotel had been fairly new then, and very grand. It had charged three dollars a day for a room. She and Evan and the rest of Todd's Touring Thespians had stayed elsewhere. When the troupe had gone on to the next stand without them, they'd moved into a slightly better hotel, but still hadn't been able to afford the Windsor.

"What was he doing there?" Diana asked. "And why should the authorities leap to the conclusion that my mother murdered him when they'd been divorced for four years. Was she caught red-handed, standing over the body with the knife?" Nothing less would convince Diana of Elmira's guilt.

Matt cleared his throat. "There was evidence found at another location." An expression of acute embarrassment flickered across his long, narrow face.

"What location?"

"The Elmira." Matt shifted in his chair and avoided meeting Diana's searching gaze.

"The *Elmira?*"

"A hotel." The rest of his explanation came out in a rush. "It was the only thing your father ceded to your mother in the divorce."

That made some sense. Diana recalled her mother telling her that her grandparents had owned and operated a hotel.

"The police had reason to suspect her, Diana. She'd threatened your father before witnesses. I don't know what evidence they found, but everything I've heard seems to indicate there's enough to convict her."

"You think she's guilty?" Disappointed to discover he was not an ally after all, Diana went very still.

"By the time they made up their minds to arrest her, she'd disappeared. What else is anybody to think? I'm sorry."

It would have been easier to bear if he'd slammed the door in her face and treated her like a pariah. Then outrage and resentment might have sustained her. Instead, Diana suddenly found she had no resistance left. The last of her strength had seeped out of her like air from a deflating balloon. She buried her head in her hands.

"Did I ever understand either of them?" she whispered, almost choking on the words. Her throat felt so tight and painful that she could barely swallow.

"You were a child when you left here." The distant rumble of Matt's voice was oddly soothing.

"I had fourteen years with them."

"Then remember those, Diana. Think of the early days."

The constriction eased a little as she let her thoughts drift back to her youth. "They were different people then. Before they had money. When I was small, we didn't live in Denver all year round. We came here only in the winter and went back to the mountains at the first hint of spring."

Life had been simple in the mining camps. They'd been poor in material things, but rich in other ways. Her father had always found time to whittle toys for her. Mother, though less demonstrative, had made sure she'd had warm clothing and something in her belly, even if she and Diana's father had been obliged to do without. Then everything had changed.

"Being rich turned my father into a tyrant." Lifting her head, she met Matt's questioning gaze. "A benevolent despot. He thought wealth gave him the right to decide everyone's future."

He'd even founded his own town near the mine and named it after himself. He'd declared himself mayor of Torrence, Colorado, but that hadn't been enough for him. At the first opportunity, he'd moved his wife and child into a mansion in the state capital. He'd wanted to be close to power, to money, to prestige.

"I was just as bad. I loved having pretty clothes and riding in a fine carriage." She gestured towards her old home, just visible through the sitting room windows. "After we moved into that house, I hardly ever saw either of my parents, and before I knew it, Father decided I should be sent away to finishing school."

"I seem to remember that you wanted to go," Matt said mildly.

"I'm surprised you even noticed my existence."

"Oh, I noticed."

Momentarily disconcerted by the admiration in his voice, she did not know how to respond. When she'd left Denver for the Young Ladies Seminary in San Francisco at fourteen, Matt had been twenty-one. A chasm had separated them. But now that she was a woman grown, the age difference seemed negligible. In fact, now that she thought about it, Diana realized that Ben Northcote was a bit older than Matt.

As if embarrassed by his comment, Matt rose and went to stand at the window. Darkness had begun to fall in earnest now, and lights winked out at them from Miranda's house. "She was his mistress before she became his wife."

Diana tensed. Even her face went taut. "Miranda said it was my father who petitioned for the divorce. That can't be right. Mother would never have betrayed him with another man."

"He had great wealth, Diana. And a ruthless streak. When your mother refused to divorce him, he found a man willing to swear he'd had an affair with her. She denied it, of course, but the judge was in Torrence's pocket. She lost everything."

"Except a hotel." Diana waited until he looked at her. "Take me there, Matt. That's where I'll find answers."

"It's getting late. Better to visit in the morning."

"I have no other place to go. Since Mother owns the Elmira, they'll have to let me stay in her quarters."

"Diana, I don't think—look, move in here. I've plenty of room."

"That's generous of you, Matt, but if you have a law practice here in Denver, you don't want to run the risk of scandal."

Her gentle reminder of just how improper if would be for a bachelor and a widow to share an abode brought a rush of color into his face. "My cook can act as chaperone. You know her, Diana.

Dorcas Johnson. She used to work for your mother."

"Dorcas is here?" She stood with a rustle of skirts and would have headed straight into the kitchen if Matt hadn't held up a hand to stop her.

"She's away for a few days, taking care of a sick friend in Argo, but she'd come back if I sent for her."

"No, Matt. Don't trouble her."

"Argo's only on the outskirts of Denver."

"I'd like to see her again. I hope I do before I leave. But her presence here wouldn't be enough to quell salacious rumors. There's simply no alternative. I must go to the Elmira Hotel."

"You're right, of course. About not staying here—because of the potential for gossip. But you mustn't go to the Elmira, either. It's in a bad section of town."

"I suspect I've lived in worse. I was married to an actor, Matt."

"Stay at the Windsor." He winced, remembering too late that her father had died there. "Or the St. James. I'll loan you funds if you need them."

Why, she wondered, was he trying so hard to keep her away from the Elmira Hotel? His very determination made her dig in her heels. "That's extremely generous, Matt, but letting you pay for a hotel room would be almost as scandalous as my staying here. Please, just take me to my mother's place."

He looked as if he wanted to continue protesting. With a visible effort, he bit back further argument. "I suppose you'll have to see for yourself." He rang for his manservant. "Hitch the horses to the trap, Gilbert," he ordered when the fellow appeared, "and load Mrs. Spaulding's belongings into the back."

Matt had been right when he'd said the Elmira Hotel was not in the best part of town. Noise, and the occasional ruffian, spilled forth from dozens of saloons and gambling houses as they retraced the route Irish Harry had taken along Seventeenth Street from the depot.

It was only marginally quieter on the street Matt turned onto. A few blocks later, he brought the trap to a halt in front of a nondescript three-story building constructed of the same red brick as his house.

"That's it. That's the Elmira."

Diana frowned, wondering how he knew. There was no hotel sign, and the windows, protected by iron grillwork, were all heavily curtained, making it difficult to see if the place was open or not. "It doesn't look very hospitable."

Her heart went out to her mother, forced to shelter in this dark, drab building after enjoying so many years in the luxury of the Torrence mansion. If she hadn't believed in the bitterness of her parents' divorce before, she did now. It had been just plain vindictive of her father to cede this place to her mother.

Before her marriage to William Torrence, Elmira had worked in the hotel her parents owned. She'd never talked much about those years, but she had once told Diana that it had not been an easy life and that she'd hated the drudgery of it almost as much as she'd later hated taking in laundry.

"Let me take you to one of the hostelries on hotel row, Diana. You don't want to stay here."

"Yes, I do. This is my mother's home." She couldn't quite keep the resentment out of her voice. "For now, it will be mine."

Reluctantly, Matt helped her down and unloaded the hatbox and Gladstone bag, the gripsack, and the tweed bag. Juggling all four, he followed her up the steps to the front door.

She expected a lobby. Instead, she found herself in a small entrance hall, more like the vestibule of a private home than a hotel reception area. Access to the rest of the building was blocked by a large oak kneehole desk positioned in front of the inner door.

"May I help you?" asked a slender young woman seated behind it. She addressed Matt, ignoring Diana. Plainly dressed and with hair the unfortunate color of Mississippi mud, her very ordinary face was made even more nondescript by the addition of a pair of wire-rimmed spectacles.

Matt cleared his throat. "Well . . . that is—"

Diana caught Matt's arm to keep him from saying more. The instincts she'd honed during nearly two years of writing for the *Independent Intelligencer* were screaming that there was something decidedly odd about this hotel. Although she intended to identify herself as Elmira Torrence's daughter eventually, she had a feeling she might learn more if she did not announce that fact just yet.

"I require a room for an indefinite stay," she said instead.

"We have no rooms available."

"I understood this was a hotel. The Elmira?"

"The Elmira is a *boarding* house, and we have eight young ladies already in residence. There are no vacancies."

"A young ladies' boarding house?" As Diana repeated the words, her uneasiness grew. She'd gotten a second wind at Matt's house and felt reasonably sure she was not letting her imagination run away from her. She might be overtired, but she wasn't naive. She had traveled with actors. She had a knowledge of the world most "ladies" lacked.

Both "hotel" and "boarding house" often meant something else entirely, especially when they were located on a street one block away from and parallel to the main street of a frontier town. They'd crossed Larimer, brightly lit with electric arc lights. That meant this was Holladay Street. Diana briefly closed her eyes. Some called it "the Row."

A burst of bawdy feminine laughter from the far side of the inner door had her eyes popping open again.

"You've come to the wrong place," the young woman said as she circled the desk to stand in front of Matt and Diana. "You'd best leave now."

Diana drew in a strengthening breath, surprised when she detected the scent of lemon furniture polish with a faint undercurrent of ammonia. She'd expected to smell cheap scent and stale tobacco smoke.

"No, not in Elmira Torrence's house," she murmured, amused in spite of herself. Her mother had always had a passion for cleanliness . . . and an intense disdain for any sort of perfume.

"My name is Diana Torrence Spaulding," she told the desk clerk. "I am Elmira's daughter."

She took advantage of the young woman's astonishment to slip past the desk and follow the sound of voices. They led her to a large, well-lit drawing room where six "boarders," dressed in elaborate, low-cut ball gowns, clustered around a grand piano. A very large, very ugly man picked out the tune of "Greensleeves" with one hand. In the other he held a foaming glass of beer.

If there had been any question in Diana's mind before, the box on the bench beside the piano player dispelled it. Carefully lettered on the outside were the words "Feed the Kitty." These were all professionals here, dedicated to earning a living for themselves and for the owner of this "hotel."

Chest tight, throat threatening to close again, Diana swallowed hard and advanced into a room that, in most respects, had the appearance of a well-kept parlor in a gentleman's home. Spacious and well-appointed, it offered visitors two bird's-eye maple love seats and numerous comfortable chairs, stools, and ottomans. The crystal chandelier cast its beams on an Oriental rug covering most of the parquetry floor and revealed that, in winter, the room was heated by a tiled, coal-burning fireplace with a heavy ornamental cast-iron fire screen. A framed, diamond-dust mirror hung above the carved walnut mantelpiece. Reflected in it was the sideboard against the opposite wall, well-stocked with liquor bottles and glasses, beer and champagne.

The giant rose from the piano bench. "You don't belong in here, miss."

"She says she does, professor." Face paste-white, eyes haunted, the desk clerk stood framed in the doorway. "She says she's Elmira's daughter."

"I *am* Elmira's daughter, and I've come back to Denver to help her."

A skeptical silence settled over the assembled company. They were a study in contrasts, Diana thought, as her gaze traveled from face to face and—inevitably, given the way these women were dressed—from body to body. The one nearest to her wore her honey-colored mane twisted high on her head and had what could only be described as an hourglass figure. Another, a plump brunette decked out in frilly pink, glared at Diana with the coldest eyes she'd ever seen. Diana looked away, directly into the grinning countenance of a saucy female with a strawberry birthmark that covered most of the left side of her neck.

"Tell her to go away, Jane," said a girl whose face was dominated by an enormous nose. When no one else spoke up to support her suggestion, she flounced off to sit on a tapestry-covered footstool, pulled up the satin hem of her green gown, and retied the garter holding up her green and yellow striped stockings.

She was just a girl, Diana thought in dismay, though she couldn't guess the exact age. None of them could be a day over twenty-five and most were probably far younger.

The piano player resumed his seat and began to play softly. The familiar notes of "Buffalo Gals" were the only sounds in the room besides the rustle of taffeta, satin, and silk.

Diana realized she had clasped her hands over her elbows and was all but hugging herself. She loosened her grip, but was suddenly very glad Matt had followed her into the drawing room.

The burly "professor" probably acted as a bouncer as well as an entertainer, nor would she give much for her chances if the two remaining women decided they wanted to get rid of her. The first was tall, with a horsey face. From the look of her shoulders and upper arms, she possessed the kind of strength farm girls develop at an early age. The last of the boarders was a pretty redhead, although the shade was far too bright to be natural. She balanced on the balls of her feet, halfway into a classic prize-fighter's stance, and looked ready to defend herself with her fists.

Ill prepared for pugilistic feats, Diana tried a tentative smile instead.

"Elmira never mentioned having a daughter." The challenge in the redhead's voice made Diana bristle.

Temper drove away trepidation and had her answering back before she could think better of it. "We haven't seen each other for nearly six years."

"Can you prove you're who you say you are?" The soft-spoken question came from the tall young woman who'd been addressed as Jane. The desk clerk's plain attire made her stand out like a weed among brightly colored flowers, but she was clearly the one with authority.

Diana supposed the request made sense. It was not unheard of for a criminal to read about someone else's misfortune in a newspaper and put forward a false claim to that person's property while he was in jail . . . or lying in the morgue.

"Well?" Jane persisted, bolder now. "Have you proof? If you can't establish your identity, you'll have to leave."

For a moment, Diana could think of nothing that would convince these people. Then she remembered what she'd tucked into the bottom of her gripsack at the last moment. She'd been about to pack it away in the Saratoga trunk when, on impulse, she'd decided to bring it with her. She'd forgotten all about it until now.

"Matt, will you fetch my luggage from the entry hall? It contains a small photograph album."

It was the one she'd carried with her to boarding school and, afterwards, on the road with the acting company. Inside were likenesses of both her parents, and two of Evan. There were as yet no pictures of Ben.

With hands that embarrassed her by their clumsiness, she pawed through the bag until she touched the soft velvet cover. A few seconds later she had the album unlatched and open to a photographer's posed picture of her parents. Her father looked stiff and solemn, her mother oddly smug.

"That's Elmira all right," the horse-faced woman said. "She must be telling the truth, Jane. How else would she get hold of this picture?"

Jane took the album and flipped through the pages, past youthful pictures of Diana and one of her friend Rowena Foxe. She stopped at Evan's likeness. "Handsome man."

Diana stared down at the familiar features. "My late husband." He'd have been twenty-eight now had he lived. A charming, green-eyed, yellow-haired Adonis, the perfection of his features marred only by a nose that was just a little too long and thin and lips that could purse into a disdainful sneer more cutting than words. "He was an actor."

Evan's profession seemed to win a modicum of approval from all the young women gathered around to peer over Jane's shoulder. Only the professor was studying Diana instead.

"Mrs. Spaulding has her mother's eyes." When he beamed at her, the expression transformed him from looming threat into gentle giant.

Jane's frown had deepened. She squinted at Diana through her spectacles as if weighing her in some imaginary balance. It did not appear she liked what she saw, but the sound of the front door opening finally forced her into a concession. "You may be Elmira's daughter, but I doubt there's anything you can do to help her."

"I won't know until I try. In the meantime, I need a place to stay."

Now that the swirling tension in the room had diminished, Diana felt the heaviness of her exhaustion descend upon her once more. She had no energy left to make decisions and the very thought of going farther than the closest bed tonight was unbearable.

"She can use Elmira's suite," the professor said.

Jane scowled but didn't contradict him.

"Diana, this place isn't safe."

"You think I'd let anything happen to Elmira Torrence's daughter?" The professor took a step towards Matt, fists clenched.

Heavy footfalls from the direction of the entry hall warned them that whoever had come into the Elmira had grown tired of waiting for service. The sound spurred Jane into action.

"Wait through there." She opened a door concealed as a floor-to-ceiling bookcase and shoved Matt and Diana through, tossing Diana's luggage after them. An instant after she'd slammed the portal shut, Diana heard a flurry of lively greetings and a burst of raucous laughter from the other side.

They were in a second, adjoining drawing room as richly furnished as the first, but here only one small lamp burned and there was no piano. They were also alone.

"You cannot stay here, Diana," Matt said. "Let me take you to another hotel." He cleared his throat and stared at the toes of his boots. "There's something you don't realize about the Elmira."

Diana closed her eyes for a moment, but it didn't help. Weariness and disillusionment sapped her strength. "I can and will stay here, Matt, because it belongs to my mother. And I know exactly what this place is." She looked him straight in the eye and didn't mince words. "The Elmira Hotel is a parlor house—a high-class brothel."

෩ාඋ

Unless you're here to tell me I may resume work, then take yourself off," Aaron grumbled. "I'm deuced tired of doing nothing."

Ben Northcote eased into the comfortably padded chair usually occupied by a nurse and stretched his legs out in front of him, flexing his ankles before he crossed them. It had been a long day, much of it spent on his feet, and it was far from over.

The man propped up against the bed pillows was Ben's brother. Aaron had been near death a mere three weeks earlier. He was still too pale, but Ben was satisfied that he was on the mend.

"You might pass the time reading, or inveigle Mother into a

game of cards."

"If I wanted to gamble, she'd be the last one I'd match myself against." Aaron let a beat pass. "She cheats."

The grin that overspread Ben's face felt wonderful. He hadn't smiled much for the last few days. Not since he'd received Diana's telegram and started trying to find out where she'd gone and why she hadn't contacted him again. His attempts to reach Horatio Foxe had proven futile. Diana's editor had not answered any of Ben's telegrams.

"I could manage a sketch pad. I know I could." The petulance in Aaron's voice dragged Ben's attention back to his brother.

"You wouldn't be satisfied with sketching. After an hour, you'd be out of bed, standing in front of an easel, brush in hand, so wrapped up in your painting that you'd lose all sense of time. You'd ignore fatigue and the next time I came by I'd find you unconscious on the floor. Do you want to undo all the good that bed rest has done you? Healing takes time, Aaron. If you try to do too much now, you may never fully recover."

His brother pouted. There was no other word for it. Aaron's clean-shaven cheeks puffed out and his lips compressed and it wouldn't have surprised Ben if he'd threatened to hold his breath until he got his way. "How much longer?"

"Another week." Aaron had almost died of his wounds and having stitched him up and nursed him safely past the worst of it, Ben did not want to lose him now through carelessness. "Give it seven more days, then resume work gradually. Half an hour the first day. An hour the next. And so on."

Scowling, Aaron folded his arms over the bandages beneath his nightshirt. The weight made him wince, but other than clenching his hands into fists, he did not change position. He was just stubborn enough to stay as he was, causing himself continued discomfort, until Ben left.

"Pigheaded fool," Ben muttered.

"There's the pot calling the kettle black! How long are you going to stay here, fussing over me, making everyone miserable, before you take yourself off and find out what happened to your Diana?"

Ben tensed at the reminder. His gaze shot from Aaron's chest to his face, half-expecting to find an expression of little-boy mischievousness there. Instead Aaron looked uncharacteristically somber.

"She's important to me, too, you know. And you promised she'd be back."

"We can't force her to return. Not to marry me. Not to serve as your muse. And her editor wants her to stay in New York. He offered her the chance to cover the sort of news she'd been hoping to write about. And a raise in pay."

Ben hadn't considered Horatio Foxe's sudden generosity a threat at the time. After all, Diana hadn't left here with Foxe. Instead she'd delayed her departure from Bangor for two additional days, to make sure Aaron was going to recover. Although they hadn't formalized an engagement, Ben had felt certain she meant to marry him. The trip back to Manhattan had been necessary so that she could put her affairs in order and pack.

"She was excited about reporting on crime and criminals." He wasn't sure why he was confiding in Aaron. His brother was not the most logical person to use as a sounding board.

"You think an assignment has put her in harm's way?"

"If she got involved in something dangerous—"

It did not bear thinking about!

"You told her you'd follow her to New York if she hadn't returned in a month."

Ben wondered which of the servants had been eavesdropping when he'd issued that ultimatum—the "deadline" Diana's telegram had referred to.

She'd said she needed to think about his proposal of marriage without the distraction of his presence, and he'd let her go, certain she'd soon come to see things his way. Her experience with Evan Spaulding had scarred her, but he thought she knew he was nothing like her late husband. Judging by the tone of the letters she'd been writing to him, she realized that. In fact, he'd expected the next one to be an answer, her agreement to become Mrs. Benjamin Northcote. But no "next" letter had ever come, only that damnably cryptic telegram.

Too restless to remain seated, Ben heaved himself to his feet and began to pace. He stopped by the window, staring up at the North Star. Although he could not see much at night, he knew that the last of the snow had finally melted. Maine's long winter was over and spring planting was imminent. This was the time for new beginnings.

"I agree," Aaron said.

Ben turned, his stance wary. He did not think Aaron had been speaking to him. But before he could confirm his suspicion, his brother's gaze shifted to the door.

"What do you intend to do about her?" Maggie Northcote demanded in a brittle voice. Ben had no idea how long she'd been standing there, listening to their conversation.

"He's going to New York," Aaron said. "He told her he'd follow her if she didn't come back on her own."

Maggie thumped the doorframe with one fist. "In a month, he said. It hasn't been a month yet. And how can he leave you, my darling, or his other patients?"

"If it will help," Aaron said, "I'll take an oath to do no painting at all for at least three days."

"Six."

"Five."

They shook on it. Then Ben turned his attention to the black-clad figure still hovering in the doorway. "A word with you, Mother?"

He took her arm and hauled her into the outer room of Aaron's lodgings in the carriage house behind the Northcote mansion. It had been fitted up as an artist's studio and was permeated with the distinctive smells of turpentine and linseed oil. Stacks of canvases lined the walls but only two had been put on display. Both showed scantily-clad mermaids. Each figure had Diana's face.

Ben turned away from them to snag the bentwood chair that customarily sat on a small pedestal at the center of the room. He eased his mother into it, then went to a sideboard stocked with crystal decanters and glasses and poured her a snifter of Aaron's best brandy.

She glowered up at him. "Do I need this for fortification?"

"I don't know. Maybe you'd prefer to throw it across the room. It should splinter with a gratifying crash."

She sipped, but her scowl remained fierce.

"I have to make sure she's all right. I intend to remind her that if she wants to work after we're married, I have no objection. How could I?"

The implied compliment failed to soften her attitude, but Ben was beyond caring if he had her approval. He shouldn't have delayed this long. His decision made, he felt as if a great weight had been lifted from his shoulders.

"I told Aaron he needed to rest for another week, hoping he'd agree to four days. He'll be fine without me here. There's no need for you to hover over him."

"If you say so, dear heart."

"I do. So, I'll be taking an early train tomorrow. I don't expect I'll be gone long, but I will take as much time as I need to locate Diana and convince her to return with me. If all goes well, we'll be married by the end of the month."

"Go, then." She knocked back the rest of the brandy in one gulp, heaved a long-suffering sigh, and stood. "We'll struggle along without you if we must."

"I'm sure you will," Ben muttered as she swept regally out of the carriage house. He just hoped she wouldn't get into too much mischief while he was away.

CHAPTER FOUR

⚘

Diana awoke groggy and disoriented and needed several minutes to remember where she was and how she'd come to be there. It was the portrait of Elmira, the same one that had once graced the Broadway mansion, that gave her the answer. It now hung opposite the bed in the owner's suite at the Elmira Hotel.

Jane had taken Diana upstairs after Matt's reluctant departure the previous evening. Diana frowned, uncertain now why she'd been so resistant to his attempts to convince her to stay elsewhere. He'd meant well. And she couldn't explain, even to herself, why she'd felt such a total lack of concern about spending the night in a whorehouse.

The unpalatable and inescapable fact that her mother owned and operated a bordello made Diana's head ache. Bad enough discovering that Elmira Torrence was a fugitive, but the additional shock must have been too much for her. It had quite undone her usual common sense.

Yawning hugely, she swung her legs over the side of the high four-poster and made her away into the attached bath. There seemed to be little point in trying to sort out all she'd learned, let alone search for answers to her many questions, before she'd had a good breakfast and several cups of coffee.

Whatever else might be said about the Elmira Hotel, it boasted the latest amenities. No chamber pots or long walks to an outhouse for Elmira Torrence! The bathroom had a large, claw-footed tub, a water closet with an elevated flush tank, and a corner washstand topped with marble. Rabbit-ear faucets supplied both hot and cold running water.

Diana's first glimpse of herself in the mirror over the sink had her retreating a step, appalled by her own appearance. "I must have been more exhausted than I thought," she muttered. Apparently, she hadn't taken time to unpin her hair and brush it free of dust. She didn't always braid it before crawling into bed, or even wear a nightcap, since she'd recently read that it was healthier to leave hair loose at night, but she rarely skipped the usual hundred strokes.

When she'd finished untangling the mess, she sloshed cold water onto her face, but her ablutions didn't do much to improve her appearance. There was something wrong with her eyes. Diana blinked and stared harder at her reflection, a queasy feeling in the pit of her stomach.

She remembered taking a light supper before falling asleep. Jane, who'd identified herself as Jane Foster, Elmira Torrence's secretary, desk clerk, and accountant, had brought up a tray. She hadn't stayed to chat, but she'd promised to return this morning and tell Diana everything she wanted to know.

Wandering back into the bedroom, Diana studied the few crumbs left on the plate. She'd eaten sliced ham, cheese, a boiled egg, and buttered bread, consumed the glass of wine that had accompanied the meal, and then scarcely had time to remove her traveling clothes and put on a nightgown before she'd fallen into a deep, restless sleep.

She'd dreamed about Ben. Vivid dreams. Erotic dreams.

As she felt color rush into her cheeks, Diana came to a conclusion that made the hair on the back of her neck prickle.

She'd had similar dreams before, but only when she'd been dosed with laudanum. Had Jane laced her wine with the potent combination of opium and alcohol? And if she had, why?

Diana wondered if she'd been wrong to think herself safe here. Still, she had not been harmed. Drugged sleep had simply kept her out of the way while the occupants of this house conducted their usual business.

The dull throb of a lingering headache made it nearly impossible for Diana to think clearly. Pressing her fingertips to her temples did nothing to help, but as she moved into the suite's sitting room she caught a whiff of something that would. She flung open the hall door before Jane could knock.

This morning's tray was larger than the one that had held Diana's supper, but she ignored the array of covered dishes to fix her gaze on the most important item, a large pot of coffee. Without speaking, she seized it and sloshed a generous portion of the reviving liquid into a cup. Her first long swallow cleared the cobwebs from her brain and eased the pain of her headache. A second smaller and more ladylike sip had her narrowing her eyes at Jane.

Once again, the young woman was dressed demurely. She looked like any of a hundred other girls who went to work in offices or as sales clerks. What on earth was she doing as second in command of a whorehouse?

"Did you sleep well, Mrs. Spaulding?" Jane asked.

Reminded of her suspicions, Diana glared at her. "I slept very poorly."

Jane busied herself uncovering the dishes of food she'd placed on a small table and did not look up. An array of mouth-watering treats nestled on warmed plates. Sausages and eggs. Potatoes and ham. Diana polished off her coffee and held the cup out for a refill. She was not worried about being drugged this morning. The Elmira Hotel's residents were done with their night's work. If there had been anything else to hide from her, they'd had plenty of time to conceal it while she slept. And if they wanted her out of the way for good, she'd already be dead.

She waited until Jane finished pouring before she went on the attack. "I would like to know how laudanum got into my supper last night."

Jane's head snapped up and their gazes met. Diana was surprised to see that the eyes hidden behind the ugly spectacles were a remarkably pretty green, and that there was more than a hint of fear in them.

"Laudanum?" Jane's voice rose to a squeak and the heightened color in her cheeks offered further proof of guilty knowledge.

"You *have* heard of it?"

"Yes. I mean . . ." Her hands shook when she returned the coffee pot to the table. It landed with a thump and a slosh. "Everyone knows laudanum is a liquid derivative of opium. It's taken by the tablespoonful to calm the nerves and ease pain."

Diana frowned as she bit into the sausage she'd filched from a plate. Women of all sorts used laudanum and thought nothing of it. "I suppose," she said slowly, "that someone might have believed they were doing me a kindness, that I needed sedating after what was clearly a series of shocks. After all, many a mother gives Mrs. Winslow's Soothing Syrup to her children, in spite of the fact that it contains a poisonous narcotic."

"It will not happen again," Jane promised, seizing on the tentative explanation Diana offered her. She seemed genuinely distressed to discover that the effect of the dose of laudanum had not been beneficial.

Diana gave her a curt nod. "Good. I do not care for opiates and my nerves are already as steady as a diamond cutter's." She pulled a small chair up to the table and sat. "Have you eaten?"

"I am accustomed to taking my morning meal a bit later, with the boarders. We serve two meals a day here, breakfast at half past eleven and dinner at five."

"And how much do the . . . ladies pay for room and board?" When Jane hesitated, Diana caught her forearm and held it until their gazes locked. "I am Elmira's daughter. I want to know what her life is like. How she makes her living."

"She never spoke of you. Not once."

"Nevertheless, I have come here to help her. I can do very little if I don't have all the facts, including those about the operation of her business. How much do the boarders pay her for a month's food and lodging?"

"Twenty dollars."

Satisfied, Diana gentled her voice. "I believe it is time you and I dropped the pretense that this is an ordinary boarding house. We both know what goes on here. What I don't understand is how my mother became the madam of a brothel."

"You'll have to ask Elmira that question."

"She sells the services of girls younger than I am." Diana felt a little sick at the thought.

"A man's not going to pay much for an *old* woman, but if it relieves your mind, most of Elmira's profits come from selling beer and wine." At Diana's look of surprise, Jane shrugged. "Beer goes for a dollar a bottle. A split of champagne costs five."

A fork full of fluffy scrambled eggs halfway to her mouth, Diana paused to give Jane a sharp look. "How much do the . . . boarders earn?"

"An average of fifteen dollars a night apiece."

Diana felt her eyes widen. A woman with a good, respectable job in an office might take home that much for a month's work, if she had a generous employer.

"Half of that goes to your mother."

"In addition to paying for their room and board?"

"Are you one of those do-gooders who'd rather see them join the other jobless, homeless souls camped out on the banks of the South Platte?"

"No, but shouldn't they be allowed to keep all they earn?"

"Your mother has expenses, Mrs. Spaulding. Upkeep on the building, hiring the professor, who is both our piano player and the bouncer, and paying for extra musicians on busy nights. They get two dollars apiece for an evening's work, and a free dinner in the kitchen. Elmira also employs three women who do not deal privately with gentlemen. I do not, nor does the cook or the night maid. There is also a boy to do odd jobs. The cook is paid twenty dollars a month, the maid a dollar a day for housekeeping and washing and extra for the ironing and mending. In addition to all that, Elmira has to bribe the police not to bother us. Just be grateful there's no mac involved!"

"Mac?"

"That's what they call a pimp in these parts. Your mother doesn't hold with turning her profits over to a man. Any man. She told me once that she gave her husband every penny she earned taking in laundry, trusting him to invest what little they didn't need for mere survival. Then he left her with nothing."

"Except this hotel."

"Except this hotel," Jane agreed. "There are three parlors on the first floor, together with a dining room and kitchen. On the upper floors are fifteen bedrooms, plus this suite. And in the basement you'll find a wine cellar and servants' quarters."

"Tell me about the boarders. Who are they? Where do they come from?"

"We don't ask. Most use working names. You met Red Katie and Honeycomb last night. And Long Tall Linda, Strawberry Sue, and Big Nose Nellie."

"What about the cold-eyed brunette?"

"She goes by Maryam. There are two others, Maybelle and Chastity."

"They all seem to dress well. Who provides the costumes?" In a theatrical company, they were sometimes the property of the troupe, sometimes owned by individual actors.

"They buy their own gowns," Jane said. "That's common practice, though some madams advance their girls money. Your mother has accounts at all the best stores in Denver, if you need anything for yourself, but since some shopkeepers charge us more than they do a respectable customer, you might do better not to let on who you are."

"Mother might have done better to stay behind the scenes, but she obviously chose not to." Jane said nothing. "Do you know where she is?"

"No."

Diana tossed her napkin aside and pushed her empty plate away. "And you wouldn't tell me if you did."

"Probably not. She's been good to me. To everyone here. She insists on baths once a day and monthly visits to a doctor." A flicker of amusement danced behind the spectacles. "But she is cruel in one respect. She won't allow any of us to wear perfume."

Diana's lips curved into a faint answering smile. Now that *did* sound like her mother. Diana could remember hearing her wax caustic on the subject of ignorant women who thought the application of a strong sweet scent could hide the stench of an unwashed body. Far too many people in the mining camps, men and women both, had gone weeks without a visit to either bathhouse or laundry.

"She might if it smelled like lemon furniture polish," Diana murmured, inhaling deeply. She should have realized right away that someone else now lived in the mansion on Broadway. There had been a foreign smell to it. Frangipani. Miranda's choice, she supposed, although it did not really suit the delicate blonde.

"How does Mother feel about the use of laudanum?"

"She permits it. How could she stop it when anyone can buy it by the quart at any drugstore?" Jane waited a moment and when Diana made no further comment, added, "She is stricter about Swiss-S. She has forbidden any of the girls to drink that. It is a concoction made from absinthe, sometimes with a few drops of laudanum added."

"Why would anyone want to take something that strong? In the wrong dosage, absinthe alone can kill." For that matter, so could laudanum.

Deadpan, Jane said, "They say Swiss-S makes a body feel awfully good from the waist up and lively as hell from the waist down."

A chuckle escaped Diana before she could contain it." I suppose I can understand the appeal, then, but it seems a dangerous choice of libation all the same."

"That is why your mother doesn't allow it here."

"Yet she permits her boarders to sell themselves." The risks were enormous. Disease. Pregnancy. Mistreatment, even death, at the hands of violent customers. *The National Police Gazette* was full of such tragic tales.

"They're better off in this house than on their own. The girls in the cribs live poor and die young."

"And these girls?"

"Can save enough to go into business for themselves, if they're frugal. Don't look so surprised. The usual charge to go up to a bedroom is five dollars for a quick date. Those who want to stay the night pay fifteen. It adds up. And some girls end up marrying their steady customers. There are worse ways to get on in the world."

Fascinated and repulsed at the same time, Diana could not contain her curiosity. "But you don't sell yourself."

"Your mother pays me a generous salary. As much as a good cook would make at one of those fancy resort hotels in the mountains, so I do well enough without. Elmira does even better." Suddenly Jane grinned. "Have you had time to examine her things?" She flung open a wardrobe packed with clothing and took a heavy jewelry box down from the top shelf.

"Why didn't she take some of this with her when she fled?" Diana asked a few minutes later as she fingered a strand of pearls. Gold glinted deeper in the case and a sapphire ring winked up at her.

"She didn't have time to pack."

Every question Jane answered raised a dozen more. Diana was

debating what to ask next when the sound of a door slamming downstairs and a male voice shouting Jane's name brought renewed color rushing into that young woman's face.

"I'm sorry. I must go."

"I thought you didn't take customers?" Diana hoped her mother's suite wasn't about to be invaded by an angry stranger. Or was he one of those "macs" Jane had spoken of. Someone out to take over the Elmira Hotel in Elmira Torrence's absence?

"He's a . . . friend." Jane didn't sound convincing. "I'll go talk to him. I'm sorry. He shouldn't have come here."

When he bellowed her name again, she darted into the hallway as if afraid to disobey the summons. Diana started to follow her, then realized she was still in her nightgown. She wasted no time getting dressed, slipping into a simple outfit of dark blue wool that buttoned down the front and could be worn without a corset.

Putting on sturdy shoes delayed her a few minutes longer, as did locating a hatpin, but she felt both precautions were necessary. Although she hoped she wouldn't need to resort to kicking or stabbing, she was prepared to take any steps necessary to protect Jane from her angry and possibly violent "friend."

A distant clock struck nine as Diana made her way through the quiet hotel, past a series of closed doors. Faint snores issued from behind one of them. Someone coughed in another room.

At the bottom of the main staircase, Diana paused to listen. The sound of raised voices led her to the back parlor, the room she and Matt had been hidden away in the night before.

The intruder was a thin, sharp-featured man with a bright shock of strawberry blond hair. He dressed like a banker and gave off the pleasing aroma of bayberry soap, but there was nothing pleasant about the expression on his face. His thin lips were compressed into a flat, disapproving line. He had his fingers clamped on Jane's thin shoulders as if he meant to shake her.

"Unhand that woman!" Diana cried, and felt like a melodramatic fool when the two of them turned in unison to stare at her with identical expressions of incredulity on their faces.

Jane broke free, shoving past him to Diana's side. "I'm so sorry, Mrs. Spaulding. I've tried to explain."

"Explain what?"

The stranger followed right on Jane's heels. He was armed only with a blade of a nose, but Diana could see the temper building in his eyes. For a moment that look reminded her so strongly of Evan in one of his temperamental rages that it took all her willpower not to turn and flee.

"Who are you?" she demanded instead, squaring her shoulders and forcing herself to glare back at him.

"This is Alan Kent," Jane said. "He works . . . worked for your father. Alan," she added, a warning note in her voice, "you have it all wrong."

"I don't think so. I just talked to Mrs. Torrence. She's very upset."

"You talked to my mother?"

"Not Elmira." Exasperation tinged his words. "I'm speaking of Miranda Torrence."

"I see. So now that my father is dead, you work for my stepmother."

"How do we know you're who you say you are?" Kent demanded.

"Alan!" Jane spoke sharply and waited until he glanced her way. "That's not in question. She brought a photograph album. Pictures of her parents. Of herself. Of her late husband."

Kent still looked skeptical, but he backed off a few steps and Diana breathed a little easier. She no longer felt physically intimidated by him, but she sensed she wasn't going to enjoy the remainder of this encounter any more than she had its first few minutes.

"Miranda says you claim you don't want a share of the Torrence inheritance, but she doesn't believe you. Why else would you show up here after all this time?"

"I came because my mother has been unjustly accused of a heinous crime."

"I don't see why you should care what happens to your mother," Kent grumbled. "From what the lawyers said, you haven't spoken to each other for six years. It has to be the money you're after. If you can't get it from Miranda, then you'll try to take over this place."

"I came to help my mother," Diana repeated, pausing between each word. "No matter what happened between us in the past, I'm still her daughter. How can I not do everything in my power to discover who really killed my father?"

"But Mrs. Spaulding," Jane said. "Your mother did kill him. The morning after the murder, the police found a bloodstained glove in her bedroom."

⊗⊘⊗

Denver City Jail had as bleak an exterior as Diana had ever seen, but the interior had been even more distressing. She came out in a rush, spitting mad and frustrated. The officious, unhelpful moron who was Denver's chief of police had decided Diana's mother was guilty and didn't care about anything but arresting her and putting her on trial.

At least he'd confirmed what Jane had already told her, that the only physical evidence against Elmira was a glove found in her suite at the hotel. The fresh bloodstains on it were assumed to be the victim's, but Diana didn't see how anyone could prove that.

Why, she had two bloodstained gloves among her possessions right now, one from the splinter she'd poked into her thumb on the ferry to Weehawken and the other from yesterday! She wasn't sure how she'd come by the second stain, but it certainly hadn't been from doing murder.

According to Jane, Elmira had not only denied killing William

Torrence, she'd also claimed the incriminating glove was not hers. No one had believed her, but Diana couldn't help but think how easily something as small as a glove could be planted among someone's possessions. And there had certainly been no shortage of strangers in the upstairs hall of the Elmira Hotel that night. There were strangers in the building every night.

After talking to the chief of police, Diana no longer had any difficulty understanding why her mother hadn't waited around to be arrested. She'd asked him what would happen to Elmira if she was caught and had been told that a woman awaiting trial in Denver was put under the supervision of the city jailer, since the City Council had yet to authorize the hiring of a police matron, and held without privacy or comfort, denied contact with anyone but her lawyer.

Taking a deep breath to steady her temper, Diana directed her gaze towards nearby Capitol Hill, where the new state capitol was under construction. Hotels for tourists, modern office buildings, private schools, and exclusive clubs had already sprung up around it.

Diana sighed. She could remember standing on top of that rounded height of land with her father when their own newly built home was one of only a few structures close at hand. A scattering of church steeples, residences, and flat-roofed business blocks had made up the rest of their view of the city, with majestic mountains rising to the west and the wide expanse of the empty plains to the east.

The memory failed to calm her, but it did succeed in redirecting her anger. This was all William Torrence's fault. Even then, when she'd still idolized him, he'd been all show and no substance. Money and prestige had mattered more to him than love. He'd boasted that he'd be the most important man in Denver one day. And the richest. And that he already had the finest house. He'd made no mention of the loyal wife or loving daughter.

Diana boarded a streetcar and paid her five cents. She gave

herself a stern lecture en route to the next hurdle. She'd be no help to her mother if she let her emotions have free rein.

The law firm of Patterson, Markham, Thomas and Campbell had the best reputation in Colorado for winning criminal cases. They had successfully defended a number of people accused of homicide. Diana, whose natural optimism had resurfaced by the time she was shown in to see Tom Patterson, felt her high hopes plummet again when that impeccably-dressed gentleman balked at the name Elmira Torrence.

"I will not represent anyone associated with the red-light district." His lips curled with distaste.

"Mr. Patterson, you don't understand. My mother is innocent. And her reasons for running the Elmira Hotel are—"

"No, you don't understand, Mrs. Spaulding. I will not take this case." The ends of his mustache twitched with the force of his refusal.

"If it's a matter of your fee—"

He abruptly lost patience with her. "Money is no object?" he snapped. "Very well, I'll represent your 'innocent' mother . . . if you pay me fifteen hundred dollars. In advance."

Diana had always thought it a literary convention to say a person's eyes bulged or her jaw dropped, but she felt both things happen to her at once. She was still goggling when Patterson had her ejected from his office.

She took several deep breaths, collected her dignity, and resolutely moved on to the next stop on her itinerary. Patterson's office was not the only business at Seventeenth and Curtis. She entered the five-story red sandstone building that housed the *Rocky Mountain News* and asked for Col. John Arkins, managing editor and part owner of the newspaper.

The letter Horatio Foxe had given Diana was addressed to Arkins, but before she could deliver it to him, he bowed over her hand with old-world gallantry. "I am delighted to meet you, Mrs. Spaulding." There was a hint of Ireland in both his voice and his appearance, and he had the dashing, almost careless demeanor Diana associated with that country. Charmed, she was unprepared for what he said next. "The last time I heard your name, it was also in connection with a murder."

"I beg your pardon?" She went very still in the chair in which he'd just seated her.

"When the Leadville *Chronicle* covered your husband's death. A great miscarriage of justice, in my opinion. Letting the man who shot him get away like that. They never did find him, did they?"

Diana had to swallow hard before she could answer. "Not that I know of." Once she'd left Leadville, she hadn't looked back. She didn't suppose the authorities there knew where to find her, even if they did have something to tell her about the man who'd killed Evan for cheating at cards.

"And this time it's your father who's dead." Arkins beamed at her with ill-concealed speculation in his twinkling eyes. "Mr. Foxe suggests we might be able to help each other, Mrs. Spaulding. He's sent several telegrams here since you left New York, asking for details on the case. I imagine he's also sent messages to you. If you have not yet collected them, the Western Union office is at Sixteenth and Lawrence."

Reading telegrams from Horatio Foxe was far down Diana's list of priorities at the moment. Anger flared up, at both Foxe and Arkins. They wanted to use her. It was the story that mattered, not her, and not her mother.

"Col. Arkins," she said through clenched teeth, "I came to Denver as a daughter, not a journalist." Her hands balled into tight fists in her lap. "At the moment I'm looking for information, not providing it. To be truthful, you are one of the first people I've spoken to."

"Henry Burnett covers the lowers."

"The lowers?"

"The hotel beat along Larimer Street and on down to the railroad station. That includes the Windsor. And the Elmira. I can arrange for you to talk to him in exchange for an interview with you, but I can tell you already what he'll say. She's the most likely suspect. Why else disappear just when the police wanted to arrest her? I'm sorry to say that there seems little question of your mother's guilt, Mrs. Spaulding."

And he called himself a journalist! "To my mind, there is a great deal of question about her guilt, Col. Arkins. Is Mr. Burnett in the building?"

"He is not, at present, in the office. Indeed, I am not certain when he'll be available to talk to you."

"When I agree to cooperate, perhaps?"

Col. Arkins shrugged. "I did you a favor once, Mrs. Spaulding. You might consider returning it."

"What favor?"

"When Evan Spaulding was murdered, your father asked me to hush up your connection to him. That saved you a lot of trouble, I expect. It would have made a sensational story—elopement, life with a company of players, murder." He shook his head regretfully. "Could have stirred up a lot of scandal at the time."

Diana walked out of his office before she said something she'd regret . . . especially if it ended up on the front page of the newspaper. A few minutes later she was back out on the wooden sidewalk, once again seething with anger and frustration. She jumped when a familiar voice hailed her from the street.

"Diana! There you are!" Matt Hastings waved from the high seat of his trap.

Forcing a smile, Diana moved closer to the edge of the wide, dusty expanse of Curtis Street. The previous night she'd been too distracted to notice how shiny and new Matt's vehicle was, or that the two black horses harnessed to it with red leather were exceptionally well matched, both to each other and to the black trap with its red trim. "Good morning, Matt."

"I've been looking for you. Miss Foster said you'd gone to talk to the chief of police and that you hoped to hire a lawyer."

Diana nodded. She hadn't mentioned her intention to call on Col. Arkins.

Matt jumped down, helped her onto the seat, then clambered back up himself. Without asking where she wanted to go, he turned the trap around and set off towards Holladay Street. En route he pointed out a two-story building at the corner of Sixteenth and Curtis. "That's the headquarters of the Pinkerton Detective Agency. The Denver office of the Pinkertons is the staging area for the entire region."

"Are you suggesting I hire a detective to look for my mother?"

"It's something to consider. And everyone knows private detectives have a reputation for being more efficient . . . and more honest . . . than local police forces."

"And no doubt more expensive," she murmured. After a moment's hesitation, she related the gist of her encounters with Denver's police chief and premier criminal attorney.

"Until your mother is found, there isn't much point in paying a lawyer," Matt said. "Besides, if you can't afford a hotel, you certainly can't manage an attorney's retainer."

Diana fingered the bank draft in her pocket but decided not to mention it. She'd hold the money in reserve. A hundred dollars would not have covered Mr. Patterson's hefty fee, but it was more than she wanted to carry around in cash. "How much do you charge?" she asked Matt.

"Oh, I'd be no good to you, Diana. I specialize in civil cases. Libel suits. Divorces. I did help Elmira with a small matter a few years ago, but there wasn't much I could do for her. Your father was her opponent in the case. He was a powerful man, Diana. And ornery when he was riled."

He turned onto Holladay Street. It was barely noon and still quiet, although the residents of the parlor houses were by now awake. The saloons were already open for business.

"Do they ever close?" Diana asked.

"A bell rings for midnight curfew, but it is usually ignored. So is the law that bans saloons and gambling houses from opening on Sunday. Of course, strictly speaking, prostitution and gambling are illegal at any time. I don't like you staying here, Diana."

"I need to be at the Elmira, at least for a while." She hopped down from the trap on her own. "Thank you for bringing me . . . home."

He winced at the word but seemed to accept her decision.

It was only after Matt drove away that Diana stopped to wonder why he'd come looking for her in the first place.

CHAPTER FIVE

೮⊃ଔ

Diana went straight up to her mother's suite, taking pains to avoid the other occupants of the Elmira. After divesting herself of hat and gloves, she settled in at the small lady's desk in the sitting room and located a pen and a box of thick, cream-colored stationery.

It had never been opened. In fact, she found no letters addressed to Elmira in the desk. There were no bills, either, or any ledgers. Diana supposed Jane handled such things, if whorehouses bothered to keep written records at all.

Keep your mind on the matter at hand, she warned herself.

She'd been going about helping her mother all wrong. The shocks she'd had, one after another, had left her disoriented. She'd felt devoid of emotions one moment, too full of them the next. She had not been thinking clearly. Now she must. She set pen to paper and started to write.

Composing an account of all she had learned so far helped Diana organize her thoughts. When she'd reread the pages, she added a brief note, signed the bottom of the last sheet and tucked the epistle into an envelope addressed to Ben Northcote. She'd mail the letter at her first opportunity.

Her mind clearer, and one small burden of guilt lifted from her shoulders, Diana selected a fresh sheet of stationery and began to inscribe a series of pertinent questions. An hour later she studied the results of her labor with considerable satisfaction. She had come to no brilliant conclusions, unearthed no answers, but she did feel she had a much better grasp of the situation.

The first question on her list was: *What evidence is there against Mother aside from the glove?*

The second line read: *When and where did Mother threaten Father before witnesses and who were they?*

Four years seemed a very long time for anyone to hold a grudge. If her mother hadn't killed her father over the divorce, what possible motive could she have had?

The next three questions involved the Windsor Hotel:

Did anyone see Mother at the Windsor that night?

Who saw Father at the Windsor before he was killed?

Why was he at the Windsor?

It was a huge establishment, filled with bedrooms, barrooms, and ballrooms. Matt had said her father had been killed in a suite. His own, or someone else's? Had he been in one of the public areas first, attending a reception or engaged in a game of pool? Or had he taken a room in secret for some nefarious purpose?

Who else besides Mother might have wanted to kill him? she wrote.

A good many people might have, she supposed. But which of them would also have had the opportunity to make Elmira Torrence look guilty by planting a bloodstained glove in her room?

The young widow profited from William Torrence's death. Diana wrote her name first. She might have had a confederate at the Elmira. Diana made a mental note to find out more about Miranda's background.

"Business rivals," she murmured. "But who?" Her father had exhibited a ruthless streak in dealing with Elmira. Had he cheated others as well?

She tossed her pen aside and used both fists to rub her eyes.

For all she knew, half of Denver might have had good reason to want William Torrence dead!

She looked at the list again. At least she had a place to start. With Miranda. Where had she been when the murder took place? Diana was contemplating just how she might find out when she heard a scratch at her door.

Jane came in without waiting for an invitation. "There are some people downstairs who want to talk to you, Mrs. Spaulding."

Jane's flushed face and nervous demeanor set warning flags flying. Diana quickly folded her list and tucked it into the pocket that already contained her letter to Ben. "What's wrong?"

"Nothing! That is, there's nothing to be alarmed about. It's just that I don't know how to prepare you."

"Who are these callers?"

"They're all prominent local madams." Jane swallowed hard. "Important people in this part of town."

Not to be ignored or trifled with, then. She stood and smoothed the wrinkles out of her skirt. "What do they want with me?"

"News travels fast on Holladay Street. I imagine they want to know what you intend to do with the Elmira when you inherit it."

"That presupposes my mother is going to be executed." Everyone seemed to assume the case was cut and dried, a notion that made her bristle with suppressed anger. "And that I am her heir, which I doubt." Elmira would have made a will. Diana was sure of it. But it seemed as likely to Diana that Elmira would leave her property to her employees as to her daughter.

"Do you want to talk to these women or should I send them away? There are five of them in the Chinese parlor. You haven't been in that room yet. It's the one in front."

"Oh, I'll see them all right. They may know something that will help Mother. But I think you'd best tell me a little about each of them first."

Jane blinked at her for a moment, then suddenly grinned. "I

can do better than that." She crossed the room to the floor-to-ceiling bookcase set into the wall next to the fireplace and touched a carved swirl just above shoulder level. A section six feet high and two feet wide swung silently out into the room. "Follow me, Mrs. Spaulding."

"If we're going to skulk about in secret passageways together," Diana murmured as she stepped through, "I think you'd better start calling me by my given name."

Jane lit a lantern that had been stored in a niche just inside the opening. Its flickering beams revealed a narrow landing and a winding metal staircase leading down. "This way, Diana. At the bottom there's a peephole into the Chinese parlor."

Diana descended gingerly and put her eye to the spot Jane indicated. "What keeps them from seeing a hole on the other side?"

"You're looking through the eyes of the portrait of Elmira that hangs over the mantel."

The idea made Diana's stomach crawl, but she was too curious about the madams who'd come to call to forego the chance to learn all she could about them. "Who is the plump blonde wearing the diamond encrusted cross at her throat?"

"That's Mattie Silks. She'll likely do all the talking. She owns two houses on Holladay Street, connected at the rear, one red brick and one frame. They say every dress she owns has two pockets, the left for gold coins and the right for her ivory-handled pistol."

"Lovely. She's standing next to a very tall woman with black hair and emerald earrings."

"That's Jennie Rogers. She runs four parlor houses. She wants to add the house Eva Lewis runs. Eva's the one standing at Jennie's elbow—she always is. There's a walkway to the rear between Eva's house and one of Jennie's."

Diana's gaze shifted to a fourth woman. "Who's the restless one pacing the parlor?" She was younger than Mattie or Jennie but not as striking in appearance . . . unless you took into account the long, black cigar clamped between her painted lips.

"That's Gouldie Gould. Her business is located on Lawrence, between Twentieth and Twenty-first Streets. She gets away with setting up there by calling herself a dressmaker."

Diana had heard the euphemism "ladies' tailor" before, but "dressmaker" was new to her. "And the demure young brunette with the white poodle?"

"Pearl Adams." Jane hesitated. "She moved here from Leadville a year or so ago. Has a lot of very rich and exclusive clients."

Diana winced at the mention of Leadville, where Evan had died, and was thoughtful as she left the peephole and made her way back upstairs. She didn't speak until Jane had closed the secret door behind them. "Those women are the leaders of this community."

"In a manner of speaking."

Diana paused long enough in her mother's rooms to check her appearance in the mirror. She adjusted the cameo at her throat, then took a deep breath and exited the suite to descend the main staircase. With Jane in attendance, she swept into the Chinese parlor as if she were perfectly accustomed to playing hostess to a room full of courtesans.

Her gaze went first to the portrait over the mantel. What she saw there had her blinking in surprise. This likeness of her mother showed an Elmira Diana had never met, a flashy, vibrant woman wearing low-cut red silk, elaborately dressed hair, and a secretive smile.

She fit right in with the other women in the parlor.

The blonde Jane had identified as Mattie Silks stepped forward. Slightly under average height, she had blue eyes, a creamy complexion untouched by rouge, and a full underlip. She gave Diana a smile that appeared friendly while she introduced herself and the others.

"Belle would have been here too," she added, "but she had a slight accident yesterday while attending the horse races in Overland Park."

"What can I do for you ladies?" Diana asked, well aware of the irony in calling them that. The air was clogged with strong perfume. Eau de Cologne warred with French violet, heliotrope with Esprit de Rose, and all four scents clashed with the stench of Gouldie's long black cigar.

"Champagne for starters," Mattie said with a low throaty laugh. "I never drink anything else."

Jane clapped her hands and to Diana's amazement a small boy in a loose blue blouse and trousers came in to wait on them. The clothes, together with the color of his skin and the way he wore his long black hair in a pigtail, marked him as Chinese, but the shape of his eyes betrayed his mixed parentage.

"A nice match for the decor," Mattie said, peering down her nose at the boy.

"This is Ning," Jane said. "Elmira hired him to do odd jobs and run errands."

"How odd?" Eva's salacious chuckle sent a cold chill down Diana's spine.

"Is he for sale?" Mattie wanted to know. "I have an acquaintance who's looking for a matched pair, and I hear the Windsor has a Chinese boy in one of the bars."

"He's an *employee*." The acerbic note in Diana's voice made more than one eyebrow arch, but she did not apologize for the show of temper.

"Go on, Mattie," Jennie taunted. "Hire him away."

Mattie's eyes darkened, and one hand covered with a black kid glove, laced, tipped, and striped in silver, crept across the folds of her dark red moire skirt to slide into a hidden pocket. Remembering what Jane had said about the pistol Mattie kept on her person, Diana held her breath, but the tense moment passed when all Mattie did was jingle a few coins together.

"I've better things to do with my money," she said, accepting the champagne Ning offered her and sipping with apparent pleasure.

It was at that moment that the name Mattie Silks triggered Diana's memory. Mattie was one of the two women who'd participated in that duel she'd heard about as a girl. She didn't know whether to be impressed or afraid.

Just as disconcerting was her realization that, although they sipped champagne and other, stronger libations, on the surface these women resembled nothing so much as a group of society matrons gathered to plan some charitable endeavor and gossip about their neighbors. To a woman, they wore gowns of grosgrain and moire, cashmere and faille, expensive gloves and shoes and hats, and jewelry that put anything Diana owned to shame. Pearl Adams in particular was decked out in a splendid ensemble right out of the pages of the latest issue of *La Mode Illustrée*.

"I hear you're paying Minnie a hundred dollars a month to lease her place," Pearl said to Jennie.

Eva looked startled. "Didn't offer *me* that much," she muttered.

"Don't intend to, either," Jennie snapped.

Diana hastily wiped the bemused expression from her face. Her momentary fancy had shattered the moment Pearl had opened her mouth. These were businesswomen. Entrepreneurs. Admirable in their own way, but *never* ladies.

Directing her piercing gaze towards Diana, Jennie said, "Don't start to think this place will get you much."

"It won't get me anything. It's my mother's business, not mine."

"Has Ed Leeves come by to see you yet?" Pearl asked.

"Who is Ed Leeves?"

Jennie snickered. "A *friend* of your mother's. He's a piece of work, Ed is. Fingers in a lot of pies."

They all thought that comment uproariously funny.

"Miss Diana here's got a friend, too," Eva said, giving her a sly look from beneath the brim of an elaborate bonnet, constructed of straw, lace, and velvet ribbons. "Matt Hastings gave her a ride in his trap this morning."

"Handy," Mattie said. "Him being a lawyer and all."

"Wrong kind for what Elmira needs," Jennie chimed in. "Not that any lawyer's going to do her any good."

"At least he'd be sympathetic," Pearl said. "He owns a dance hall up to Torrence."

This was news to Diana, but not a subject she chose to pursue at the moment. She was more interested in getting information on her mother's predicament. "Everyone seems to assume my mother will be convicted of murder. Why don't you tell me why?"

"She threatened your father," Pearl said. "Everybody knows that."

"When? Why? With what?" When no one answered, she turned to Jane. "Do you know anything about this alleged threat?"

Jane shook her head, her face twisted with emotion. "If only I'd seen her come in that night. Then we'd *know.*"

"Distracted, were you?" Jennie imbued the words with enough sarcasm to make Jane flush.

"The hotel was reserved all that night for a private party. A rich cattleman in town for the week took over the whole place to entertain friends. Since I wasn't needed at the door, Elmira said I might have a visitor of my own. You met him, Diana. Alan Kent." Hot color rushed into her cheeks when she said his name. "He's a nice young man," she added defensively. "We didn't do anything but talk."

As one, the madams laughed.

"Something wrong with him then!" Eva slapped her knee and hooted.

"Do any of you know anything about my mother that could help her case?" Diana asked. What Jane did with Alan Kent was none of her business.

"None of us like your ma much," Mattie admitted.

"She's got a snooty way about her," Jennie agreed.

"But she's a good businesswoman. Built up something mighty fine here." Gouldie looked at each of the others as if gathering support. "None of us want to see Ed Leeves take it over."

"What *do* you want?"

"Going out of business would be okay," Mattie said with another low chuckle.

"Or you could sell to one of us," Jennie countered.

"I've told you. I can't sell what isn't mine." She could close the place down. "Keeping a lewd house" was against the law, punishable by arrest and a hefty fine. But in spite of the nature of her mother's business, Diana was reluctant to cut off Elmira Torrence's only source of income arbitrarily. "Wouldn't it be better to prove she's innocent? That way things would go back to the way they were."

"Easier said than done." Gouldie puffed out a billow of smoke and narrowed her eyes at Diana. "What did you have in mind?"

"At the moment I'm just gathering information. You can help me there, if you will. You . . . hear things."

"That we do," said Pearl, sending Diana a conspiratorial wink. The poodle, resplendent in a jeweled collar attached to a lead made of gold links, gave a yap of agreement.

Diana started to ask if any of them had known her father, then rephrased the question. "What do you know about my father's enemies? Who would have wanted to kill him?"

"Your friend Matt Hastings, for one," Mattie said. "He and your father were partners in a mine in Torrence for awhile, until Torrence cheated him."

"Could be anyone Torrence ever did business with," Pearl said. "He was a nasty piece of work."

"Do you base that opinion on personal experience?" Eva taunted her.

"He never came to my place. Not once. But I used to visit with Elmira now and again. She sure had reason to know what he was like."

"Did my father ever visit her here?" Diana asked.

"Never set foot on Holladay Street as far as I know," Jenny said. "Too snooty by half."

"But he used to own the Elmira," Diana protested.

No one said anything.

"Why was he at the Windsor that night?"

"Had a mistress there," Mattie told her. "That's what I heard from one of my regulars, anyway."

But no one knew who she was or where she'd gotten to, or if they did they weren't admitting it. The best anyone could do was give her the name of the assistant manager who'd called in the police when the body was found and make a few suggestions on the best way to get information out of him.

Pearl Adams was the last to leave. She turned back at the door to offer one last piece of advice. "Watch your back, honey," she warned. "I figure Elmira killed him, but if she didn't, then there's someone out there who wants everyone to keep on thinking she did. Man like that's not goin' to take kindly to you provin' otherwise."

ഇറയ

Where is she?" Ben Northcote's hands itched to circle Horatio Foxe's scrawny neck and squeeze until his eyes bulged.

Foxe shot to his feet behind the bulk of an oversized oak desk. The cheroot he'd had clamped between his yellowed teeth dropped unnoticed into the clutter of papers covering most of the scarred wooden surface.

After a long, sleepless journey by rail, Ben had reached Diana's boarding house on Tenth Street only to be told that she'd left eight days earlier, bag and baggage. Her landlady, Mrs. Curran, had confirmed what she'd said in her reply to Ben's telegram. Diana had departed in company with Horatio Foxe. Mrs. Curran had no idea where they'd gone.

"She'd had bad news of some sort," Mrs. Curran had added.

Hearing that, Ben had lost no time hailing a Hansom to take him to Park Row, where most of the city's major newspapers, as well as the *Independent Intelligencer,* based their operations.

"Where is she?" Ben slammed the door closed behind him, making the glass rattle ominously, and strode across the room. He gave Foxe no opportunity to escape before he slammed both hands flat amid the litter on the desk. A thin plume of smoke was already rising from the haphazard pile of papers.

Ignoring it, Foxe puffed out his chest. His shoulders went back and his head shot forward. "Confound it, Northcote! You've no call to come busting in here and raising a ruckus. I've done nothing to Diana Spaulding but try to help her out."

"Where is she, then? Why hasn't she written?" Ben backed off, but his clenched fists underscored the threat in his voice. "I'm prepared to beat the truth out of you. In fact, I'd enjoy it."

The smaller man winced. "That won't be necessary."

"Talk fast, then, before I give in to the impulse to toss you out that convenient bank of windows behind your desk."

"She's in Denver."

He snatched up his smoldering cheroot, slapping at the corner of a telegram and a sheet of foolscap until he'd extinguished all the stray embers. When he was certain nothing else would catch fire, he dropped back into his chair and regarded Ben warily over the glowing tip of the cigar.

"Be sure you tell her that when you see her. That you had to threaten me before I told you anything. Although, technically, all I promised was that I wouldn't *write* a word about her business to you when you contacted me."

"Denver?" Ben prompted him. *Why Denver?* he wanted to shout. It was like a knife in the heart to learn she was so very far away. The distance made her lack of communication even more inexplicable.

"That's where she was bound when she left here. Denver, Colorado."

"Why?" Deprived of the physical release of pommeling Foxe, Ben was reduced to cowing him with a fulminating glare. It was a poor substitute for action.

"I take it you don't know anything about her parents."

Ben felt a stab of dread. "Family matters," her telegram had said. But for some reason he'd expected that to mean the late, unlamented Evan Spaulding. "Her parents? They cut her off. She doesn't like to speak of them."

"No, she wouldn't. Oh, sit down, man! You'll give me a crick in my blasted neck staring up at you."

Grudgingly, Ben complied. That this was about Diana's parents threw him into even greater confusion. It made no sense to him that she hadn't asked for his help or advice when she'd all but agreed to marry him. Surely whatever skeletons resided in her family's closet were no worse than the many secrets the Northcotes kept.

Foxe tipped his chair back and took a moment to collect his thoughts before he asked, "Ever hear the name William 'Timberline' Torrence?"

"No."

"Diana's father. Mean cuss, from what I hear. M'sister met him once." Foxe blew a smoke ring at the ceiling.

So she'd been born Diana Torrence. It seemed strange to think of her as anyone but Diana Spaulding, though he did think Diana Northcote would suit her even better. "Did Torrence send for her?"

Ben supposed she'd have rushed off to Denver if her father had dangled the hope of a reconciliation under her nose, although that didn't explain why she had been so terse in her telegram. Or why she'd apparently instructed Horatio Foxe not to reply to any of Ben's predictable demands for information.

Foxe's chair landed on all four legs with a thump. He took the cigar out of his mouth and ran ink-stained fingers through a shock of sand-colored hair. The ironic gleam in his eyes had been replaced by a somber expression. "Torrence was murdered."

"Good God!" Ben came to his feet in a rush, then stood still, arms akimbo, at a loss what to do or say next.

"It gets worse."

By the time Foxe finished providing details, Ben stared unseeing at the tall buildings visible through the office window. Why hadn't Diana told him what had happened? Surely she didn't believe he'd think less of her for anything her parents had done? That was insulting to him.

"I haven't heard from Diana since she left New York," Foxe said after a short silence, "but I have learned a bit more about her mother's situation. Seems she's been running a bordello ever since the divorce. I don't mind telling you I'm a little worried about Diana. Must have been a shock when she got there and found out about *that.*"

It certainly took Ben aback. He lowered himself into the chair once more and met Foxe's penetrating stare. "Diana is a remarkably open-minded female, and I have reason to know she can look at a 'soiled dove' and see an individual woman."

Foxe's eyes narrowed. "Could you handle learning something like that about *your* mother?"

Ben didn't answer. He didn't even try to imagine such a situation. "What about the murder charge?"

Foxe shrugged, but there was a worried look on his face. "Elmira Torrence took off before the police could arrest her. She's disappeared without a trace." He extinguished the stub of his cigar and began to swivel his chair back and forth.

"If there's something more, spit it out." Ben couldn't think of much that would be worse than the murder of one parent by the other, but something was obviously preying on Foxe's mind.

"Denver grew fast, and so did its underbelly." He stopped swiveling and met Ben's gaze head on. "Politicians and lawmen are well paid to look the other way when it comes to what goes on in the saloons and gambling halls and brothels. According to my sources, Elmira Torrence has long-standing ties to one of the most influential of these . . . gentlemen, a fellow known as Big Ed. Edward Leeves. They grew up in the same small town. Both his parents and hers were in the hotel business. Elmira hooked up with him again after her divorce. If she's been involved in his business ventures, above and beyond running a whorehouse, and Diana pokes her nose in where it doesn't belong in an attempt to locate her mother . . . ."

Ben bolted to his feet as Foxe let the thought trail off. Diana *would* "poke her nose in" and they both knew it.

"You can get to Denver in five days if you leave right away and travel straight through. Diana herself can't have reached there sooner than Wednesday or Thursday."

This was Saturday. Ben met Foxe's grim smile with a grimace of his own. There was no telling how much trouble Diana could get herself into with an entire week's head start.

"But I suppose you can't just drop everything and go after her," Foxe said with mock sympathy. "Not with your responsibilities at home, and all." He tipped back in his chair, chewing on the end of an unlit cheroot. "How is your brother?"

"Better."

The curt reply seemed to amuse Foxe. "Good. Good. Well, you go on back to Maine and take care of him and your other patients. Perhaps I'll go West and lend Diana a hand. There's a story in it, and she won't want to write it." He nodded, as if coming to a decision, and slanted a sidelong glance at Ben. "Shall I tell her you'll be waiting for her when we come back East? Perhaps I can suggest that she send you regular reports by telegram in the interim."

Ben held onto his temper by a thread. "Telegrams and letters are most useful, but no substitute for talking to someone in person."

"Indeed. For that reason neither would do your brother much good if you were in a distant city when he needed medical assistance. Are you sure he's in the care of a competent physician?"

Ben remembered Aaron as he'd last seen him, on the mend but so determined to get back to his painting that he might well break his promise to take things slowly. He pictured Maggie, so wrapped up in her own fey world that he wasn't entirely certain she'd notice if Aaron had a relapse.

"You took an oath as a physician." Foxe's whispered taunts echoed the voice of Ben's own conscience. "You have an obligation to your patients, as well as to your blood kin."

"I made a promise to Diana, too. And to myself."

"Ah, yes. Our strong, brave, self-sufficient Diana, so determined to see things through on her own. When it comes right down to it, Northcote, I don't believe you really have any choice at all."

∓∓∓

Ning?" Diana called, stepping out onto a back stoop.

He was too far away to hear her but she could still see him. The blue blouse was distinctive. He'd be easy to follow, she decided, and if she caught up with him now to ask him to do a small favor for her, it would save him the trouble of another trip later, when he got back from running Jane's errands. Diana delayed only long enough to borrow a shawl from the peg just inside the kitchen door before setting out in pursuit.

The boy moved faster than she'd anticipated, and she had to scurry to keep him in sight. He slipped down a side street, hurried along a narrow lane, and turned again into an alley crowded with two-story wooden buildings. Diana rounded the last corner and looked about in bewilderment. Orientals in blue cotton were everywhere. Men and women as well as boys and girls. Ning had vanished, a needle in a haystack, lost in a crowd of similar faces.

Diana froze, feeling as if she'd stepped into another country. Even the smells were different here. Herbs she didn't recognize by sight or scent were offered in the shop nearest her. From the store just beyond came a tantalizingly exotic aroma of cooking food.

The buildings were jammed together, a church up against a restaurant, a saloon beside a laundry. As she moved slowly forward, entranced by her surroundings, she caught a whiff of borax, sulphur, and lye, all of which were used in bleaching.

A clatter arose, signalling the approach of a train. She heard it slow as it prepared to stop at the nearby depot. The engine groaned and spewed noxious smoke into the air.

When the din died away, Diana found herself listening to voices, all speaking in a foreign tongue. The high-pitched, singsong words did not seem threatening, but she'd taken only a few more steps before she smelled a faint, sweet odor running beneath all the other scents.

She knew at once what it must be. One of these close-packed buildings housed an opium den.

Suddenly all the horrific tales Diana had been told about "Hop Alley" came flooding back to her. She'd been away at school during Denver's notorious Chinese riot, but she'd heard the stories. San Francisco had a large Chinese population of its own, and its residents had followed events in Colorado with considerable alarm.

She stopped, looking for a way back to Holladay Street. It couldn't be more than a block away, but she was hemmed in by buildings and people, and every eye, or so it seemed to Diana, was watching her to see what she would do next.

A band of youths began to close in on her. They moved with the matching strides of a pack of wolves on the hunt. The one in the lead grinned, but it was neither a pleasant expression nor a reassuring one. She almost expected to see fangs flash.

"I am looking for a boy named Ning," Diana announced. The words came out sounding a bit breathless but at least she'd spoken clearly. "He works for my mother."

Did they understand English? They certainly didn't trouble to speak it. The youths exchanged several comments in their own language, leaving Diana at a loss to translate the remarks. When they laughed, she decided she didn't *want* to know precisely what they'd said. Their lack of respect was clear enough.

"Ning," she said again. "He works at the Elmira Hotel."

"Long gone," a nasal voice informed her.

Diana whirled around to find a man dressed in colorful silk

robes standing in an open doorway. It had been closed when she passed by. The Chinese characters above it were flanked by English words: GUN WA CHINESE REMEDIES.

"I am Gun Wa, the great Chinese physician," the man said. "If you have the entry fee, you may take the underground passageway to Holladay Street."

One of the boys voiced a loud protest in Chinese. Gun Wa shouted back in the same language.

"Or I can be leavin' you to them."

Diana's eyes narrowed. The sinister leer accompanying the offer made her skin crawl, but there was something odd about his accent. For just an instant, he'd sounded more Irish than Chinese.

"A passageway?"

"Ten dollars to go through to safety, and for fifty cents more I'll throw in a rare herbal remedy, guaranteed to cure anything." From the silken folds of his wide sleeves he produced an amber bottle about seven inches high.

Pockets inside the lining, Diana thought. A theatrical trick.

Behind him, the interior of the building was in darkness. Diana had no idea what she'd be getting into if she entered. Would she ever come out again?

"I don't have ten dollars," she said in a small voice.

He looked her up and down. "Jewelry?"

"I have a bank draft I haven't cashed yet. I don't suppose you'd extend credit?"

She was uncomfortably aware of the band of youths at her back. When she heard a rush of footsteps coming her way, she opened her mouth to promise Gun Wa the entire hundred-dollar draft if he'd help her escape.

A small, blue-clad figure barreled into her before she could vocalize the offer. "Mrs. Diana!" Ning cried, grabbing her hand. "You come with me now."

As if by magic, the crowd melted away. The older boys stepped aside to let them pass, satisfying their pride with a few incomprehensible taunts. Gun Wa disappeared back inside his shop.

"You don't look back." Ning said, walking faster. "Tough place," he added as they left Hop Alley behind. "They knock a man in the head for two bits."

"That Gun Wa," Diana said, taking one last look over her shoulder in spite of Ning's warning. "Is he really a physician?"

Ning's big round eyes laughed up at her. "He not even Chinese."

CHAPTER SIX

§ﾝ᠒

Diana and Ning were almost back at the Elmira before the boy spoke again. "You say you look for me."

"Yes. I thought you were going to one of the shops on Larimer Street for Miss Jane. There was something I wanted you to pick up for me."

It seemed unimportant now, but she'd intended to ask him to buy copies of the *Times,* the *Tribune,* and the *Republican.* She thought she might be able to discover, by reading the stories those Denver newspapers ran, which one would be most sympathetic to her mother's cause. There had really been no need to chase after Ning. It had been a foolish, almost disastrous impulse. She could have purchased the latest editions herself. She would, when she went out again this afternoon.

"Best herbs in Hop Alley," Ning said, as they passed through the back door into the Elmira's kitchen.

The cook, a sour-faced, rail-thin woman named Louise, looked up from a range with six lids and a large oven, then quickly averted her eyes. Jane was there, too, supervising the night maid as she loaded covered dishes onto a tray. Ning produced a newspaper-wrapped parcel from inside the front of his shirt and presented it to Jane.

"I help serve morning meal now," he said.

"Tell me about Ning," Diana said when he'd disappeared into the dining room.

Jane hesitated. "What do you want to know?"

"Is he an orphan?"

"As good as. His mother was a prostitute. She's dead, but her sister lives in Hop Alley. God knows how *she* makes her living."

"And his father?"

"No one knows who he was. A white man, obviously."

"Is that his only name? Just Ning?"

Jane frowned as if trying to remember what she'd been told. "It's a nickname, I think. They called him after the province in China his family came from. Ning's the short form. We probably couldn't pronounce the real thing. Are you planning to eat with us this morning?"

Diana accepted the change of subject and the invitation to join the others in the dining room. The clock was just chiming the half hour when she and Jane sat down at the table. The others had already taken their places.

This was the perfect opportunity to become better acquainted with her mother's "girls," Diana decided. So far, she hadn't exchanged more than a few words with any of them. To avoid interfering in the bordello's business, she'd spent most of the previous afternoon and evening in Elmira's private suite.

She sent a tentative smile in the direction of the two young women she had met for the first time yesterday. Maybelle was a skinny little creature with straw-colored hair while Chastity, a brunette with dark eyes and full lips, had a more voluptuous figure. As were they all, these two were simply dressed in respectable garments that made them look as if they *were* just residents in a young ladies' boarding house. More of Elmira's influence, Diana assumed.

When Georgia the night maid, who appeared to work all day,

too, had placed the last of the platters filled with food Louise had prepared on the table, Jane cleared her throat and said grace. "Elmira insists," she explained when she lifted her bowed head and caught Diana's look of surprise.

Red Katie, to Diana's right, passed the eggs. Diana helped herself to a generous portion and continued to add to the bounty on her plate as one dish after another came her way. Consuming a hearty meal before she faced her next challenge wasn't a bad idea. In fact, she had the feeling she'd need all the strength she could muster if she was to carry out her plan for the afternoon.

First, however, she must discover what she could learn from the women at the table with her. For the most part they were ignoring her, carrying on private conversations in soft voices while they ate.

"One ounce of white wax, two ounces of strained honey, and two ounces of juice of lily bulbs," Long Tall Linda said to Honeycomb. "Melt 'em and stir 'em together and you get a first-rate remedy for wrinkled skin."

Diana turned to Red Katie. "I believe my mother was framed for my father's murder. If she was, anything any of you may have noticed that night could be significant."

Red Katie shoved a lock of hair behind one ear and gave her a hard look. "We were busy. All of us."

"Not every moment, surely."

"Had to entertain for a private party," said Strawberry Sue. "All the guests had brass checks, so neither Elmira or Jane had to be here. The professor just locked the door after they were all in."

"Brass checks?"

"Tokens," Red Katie explained. "Usually they have a design on one side and lettering on the other."

"They are used as a medium of exchange," Jane said. "A customer can purchase one to give to a girl for one silver dollar, or buy six for five dollars. The girls turn in their tokens in the morning and receive cash in return. Very handy for making sure the fee's been paid."

"How is it done otherwise?"

"Fella pays up front for what he wants," said Big Nose Nellie. She looked even younger in daylight and without cosmetics. "Then he comes in and picks his girl. But sometimes they pay for one thing and want another."

"Now a usual Wednesday night, we'd have had some free time," Maybelle said. She had a nasal voice that grated on the nerves. "Even be bored sometimes."

"How do you pass the time when you have no customers waiting?"

"The professor plays tunes for us," Red Katie said. "Piano. Harmonica. And he whistles some, too."

"Where is he this morning? Does he live elsewhere?" It occurred to Diana that she didn't even know his real name.

"This is his day to get a haircut," Jane said.

"And we play games," Maybelle interrupted, answering Diana's original question about pastimes. "Pigs in Clover. Pan."

Diana knew the first. The object of Pigs in Clover was to manipulate five little lead pellets into the center cavity of a round, glass-covered box, a trick more difficult than it sounded. "What's Pan?" she asked.

"Panguingui," Jane said. "It's a card game."

"An excellent card game." Katie twirled a lock of her bright red hair around one finger as she explained. "It uses twelve decks of cards and is nicely complicated, but the best part is that a player can leave at any time and return again later to take up where she left off."

"No Pan that night," Big Nose Nellie said, "but I did see Elmira come in. Must have been around midnight."

Diana's heart rate speeded up. Had that been before or after the murder? She wasn't sure. Her father's body hadn't been discovered until the next morning. She'd have to find out when he'd last been seen alive the night before.

"You saw her come in?" Jane echoed. "You never said so to the police."

"Why should I? Besides, no one asked me till now."

"What else did you see?" Diana bent forward, perching on the very edge of her seat, eyes riveted to Nellie, who sat across the table from her. "Was she acting oddly? Did she look strange in any way?"

"Was blood dripping off her hands?" Maryam's sarcastic tone was like a blast of frigid air blowing through the room. Once again, incongruously, she was dressed entirely in a soft shade of pink.

Nellie made a childish face at her. "She looked just like she always does." Then her brow furrowed as if in bewilderment. "She was wearing those pretty gloves of hers, the ones with the lace trim, but that wasn't what the police took away."

"What did the glove the police found look like?" Diana scarcely dared breathe while she waited for an answer.

"It was kid," said Red Katie. "The bloodstained glove was plain cream color kid, same as everybody owns."

"Then I could be right. Someone might have put that glove in Mother's suite to incriminate her. And it needn't have been the night Father was killed. It could have been the next day. Any time before the police arrived."

Maryam's snort cut short Diana's musings. "All the world was here that morning. Soon as word got around that he was dead. Condolence calls." She laughed.

Thoughtful, Diana took a sip of her coffee, found it had gone cold, and set the cup aside. "You exaggerate, I am sure. What visitors called? And where did Mother receive them?"

"In her suite," Red Katie said, regarding Diana with new respect. "You're right. Someone could have framed her. But why would they?"

"You think it was one of us," Maryam said in a flat voice. "Blame a whore. Why not?"

"I'd rather blame the person who actually did it."

"Mattie Silks came," Katie said. "And Pearl Adams. Ed Leeves."

"Not Miranda Torrence?"

"Not likely she'd set foot in here," Jane said.

"No, I suppose not. But now we have a place to start. Nellie, you must come with me to the police. We will tell them what you saw and you can explain about Mother's visitors, too. That should persuade them to look at other suspects."

After a stark moment of silence, during which Nellie simply goggled at her, Jane coughed delicately. "I'm sorry, Diana, but neither what Nellie saw nor our speculations will help Elmira."

"Why not?"

"Because the police won't take my word for anything," Nellie told her. "I'm a whore, remember?"

"They wouldn't believe Elmira when she denied being at the Windsor Hotel, or when she said that glove wasn't hers. Why should they believe one of us?" The question came from Honeycomb, who punctuated her comment by popping a last piece of toast into her mouth. Her hair was down this morning and was long enough for her to sit on.

Were they right? Diana hoped not, but wasn't that why Elmira had felt she only had two choices—allow herself to be arrested or run away?

"We're soiled doves," Long Tall Linda said. "Dishonest, dirty, and beyond redemption."

"No, no," Red Katie said. "Frail sisters." Under cover of the general laughter, she leaned close to Diana's ear and whispered, "Those are the terms the do-gooders use, the ones trying to reform us."

"How do you refer to yourselves?"

"I like brides of the multitude," Katie said after thinking about it for a moment.

"Ladies of the Line is better," said Maryam.

"No. Sporting women," Sue chimed in with her infectious grin.

"Boarders." Jane's disapproving tone and stern expression put an end to the banter. "You know how Elmira feels about the subject. Young women who live in the Elmira Hotel are boarders."

⊱⊰

"The hotel has three hundred rooms on five floors, all with fireplaces," boasted Diana's guide, an assistant manager at the Windsor, who'd told her to call him Charlie. His jowly face was perched on a thick neck tightly contained by a starched collar and a four-in-hand tie. "Amenities include a swimming pool and steam baths, three elevators, gas lighting, steam heat, two artesian wells to provide water, and mercurial alarms set in the ceiling of each room to notify the desk if the temperature rises above 120 degrees." He used one thick finger to indicate a small device some twelve feet above their heads.

Diana poked her head into the bathroom and saw that her father had taken a suite with its own tub.

"One of sixty in the hotel," Charlie said in a cheerful voice when he noted the object of her interest.

He should sound pleased with himself, Diana thought. He was making a nice profit giving fifteen-minute tours of the murder scene at a dollar a head. It was an outrageous fee, considering that four bits more paid for an entire night's lodging at that other Windsor Hotel, the one in Bangor, Maine.

Diana sighed. The strangest things made her think of Ben. She missed him terribly and wished he were here to help her question Charlie, but there was no sense in crying for the moon. She was on her own and must make the best of it.

"Was the man who was murdered a visitor to Denver?" she asked Charlie, feigning ignorance and trying to convey a hint of nervousness at the same time.

"Oh, no, madam. He had a house here. But Mr. Torrence used the Windsor for business meetings, since he didn't keep an office in Denver. He had a silver mine and other interests in a little town in the mountains—place he named Torrence after himself. I'm told he was planning to conduct interviews here the next day."

How long would it be, she wondered, before the owners of the hotel heard about Charlie's activities and sent him packing? Still, his greed served her purpose. She smiled, prepared to get her money's worth. "What post did he have open?"

For a moment Charlie looked annoyed, though whether at her for asking or himself for not knowing the answer, Diana could not say. "What does it matter? When word got out he'd been killed, no one showed up."

"A pity there were no papers lying about for you to examine. Surely he'd made notes on the subject."

Charlie fiddled with his tie. "None I saw."

"What happened to the things the police took away?"

"Widow got 'em all, I expect." Nervous fingers shifted to his collar and he ran one under the edge, as if he wished he could loosen it. His face shone with sweat.

Outside, the temperature had been climbing towards eighty degrees when Diana arrived at the hotel, though a light breeze had kept the day comfortable. In this unused, closed-up room, however, where the sun had been pouring in all morning through large east-facing windows, it was decidedly stuffy.

Uncomfortable enough to explain Charlie's obvious fidgeting? Diana didn't think so.

"Where exactly was the body found?" she asked.

"I'll show you." Charlie mopped his brow with a handkerchief and, recovering his aplomb, strutted up to the oversized bed. He pointed to a spot beside it. "You can still see a few bloodstains on the Brussels carpet if you look close."

Since his suggestion made her queasy, Diana stayed put. She had hoped to be able to examine this crime scene with the same detachment she'd maintained on assignment for the *Independent Intelligencer* in Manhattan.

In a strained voice, she forced out her next question. "At what time was he found and by whom?"

"One of the maids discovered the body when she came to clean the room at around ten the next morning."

"Newly stabbed?" Diana asked. If that were the case, then her mother hadn't done it.

But Charlie shook his head. "He'd been dead awhile. Police think twelve hours or more."

Before midnight, then. That was not good for Elmira's case. "So, a maid found him. Poor creature. What a shock that must have been for her."

"Had hysterics over it." Charlie rocked back onto his heels and flashed a grin at Diana over his shoulder. "An elevator operator heard her screaming and came to investigate. Then he called me."

"So you saw the body before it was taken away?"

"Oh, yes." Warming to his topic, his earlier uneasiness apparently vanquished, he rubbed his pudgy hands together. "Lying on his back, he was, eyes open and staring at the ceiling. He'd been stabbed two or three times and still had the blade stuck in his chest."

Diana's stomach churned at the graphic picture he painted, but she forced away the knowledge that they were talking about her father. She was a reporter. This was just another crime. She must maintain her composure until she had the whole story.

To give herself time to regain control of her seesawing emotions, Diana returned to the parlor of the suite. Why had her father been killed in the bedroom if he'd used the suite for business meetings? Were the madams right? Had these rooms at the Windsor really been a love nest?

She turned on Charlie. "Did he have a . . . companion living here?"

"Certainly not! This is a respectable hotel."

Diana had deliberately let good old Charlie think she was a wealthy hotel guest with a ghoulish interest in murder. Since the crime, several others of that ilk and a few local society women, as well as numerous curious gentlemen and at least one bordello keeper, had taken advantage of the "tour" he offered. Diana had no doubt there would be more, especially if her mother were caught and brought to trial.

"The maid who first found him—does she have a name?"

"Name? What do you want to know that for?" Suddenly wary, Charlie's deep set brown eyes hardened into a suspicious stare.

"I'd like to talk to her."

"Why?"

"Maybe she knows more about what went on in this suite than you do."

"That's it!" Face flushed, he made little shooing motions at her. "Nobody knows anything else. You've seen all there is to see. Time to go."

"I don't think so." Evading him, she ensconced herself on the sofa and sent a glittering smile in his direction. "Why don't you sit down, Charlie, and make yourself comfortable while you answer the rest of my questions?"

"What? What?" Dancing in agitation, his face rapidly turning puce, he cast a nervous look towards the door to the corridor.

"Sit down." She pointed to the chair opposite her. The school marm tone and the jabbing finger had him scurrying to obey.

"Who are you? What do you want?"

"Information, Charlie. That's all."

"Hell's bells! You're one of those female newspaper reporters, aren't you?"

"I have had a few things published." It was a relief to tell part of the truth, and better still that her profession seemed to scare him.

"Don't tell me you're from the Pinky?"

She smiled slightly as she realized he meant the pink-paged *National Police Gazette.* "All right. I won't tell you that." She reached into a pocket, pulled out a cloth-covered notebook, and flipped it open to a blank page.

"Doomed. I'm doomed."

"Not if you cooperate. There's no need for anyone to know about your lucrative little sideline so long as you answer my questions honestly. Now, you were about to tell me the name of the maid who found the body, and where I can find her."

He didn't even offer token resistance before providing the names of the maid and the elevator operator and the location of their lodgings. Both had rooms in the "Little Windsor."

"It's just across the alley," he said, "a three-story building connected to the hotel by a tunnel. We keep it just for hotel staff. Many of them live there. Very convenient."

"Very." Diana tapped one end of her pencil against her chin and looked Charlie right in the eyes. "Just as a mistress living in these rooms would have been very convenient for Mr. Torrence."

"Why won't you believe me? The Windsor is a respectable hotel!" She maintained eye contact until he grew flustered and looked away, once more running a finger under his too-tight collar and swallowing hard. "I *told* you. Mr. Torrence hired the suite for business meetings. He had no office in Denver."

"He had a house. He could have met colleagues there."

"Home is for the family!" Charlie sounded so sincerely affronted that she almost believed him.

"Most influential men aren't averse to inviting business acquaintances to dinner. Are you implying he had unsavory associates? I delight in scandal, Charlie. And," she added in a sly voice, "I can make a story out of an assistant manager who gives tours of murder scenes if I have nothing better to write about."

"Scandalous enough what did happen," he shot back. "Mr. Torrence, a highly respected member of this community, a pillar of society, was killed by the faithless female he'd divorced for adultery." He lowered his voice to a conspiratorial whisper. "She keeps a bawdy house."

"Nothing so fatal as a fallen woman," Diana muttered, but she managed to keep a look of salacious interest on her face.

Charlie's head bobbed up and down and his worried expression cleared. "Torrence met her here more than once. His former wife. I saw them together."

"He met her *here?* In this suite?"

"Well, no. Not that I know of. How would I? But once they were in the main dining room and another time in the ballroom and I heard them shouting at each other."

"When? How long before the murder?"

"Oh, well . . . it was sometime last year. Near Christmas. But there was always bad blood between them. She'd hated him for years."

Diana thought about asking just how long Charlie had known her parents but decided to keep her focus on the key issue. "Did she threaten his life?"

"She said she'd make him pay for the way he'd treated her."

Not the same thing at all, Diana thought, relieved. "Did you see Elmira Torrence here the night of the murder? Did anyone?"

"Well, she must have been here, mustn't she? She killed him."

"But how did the police decide she was the one who did it? Was there some evidence left here? Something of hers? *Did someone see her?*"

"When they went to her . . . er . . . place of business, they found clothes spattered with blood."

A glove, Diana thought irritably. A single glove that might have belonged to anyone. It made much more sense to believe some enemy of Elmira's had planted that glove in her suite. She had business rivals—witness the other madams. And then there was the mysterious Ed Leeves.

"If no one saw her in this hotel that night, how can you be so sure she's guilty?"

"Stands to reason," Charlie insisted. "She ran away, didn't she?"

Diana ground her back teeth together and fought to hold onto her temper. "Did the second Mrs. Torrence know her husband kept these rooms?"

Charlie blinked at her, as if taken aback by the unexpected question.

"Why come here rather than rent office space or use his lawyer's office? In fact, since Mr. Torrence was so wealthy, I find it odd he did not own a single building in Denver's business district."

"Whether he did or not, he liked to stay at the Windsor."

"He chose to do . . . business . . . here often?" Diana hoped a sugar-sweet tone would conceal her growing disgust. Had her father brought Miranda here when he was still married to Elmira?

"Business. Yes, that's it exactly." Charlie had his handkerchief out again and was patting his damp forehead. The nervous way his eyes darted from the grandfather clock to the door told her he was beginning to worry about accidental discovery almost as much as he feared her threat to expose him. She'd already kept him longer than the fifteen minutes she'd paid for. If he was thought to be shirking his responsibilities, even if he wasn't caught giving tours, dereliction of duty might cost him his job.

Diana regarded him in a silence so thick it vibrated, wondering if there was more he could tell her. Probably not. Whatever his reasons for hiding the identity of her father's mistress, he wasn't about to reveal her name to someone he thought was a reporter.

Diana's hands, which had started out primly folded in her lap, were tightly clenched. It took a concentrated effort to relax her grip, finger by finger. Flexing to restore circulation, she fixed Charlie with a stare that brooked no disobedience and demanded the one remaining thing he could do for her: "Take me to the maid who found the body."

Both the maid, an Irish girl named Maeve, and the elevator operator, proved cooperative after Charlie told them they *had* to answer her questions. Unfortunately, neither of them had anything to add to what she'd already learned. Sam, the elevator man, had been curious enough to talk to several other hotel employees who had been on duty the night of the murder. He was happy to relay the information that no one had seen anyone, not even William Torrence, go into William Torrence's suite. Nor had anyone been seen leaving. No one would admit to knowing anything about a mistress.

Diana left the Windsor on the Larimer Street side and walked back to the Elmira. It was only a short distance, and all along solid plank sidewalks that kept pedestrians out of the muddy street. In broad daylight the journey was safe enough on foot and could be accomplished in less time than it would take to flag down a hack and ride through traffic.

Diana had plenty to mull over on the short trek. First, that the so-called evidence could have been planted. Second that *someone* was lying. Bribed to, no doubt. And third, though she didn't like this train of thought, that if her mother had murdered her father and fled on foot, it wouldn't have taken her long to cover the distance back to her own hotel. Diana would not have liked to be out in this neighborhood alone at night, but after four years of living on Holladay Street, Elmira would have been accustomed to it. She *could* have killed William Torrence.

Diana felt reasonably certain her father *had* entertained a mistress in that suite at the Windsor Hotel. She might not have seen her father for six years and might have been away at school for four years before that, but she felt certain that some things did not alter.

A place her father had intended to use only for business would have been plain and practical. If he'd wanted a setting that would relax an associate, he'd have arranged to meet him for a meal in one of the private dining rooms offered by Denver's many restaurants. He'd splurged on the mansion to assure his own comfort and prestige and because such luxury was sure to please a wife. It followed that if he'd wanted to impress a mistress, he'd take a suite at the Windsor for their assignations.

Diana examined her logic, found it sound, and moved on to

the obvious question—had William Torrence's mistress also been his murderer? Unlikely, she decided. Why slay a goose that was laying golden eggs? Murder *Miranda*, perhaps, in the hope of taking her place, but not Diana's father.

She stopped on the doorstep of the Elmira Hotel to look out over Holladay Street, so lost in thought that she was only dimly aware of the other buildings and the traffic passing by. The mystery woman might have been a witness to the murder. She might just as easily have been the reason for it.

Her existence had given someone besides Diana's mother an excellent motive for murder. The second wife who discovered she had a rival might well be driven to drastic measures, especially if she feared she was about to receive the same treatment as the first. It was not impossible. Diana had read somewhere only recently that three in every thousand marriages now ended with a judge's ruling, and that the highest incidence of divorces was in the western states. Besides, Miranda had been the one with most to gain if her husband died.

Diana felt a rush of triumph as she considered the conclusion she'd reached. She was sure she was right. Miranda had to be the one who'd murdered William Torrence.

Now all Diana had to do was prove it.

CHAPTER SEVEN

ଛୠଔ

A brick wall marked the property line between Matt Hastings's house and the Torrence mansion. The long, narrow lots made up for their lack of frontage with space at the back for gardens and other plantings. Matt's mother had put in apple trees. Diana remembered scaling the wall as a child to climb one and gorge herself on the fruit.

It was too early in the season yet for blossoms, but the trees looked as if they were beginning to bud. If the present warm spell continued, color and scent would soon burst forth. Then again, this being Denver, there might well be another snowfall first.

Matt appeared to be an optimist. When Diana had unexpectedly arrived on his doorstep at three in the afternoon, he'd ordered Gilbert to bring tea out to them at the wrought iron table and chairs beneath a rose arbor. Gnarled brown branches twisted up the sides and over their heads, bare of all but thorns, but it would be a charming spot once blooms appeared.

"Lemon?" Matt asked. "Sugar?" The only fragrance in the garden came from the tea tray.

By rights, Diana should have offered to pour, but he seemed intent on playing the good host. "It's fine as it is. Is Dorcas still away?"

"Until tomorrow."

While Gilbert set out more trays, Diana searched for the right words to broach an awkward subject. The appearance of Miranda's maidservant in the yard next door provided the opening she'd hoped for.

"Have all the servants my mother employed been replaced?" She reached for one of the little cakes Gilbert had brought and smiled when she tasted cinnamon.

"I must confess I do not know. I don't pay attention to the domestic arrangements of the neighbors. Mother could have told you," he added after a moment.

While Diana and Matt watched, the maid attached a half dozen pillows to a line placed where a current of air would stir it and set to striking the pillows with a carpet beater. Each blow raised little puffs of dust.

"That man Miranda employs has a frightening aspect," Diana said. "Not that physical appearance necessarily reflects character, but there was meanness in his eyes." She shivered. "And the boy with him had a feral look about him."

"Bodyguard," Matt muttered, his distaste clear, "and his son, I believe. You should have seen the last one. He looked like a cross between a melodrama villain and an underworld thug. Carried two pistols hung on his hips and wore a permanent sneer on his face." At Diana's surprised glance, he flushed, then cleared his throat. "It seems I do notice some things about the neighbors."

"Did my father need an armed guard? Does Miranda?"

"The rich sometimes think they do."

"And the maid?" Diana shifted her gaze to Miranda's back yard. The young woman had finished her chore and was just disappearing into the house.

Matt obligingly squinted in that direction. "Well, she's new. The previous one was a redheaded Irish lass. Miranda seems to have considerable difficulty keeping female staff."

"How new is this one? Since my father's death?"

"I'm sure I don't know, Diana." He watched her as he took another sip of tea. "Why this sudden interest in Miranda's servants? From what my mother used to say, it's next to impossible to hold onto a good housemaid. As soon as they're properly trained, they run off. Get married. Take another job. Sometimes they just disappear."

"My interest is in Miranda." She selected another cinnamon-flavored tea cake. "Tell me about my father's second wife, Matt. Who was Miranda Torrence before she married him?"

Matt frowned and returned his cup and saucer to the table, avoiding Diana's eyes. "The wedding took place in Torrence. That's where he met her. She was a Miss Chambers then."

"And you own a . . . business in Torrence. Or so I hear. You must know more than her maiden name."

He said nothing, but his reluctance was almost palpable.

"It's important, Matt."

"Why?" His eyes fixed on her as he waited for an explanation.

Diana drew in a deep, steadying breath and then told him what she'd learned during her visit to the Windsor Hotel. "Miranda had as much reason to kill Father as my mother did," she concluded.

"You think *Miranda* is a murderess?"

"That makes as much sense as accusing Mother of the crime."

"And just how do you intend to prove it? She says, or so I've heard, that she was home all that evening. Her servants will no doubt verify her claim."

"The servants we've just discussed?"

Diana wished she could interpret the blank expression that now hid Matt's thoughts from her. Did he believe her? Would he agree to help her?

"Perhaps you can locate the previous maid," Matt said, "but I wouldn't count on finding her."

A horrible thought crossed Diana's mind. Had Miranda disposed of a maidservant as well as a husband? What if it had been her former maidservant William Torrence had meant to entertain in that hotel suite?

Diana quickly dismissed that notion, remembering the expense her father had gone to. He'd never have spent so much on a servant. But she could not eliminate the possibility that a girl working in the Torrence mansion might have known more about the activities of her betters than was good for her.

"Miranda could have had her bodyguard do her dirty work for her," she mused aloud.

"He'd have beaten your father up, or shot him. Torrence was stabbed. There was passion behind it."

"It was personal," Diana agreed. "That argues for my mother or Miranda or Father's mistress. I need your help, Matt. I doubt Miranda will talk to me, and I have no evidence substantial enough to take to the police. Not yet. But *you* could question her. And talk to her servants, past and present. One of them may know something about the woman who was with my father the night he died. There was someone there. Or expected. I'm sure of it."

He pondered this suggestion while finishing his tea and eating the last of the cakes. "Unless you can identify this hypothetical woman, you have no hope of proving Miranda had any reason to want her husband dead. And for all you know, your mystery mistress, if she exists at all, is respectable and married, someone in Denver society who doesn't want to be found."

"Someone knows who she is and how to find her."

He looked as if he were about to argue, then glanced at her face and changed his mind. "All right, Diana. I will do what I can to help. I'll ask Gilbert to question Miranda's servants."

The words were the right ones, but Diana had the feeling he was only saying them to placate her. His attitude puzzled her. He seemed curiously inclined to defend Miranda Torrence.

She *was* pretty. Blonde. Shapely. Petite. Although Diana had never considered herself a particularly large female, she had felt like a giantess next to the other woman. Miranda was just the type to bring out protective instincts in a man.

"Walk with me, Diana?" Matt stood and offered her his hand. There was, she saw, a gravel path meandering through the apple trees. She did not remember that from her girlhood.

They strolled in silence for the first circuit. Then Matt slowed his loose-limbed stride and stooped a bit so that she couldn't help but be aware of the serious expression on his face.

"You can't deny Elmira quarreled with your father. Or that she ran away from the police."

"Wouldn't you, if you'd been framed for a crime you didn't commit and knew everyone would believe the worst of you because of your profession?" She rushed on before he could answer. "Please, Matt. Help me discover what really happened that night."

"Miranda—"

"All right. It could be someone else. An old enemy. Someone like—"

"Me? There's something you should know, Diana. You're looking for people who had reason to hate your father. I'm one of them."

"I was told you were partners with him once." With a cold, sinking feeling in her stomach, Diana realized she should have considered her old neighbor a serious suspect from the moment she'd learned that he'd been cheated by William Torrence in a business deal. Even a gentle soul could kill if the provocation was great enough.

Matt's voice was completely uninflected. "A bad decision on my part. I came to regret it even before he tricked me out of all my profits and dissolved the partnership."

"I'm sorry."

"If it hadn't been for another investment and the fact that I could earn an income from the practice of law, my mother and I would have been destitute." This time the bitterness did leak through. "Can you be certain I haven't been biding my time all these years, waiting for an opportunity to take revenge? Your father cost me a great deal of money. I was able to recoup my losses elsewhere, but still—"

"Are you telling me I should set the Pinkertons on you?" The suggestion came out more sharply than she'd intended.

"I'm saying you can't be too careful. If I *did* kill him, what would stop me from murdering you to keep my secret?"

"Did you stab my father to death?"

"No."

"Neither did my mother. Help me discover who did."

With a resigned sigh, Matt raked one hand through his hair. "I'll help. But only if you promise me you'll be careful who you talk to. Asking questions of the wrong person in this town could get you killed."

෨෬

Jane Foster's bedroom was under the eaves of the Elmira Hotel. Like the others living there, she usually slept late. She was barely awake when Diana rapped at her door at ten. She opened it still wearing her nightgown, her eyes for once unshielded by glass.

"Diana, what is it? Is something wrong?"

Set on what she had to say, Diana brushed past her mother's assistant into the small, plain room without waiting for an invitation. During a long, restless night, she'd decided that she was not about to take Matt's advice. She had to keep asking questions of anyone she could find who'd known her father, as well as of her mother's acquaintances. She could not sit idly by and trust anyone else to investigate, especially someone who was not as convinced as she was of Elmira's innocence.

"You seem to know my mother better than anyone else, Jane. Therefore, you're the best one to help me figure out where she's hiding."

Jane fumbled with one hand for the spectacles she'd left on the bedside table and jammed them into place on the bridge of her nose, blinking rapidly. "I'm still groggy. Give me a moment."

She poured cold water from ewer into basin, then splashed it onto her face, muttering all the while. As nearly as Diana could tell, she was comparing the coldness of the water to what sounded like "old man Whittud's heart."

"Who?" she asked, amused by the young woman's grumpiness. At a guess, Jane would not be fond of rising early even if she were not in a business that required her to stay up half the night.

Her voice muffled by a towel, Jane said, "The miserly bastard who owned half the town back home. My mother used to work for him."

When she disappeared behind a screen draped with gauze underwear and pink hose to use the chamber pot, Diana surveyed her surroundings. Jane lived comfortably, if more simply than her employer. She had no private bath with running water, but there was a three-quarter size brass bed, a dresser and a commode, a rocker and a straight chair, a thick rug, a lamp, lace curtains, and a writing desk. A large trunk presumably held her clothing, cash, and personal belongings. Only three of the latter were on display, well-thumbed copies of two books by Catharine Beecher, *Physiology and Calisthenics* and *Miss Beecher's Housekeeper and Healthkeeper,* and a photograph of Alan Kent in a gold frame. The picture had been placed in a prominent position on the dresser, making Diana wonder if the two were closer than she had supposed.

Jane reappeared, wrapped in a pale yellow silk dressing gown, and still blinking. "Perhaps Mr. Leeves could help." She sounded doubtful, and almost immediately shook her head. "No, better to leave him out of this."

"Mr. Leeves," Diana repeated. "Ed Leeves?" His name had come up before, and always with an exchange of knowing looks. "Exactly who is he?"

"He's an entrepreneur. He owns everything from gambling dens to saloons, and he controls at least a dozen hackmen." At Diana's lifted brow, Jane elaborated. "Drivers pick up tourists at the depot. They're in a position to make . . . suggestions."

"Ah, I see."

"He's also an old friend of your mother's. She told me once that she's known him since she was just a little girl."

"Is he, er, her lover?" That was what the madams had implied.

Jane looked uncomfortable. "I couldn't say."

It was an odd notion, her mother with someone other than William Torrence, but Diana didn't suppose it mattered what kind of relationship Elmira might have with this man. All that counted was locating her and proving her innocent of murder. "Where can I find Mr. Leeves?"

"He spends most of his time at the Catspaw, one of his saloons."

"Then let us beard the lion in his den, since I can scarcely command his presence here."

"It's Sunday," Jane objected. "The saloon will be closed."

"So much the better," Diana declared.

Jane still looked worried. "You can't just barge in. Besides, here in Denver, women—even fallen women—aren't encouraged to frequent saloons."

"I need to talk to this man, Jane. There must be a way."

She didn't bother to add that spending time in a saloon would not be a new experience for her. Evan had dragged her into more than one, the sort that had gambling hells on the floor above. He'd called her his lucky charm when he was winning at cards, and less flattering names when he lost.

"You'd better ask the professor," Jane said.

"I will if you'll tell me how to find him."

"His quarters are in the basement. I thought you knew."

"I don't even know his real name."

"It's Alfred," Jane said, opening her trunk and taking out dumbbells, clubs, and pulleys. "Alfred Burke." Abandoning any further effort to dissuade Diana from her plan, she began what was obviously a well-established morning regimen of healthful exercise.

Diana found the professor in the kitchen. He heard her out, then sent Ning off with a message. By the time Diana had finished beefsteak, toast, and her fourth cup of coffee, word had come back from Ed Leeves that she should meet him at a building he was converting into a new gambling club.

A short time later, Diana and Jane, the latter resplendent in her best bombazine and a fetching flower-encrusted straw hat, were ready to leave for that appointment. "You don't have to come with me," Diana said.

But Jane seemed to have undergone a change of attitude. "It is an excellent day for an outing, and I find I am curious about Mr. Leeves. He and Elmira always met away from the hotel, you see. I've only met him once, and then only for a moment."

It was a nice day. Several of the boarders had gone out right after breakfast, intent on a breath of fresh air and a bit of exercise before the customers started arriving at two. But Diana had no more than opened the front door when she became aware of a great commotion just down the street. She heard hoofbeats and the rattle of wheels mixed with screams of outrage and panic. Then colorful oaths uttered in high-pitched female voices filled the air.

Big Nose Nellie sat in the middle of Holladay Street, legs splayed, her skirts in disarray and her bonnet dangling by its ribbons. She shook her fist, cursing a blue streak, as a nondescript wagon of the sort known as a dog cart disappeared around the nearest corner.

"Are you hurt?" Diana demanded, rushing to her side. There was a streak of blood on Nellie's forehead and a scrape on the back of her hand, but otherwise she did not seem badly damaged.

"Only my pride," Nellie grumbled. "Damn fool!"

"He aimed right at you!" Maryam said.

"Couldn't have. What'd be the point?" Long Tall Linda sounded grumpy, as if she resented Nellie being the center of attention.

Hands on hips, Maryam regarded the taller woman with a

sardonic gaze. "Oh, no. No one would ever want to hurt a prostitute."

"Coulda been a preacher," Honeycomb speculated. "He was all dressed in black, you know the way they do."

"Half the men in town wear black on Sunday," Jane reminded her. "And I'm sure no harm was meant. Just a careless driver. Or someone who got roostered and didn't know what he was doing. Drunk," she translated, for Diana's benefit.

Long Tall Linda helped Nellie to her feet, and the girls moved en masse towards the Elmira.

"She'll be fine," Jane said, catching Diana's arm as she started to follow. "We'd best be on our way. You don't want to keep Big Ed waiting."

"Was Maryam right? Are the girls threatened with physical harm by the self-righteous bigots of this community?"

Jane shrugged. "We're usually safe enough, as long as we stay on Holladay Street. Respectable folk don't come here," she added with a quick grin, "unless they want to do some sinning themselves. And we aren't 'worthy' enough for the ladies' societies to bother with."

Diana frowned, caught off guard by a stray memory. Elmira, in her respectable past, had once tried to explain to her daughter how the Ladies' Relief Society, to which she belonged, determined which poor people to assist. Most charitable organizations seemed to equate groveling and confessions of wickedness with worthiness. And their idea of helping abandoned and impoverished children was to send them to an orphans' home and indenture them at an early age.

Her mother's view of such things, Diana imagined, had undergone a change in the last four years.

❧❧❧

The three-story building Ed Leeves was in the process of renovating was on Glancey Street near the ball park, far closer to the Torrence mansion than it was to Holladay Street. Diana and Jane traveled by streetcar, since the tracks of the Denver Tramway Company went everywhere in the city for the same five cent fare.

"This place looks familiar," Diana murmured.

"It used to be Thatcher's Collegiate Institute, a girls' school," Jane said.

"Good gracious! I came close to being enrolled here when I was fourteen, but Mother heard that the teachers discouraged female students from any contact with young men. She said I'd never find a husband that way."

"The last year or so, it's been a second-class gambling house. I hear Mr. Leeves means to make it into a first-class place."

Diana was scarcely listening. "Mother wanted me to marry a doctor or a lawyer," she murmured. Since Ben Northcote was a physician, Diana supposed her mother would approve of him.

She suppressed a sigh. If Elmira Torrence was executed for killing her former husband, she might never meet Ben. And Ben? How was he going to react to learning that Elmira owned a whorehouse, let alone that he'd asked an accused murderer's daughter to marry him? She thought he loved her enough that neither fact would make any difference, but the strength of the bond between them would surely be tested if Elmira turned out to be guilty.

Ed Leeves himself was the second surprise in store for Diana on Glancey Street. She'd expected him to be a big man, given his nickname. In truth, without his highly polished, custom-made boots with the two inch heels, he'd have been only a little taller than she was.

A lean, hard-muscled man in his fifties, Leeves looked as if he'd be equally at home riding the range, dining with politicians, or running one of the gangs of New York. The words "urbane" and "ruffian" both came to mind as Diana studied his face. He had a mane of light flaxen-colored hair, a beard that looked soft and smooth as silk, and snapping black eyes that stood out in stark contrast to the rest of his coloring.

"Elmira's daughter," he said, regarding her with a cold, assessing stare. "Interesting."

"I need to talk to her, Mr. Leeves." The note of pleading in her voice appalled Diana but she did not know how else to proceed. Leeves presented no overt threat, but an aura of danger seemed to surround him. She'd not want to meet him at night in a dark alley.

"You and a great many other people are looking for your mother," Leeves said.

"If you know where she is, I'd appreciate it if you'd let her know I'm staying at the Elmira."

He continued to study her with his intense, disconcerting gaze until it was all she could do not to squirm.

"Let me show you around the place," he said abruptly.

Diana blinked in surprise. Did he mean to take her to her mother, after all?

But Leeves had meant his invitation literally. For the next half hour, he conducted her on an extensive tour of the premises. Diana and Jane saw the public and private dining rooms on the first floor and the saloon and gambling rooms on the second. Red velvet carpeting and draperies and oak-paneled walls dominated the decor, accented with massive portraits of half-naked women.

Diana could not help but think of Aaron Northcote's artwork as she encountered one scantily clad female figure after another. "Have you ever considered using pictures of mermaids?" she heard herself ask.

Jane sniggered. "The purpose of the paintings is to give the patrons ideas. There are apartments on the third and fourth floors, are there not, Mr. Leeves? Available for customers' liaisons with the female staff of the club?"

"I am planning a variation on that theme," he said, watching Diana for her reaction. "An innovation, if you will. There will be a private entrance on the north side through which patrons may bring their own companions. Couples will entertain themselves in private dining rooms on the lower level and in private . . . parlors upstairs. With the pull of a bell, a customer can order food and drink served by the most discreet of waiters."

"Hardly innovative," Diana said. "I hear men smuggle mistresses in and out of Denver hotel rooms all the time."

The smile Leeves gave her sent a chill down her spine and forcibly reminded her of Matt's warning. He was right. Asking questions of the wrong person *could* be hazardous to the health.

They passed through what would be the main saloon, stopping to admire a white and crystal bar Leeves assured them would be the envy of every saloon keeper in Denver, before entering an even larger room.

"The roulette wheels will stand there," Leeves said, gesturing to his right, "and the Heironymous bowls opposite."

Heironymous was a dice game, Diana recalled, played with three dice and two wooden bowls, the smaller ends of which were connected by a tube. Evan had told her once that the percentage in favor of the house was enormous.

"Six faro banks against this wall," Leeves continued, pointing.

"I'm told faro is popular because gamblers don't believe the dealer can be crooked," Diana said.

"I only run square games," he said bluntly.

She said nothing. She hadn't a doubt in the world that Mr. Leeves would make a good profit, one way or another.

Diana had never understood the urge to play cards, throw dice, or spin a wheel and bet money on the outcome, but she knew all too well how powerful the compulsion to gamble could be. She also knew how easy it was for a dealer to use a tiny needle set in his ring to mark a new deck of cards. Evan had dealt faro in Leadville for a time. It had been the last gainful employment he'd had before he was killed for cheating at poker.

"I plan to have four tables for hazard and craps," Leeves said, "one table for twenty-one, two for stud poker and two for draw poker."

Diana turned her best smile on her host. If she was going to push him for information, she needed to try harder to engage him in polite conversation. "I am surprised to hear you give equal space to both, sir. Stud poker is much more popular than draw."

"You seem well acquainted with gambling dens, Mrs. Spaulding."

"My husband was, Mr. Leeves."

"Ah, yes. Your husband." Something in the way he said the word increased Diana's uneasiness. Had Leeves met Evan? It was possible. They had spent a month in Denver three years ago. Evan had probably passed most of his free time gambling. After all, he'd won enough to start his own acting company . . . only to lose it again, and his life, before the year was out.

"What provision do you make for losers?" she inquired. "Or do you simply turn them out into the street?"

"Anyone busted in my house goes away with a brass check good for drinks at the bar, a night's lodging, a meal, or a visit to the Elmira."

Diana was sorry she'd asked.

"A very posh place it will be," Jane said in admiring tones.

Diana had to agree. A far cry from the hells she'd visited with Evan. She had a sudden vivid memory of one gambling den. She couldn't recall in what town it had been, although she did remember that it was above a saloon.

It was a Saturday night and the place was crowded with men who'd worked hard all week. Miners. Clerks. Railroad laborers. There were no fashionably dressed dandies in that crowd.

Evan insisted she stand behind him, for luck. That gave her far too much time to observe the dealer, a rough-looking young man who'd left off his necktie in order to show off his diamond stud. A lookout was posted at the dealer's side to watch for cheating. He was smoking the most foul-smelling cigar Diana had ever encountered.

There was little conversation. The loudest sounds were the

clinking of ivory chips and the rattle of roulette marbles. Once in a while someone shuffled his feet, or expectorated loudly, but for the most part every man's focus was on his cards or his dice or the spin of the wheel.

And then Evan started to lose. He refused to drop out of the game, even when his last chip was gone.

"What if I wager my wife?" he'd asked the gray-bearded gambler who held the winning hand.

Diana returned to the present with a start, uncertain how they'd gotten back to the entrance of the club. "Thank you for the tour, Mr. Leeves," she murmured, scrambling to gather her scattered wits.

"I could tell you enjoyed yourself, Mrs. Spaulding." He bowed over her hand, turning it so that he could kiss the inside of her wrist.

She found the contact distasteful but forced herself to endure it.

"If there's ever anything I can do for you . . . ."

"Do you believe my mother killed my father?" she blurted.

He smiled, and she found herself, unexpectedly, charmed. "I don't care one way or the other if she did, but I have no intention of letting her stand trial for murder. I have a different plan for Elmira's future."

"What plan?"

His dark eyes held hers so that she could not possibly mistake how serious he was. "I intend to marry her."

CHAPTER EIGHT

ᏚᏅᏟᏒ

Very early the next morning, when the sun had barely risen and Diana was still abed, the sound of her door creaking open brought her wide awake, her heart pounding and her breath caught in her throat. With the entrance to the suite secured and the professor on duty all night downstairs, she had not felt particularly vulnerable at the Elmira, but the warnings she'd received, first from Pearl Adams and then from Matt, must have been lurking just beneath the surface of conscious thought.

In the dim light filtering through the curtains, she could not tell who had come in, but when she heard the soft footfalls approach, then stop, as if the intruder had paused to study her, she had to fight a nearly overwhelming temptation to pull the covers over her head and hide.

Instead she whispered, "Who's there?"

Someone sat on the foot of the bed. Someone heavy. "I'm told you've been looking for me," Elmira Torrence said.

"M-m-mother?" Diana sat bolt upright. Shoving the feather pillow out of her way, she scooted back until her shoulders touched the headboard.

"Have you forgotten my voice?" A muffled laugh followed the

sarcasm. Even muted, there was no mistaking that distinctive bray. The raucous sound had embarrassed Diana too often in her younger days.

Questions crowded into her mind, tripping over one another in the crush. Diana did not know where to begin. She had not expected her mother to appear like this, without warning, although she wasn't sure it would have made any difference had she been given plenty of notice.

"How did you get in here?" she blurted.

"It's *my* bedroom. And my hotel."

"Yes, but—"

"Haven't you discovered the stairway in the wall? You were always a great one for ferreting out secrets when you were a girl."

"I didn't know the stairs went on beyond the peephole into the Chinese parlor."

"Then you're not as clever, or as curious, as I thought you'd be. How do you suppose you're going to be of any help to me?"

Diana sighed. She'd forgotten one little thing about her mother. There was no pleasing her. Ever. And God forbid Mother should ever utter a single word of praise for her only child!

"Well, you're here now," Elmira said shortly. "And I'm here. So we may as well discuss the situation. I did not kill your father." Bitterness crept into her voice. "If I was going to kill anyone, it would have been Miranda."

"Who did kill him?"

"How should I know? I wasn't there. No, don't light the lamp. We've enough light without it."

Diana let her hand fall away. It was getting brighter in the bedroom as day broke outside. She could make out her mother's distinctive profile. The way her nose and chin angled away from her mouth gave her just the slightest resemblance to a rat.

"Where did you go the night Father died?"

"I had an appointment to meet Ed Leeves. He sent me a note telling me he'd be at a place we go to sometimes. He never showed up, so I can't prove I was there either."

"What excuse did he give when he called the next day?"

Elmira's brows lifted. "You *have* been busy. He said he'd never sent any note."

"Do you believe him?"

Elmira didn't answer.

"Mr. Leeves told me he's going to marry you," Diana informed her.

"Did he now?" A hint of surprise in her voice, Elmira shook her head. "We'll see about that."

Diana frowned. "Wasn't he the one who told you I was here?"

"Never mind how I knew. What's this about you trying to find out who killed Will? It's no good, Diana. You won't succeed. Too many people had reason to hate him, yourself included."

"But how many would want you blamed for his death? How many could get in here to leave a bloodstained glove in your room?"

"Enough. He was a cheat and a thief, and I aided and abetted him until he turned on me."

"You helped him cheat Matt Hastings?"

Elmira sighed gustily, but Diana could not tell if it was a sound of regret or merely impatience. "I put Matt's mother up to encouraging him to invest in one of Will's mines, one I knew wouldn't produce nearly as much high grade ore as Will claimed."

"How could you do that? Betray a friend. Defraud someone, especially someone you knew. It wasn't as if you and Father needed money."

"Don't be naive, Diana. Money is the only thing your father ever cared about. Getting it and keeping it. The original mine, the Timberline, was a bonanza, and it's still producing high-grade ore, pouring a steady stream of cash into coffers that now belong to Miranda. And in the early days here in Denver, he gobbled up real estate, which yielded a fine return on the investment, but when he decided to get rid of me and marry that blonde hussy, he took steps to make sure I was left penniless. He wasn't about to share anything."

She stood and began to pace. In the steadily increasing morning light, Diana could see further proof of how much she'd changed. At fifty-three, Elmira's red-brown hair was streaked with white. She was also heavier than Diana remembered, and she'd not been a small woman to begin with.

"I think he expected me to vanish, or to kill myself to avoid the disgrace of the divorce and the insult of being the owner of this hotel. I didn't oblige him. Once I lost my position in Denver society, I decided I might as well make my money any way I could. Instead of giving up, I came into my own. I've become rather wealthy in the process."

"And Ed Leeves?"

"He helped me a bit at the start."

"Why?"

"We knew each other when we were young. Our families were friendly rivals in the hotel business. Legitimate hotels," Elmira added with a slight smile.

"Would he have killed Father? For you?"

"He's not that big a fool. Besides, he knew my plans. I was about to take my revenge on Will where it would hurt him most, in his pocketbook. Legal action, not physical retribution. He owed me, Diana. For fourteen backbreaking years, I took in laundry to make ends meet." She shuddered at the memory. "I staked him. Will would never have struck it rich if not for the money I earned."

Diana got out of bed and slipped into a robe, but she made no attempt to interrupt her mother's ranting. She'd learn more this way, she hoped, than from asking a dozen questions.

"He should have honored his marriage vows," Elmira muttered.

"I did." Without warning, she spun to face Diana, wide-spaced blue eyes snapping. "Did Evan Spaulding?"

"Did Evan what?"

"Honor his marriage vows," Elmira repeated impatiently.

Diana hesitated, then shook her head. She'd been bitter about the repeated betrayals once, but she'd put those resentments behind her long ago. Like her mother, she'd come into her own. Unfortunately, she had not made nearly as much money at it as Elmira.

"Did you send him to your father? No, I can see by that confused look on your face that you didn't."

"Evan went to see Father? When?"

Elmira shrugged. "When Todd's Touring Thespians played in Denver. I went to a performance, you know. They were dreadful."

"Never mind that. We were here about three years ago. You were already divorced. How did you find out that Evan and Father had met?"

"I had my ways. But if I were you, I'd be more interested in what it was they talked about."

Had Evan tried what Diana had refused to attempt, a reconciliation? Such a move seemed out of character. By that time he'd long since stopped caring about making her happy. But he might have assumed that if she were reunited with her father, she'd be reinstated as his heir. Satisfied that this cynical explanation made perfect sense, Diana pretended indifference.

"Whatever he wanted," she said, "he didn't get it, and he never bothered to mention their meeting to me."

Elmira gave her a hard stare, then turned away to open the window curtains and let in the sun. Silhouetted there, she was an imposing sight. She was two inches taller than Diana and, at 5'7," had also been taller than her short, burly husband. But when Diana stepped closer, she saw more ravages wrought by age and hard living. Her mother's face was deeply lined and the high color in her cheeks came from broken capillaries.

"I'll have to leave soon," Elmira said, "before anyone else wakes up."

"Where are you hiding? How can I contact you? I believe Miranda killed Father and framed you. Matt has promised to help me prove it."

"Matt Hastings? You trust him?"

"Is there some reason I shouldn't?"

Elmira considered the question for a moment. "I don't know. I've learned the hard way not to trust anyone."

"He's a lawyer, Mother. If you're caught—"

"I don't intend to *be* caught. Do you think I could stand to be cooped up in a stone-floored cell with no light at night and no furnishings but a lumpy mattress stuffed with musty straw and a backless bench?"

"You can't hide forever." Aware her mother was about to bolt, Diana's desperation grew. "Will you let Matt defend you, if it becomes necessary?"

"It wouldn't matter who defended me if I came to trial. Whoever framed me did too good a job. If I'm caught, I'll hang. I could be put on trial as soon as the day after I was brought in. The proceedings might be stretched out a day or two, but in the end a jury would convict me, a judge would pass sentence, and within a week of my capture, I'd be dead."

"Petition for a reprieve could—"

A bitter laugh dismissed that idea.

"We'll start before the trial, then. And put ads in all the papers to ask for information—"

"You don't understand, Diana. I wouldn't really be on trial for murder. I'm guilty of the far worse sin of turning adversity into profit. I'm the shameless hussy who failed to slink quietly away. Society matrons will tell their husbands how to deal with the likes of me! I must be made an example of, to dissuade others from taking the same path."

Diana didn't know if her mother was right about that or not, but she could see that Elmira believed what she was saying. "Then there is only one sensible course. You cannot stay in Denver without running the risk of being recognized. Therefore you must leave. Go to New York. I'll follow and—"

"No, Diana. But you should go. Return to your own life. Leave me to mine."

Elmira had asked no questions, Diana realized. Did that mean she didn't care what her only child had been doing these last few years . . . or that she already knew? She supposed it didn't really matter. "Mother, let me help you."

"You can ask Matt Hastings to represent me if you insist on hiring a lawyer. That's your business," Elmira said as she opened the wardrobe door, "but don't expect me to pay him. I've got other plans for my money."

She removed the jewelry box from its shelf and tucked it under her arm. Then she reached deeper into the space where it had been and a moment later came out holding an enormous wad of large denomination bills.

"They won't find me, Diana, unless I want to be found."

With that she walked out of the bedroom. Diana followed, eyes widening as Elmira removed large sums of money from two more hiding places and stowed all of it on her person. She was heading for the secret panel in the wall before Diana gathered sufficient wit to form a sentence.

"You're not coming back, are you? Not even if I find the real killer." It sounded more like an accusation than a question. Perhaps it was.

"Why should I?"

"For the girls." *For me.*

"They can fend for themselves."

"And the hotel?"

"Close it. Burn it down for all I care." She hefted the jewelry box. "I have all I want out of it."

"So everything has been about money?"

"What else? Your father taught me well."

"But you take such good care of your employees. I thought—"

"Healthy girls can charge more. That's just good business."

She reached into the pocket of her skirt and retrieved one of the wads of cash. Peeling off a half-dozen bills, she tossed them at

Diana, watching as they fluttered to the carpet.

"Go back to New York, Diana. I don't need you."

ഉറ

Diana might have considered following her mother's advice if her first stop the following morning hadn't been the Western Union office. Her intent had been to send a message to Ben, but she abandoned that idea once she read the telegrams from Horatio Foxe that had accumulated over the last few days.

He'd sent two that had missed her on her way west. Forwarded on, they warned her that her mother owned a brothel and to beware of a man named Ed Leeves. *Too late,* she thought crossly. The telegrams Foxe had dispatched direct to Denver, save for the most recent, all contained the same message: CONTACT ME WHEN YOU ARRIVE. Since she'd gotten in late Thursday and this was only Monday, Diana couldn't understand why he seemed so desperate to hear from her.

The last telegram, sent on Sunday morning, offered at least a partial explanation. The message it contained would have cheered Diana in normal circumstances, telling her as it did that help was on the way. Perversely, her first reaction was to resent the interference. This meant she couldn't leave Denver, even if she wanted to, and that she'd have at least a few more days on her own before anyone from the East Coast could possibly arrive.

She left Western Union without sending any telegrams of her own. If she had to stay, then she might as well put into effect the plan she'd conceived before her interview with her mother: find a newspaper reporter who'd be sympathetic to Elmira's cause.

Hours later, temper simmering just below the boiling point, she hurried along the last stretch of Larimer Street before the turn that would take her back to the Elmira. No one at Senator N. P. Hill's *Republican* had been liberal-minded enough to consider that a brothel keeper might be innocent of murder. The editor of the evening *Times* had laughed Diana out of his office, and Eugene Field of the *Tribune* had turned out to be an old acquaintance of Horatio Foxe's. That had not been a good thing.

The only other daily was the *Hotel Reporter,* another dead end. The *Sun* was for coloreds. The *Herald* published only in German. Of the weeklies, *Opinion* was a slim possibility, if she could locate the publisher, but there was no sense approaching the *Colorado Farmer,* the *Live Stock Journal,* the *Mining Register,* the *Labor Enquirer,* or the *Churchman.*

She glanced at the watch pinned to the bosom of her Modjeska jacket. Three already. Not only had the entire day been a waste, but now she'd gone and broken her word to a little boy.

She turned at last onto Holladay Street and quickened her pace, although she was already a bit breathless. Yesterday, after her visit to the old girls' school, Diana had talked again with Ning. Upon learning that he'd never been taught to read or write, she'd vowed to remedy that situation. She'd given him his first reading lesson on the spot and promised him his second this afternoon at three.

A stitch in her side was a painful reminder that she was rushing too fast for a woman wearing a corset. She slowed her speed, but pushed steadily on. She'd made Ning a promise, and she didn't want him thinking she'd broken it. The boy had grown far too accustomed to adults who treated him like a piece of furniture— useful, decorative, but essentially worthless and easy to replace.

Puffing more than a little, clutching her side with one hand and her mesh bag with the other, Diana climbed the front steps of the hotel. The bag contained copies of the *Rocky Mountain News* for the entire week of the murder.

In desperation, she had returned to Col. Arkins's premises at the end of her quest. Since this was Monday, the only day he did not put out an edition of his newspaper, he had not been in the building. She'd managed to make an appointment for the following day to talk to Henry Burnett, the reporter who covered "the lowers." She hoped he'd be able to add some significant detail to her knowledge, but she wasn't counting on it. It was more likely that he'd already put everything he knew into the published story of the discovery of her father's body.

Jane was at her accustomed post in the entryway, since the Elmira had been open to custom for more than an hour. "You have a visitor," she said in a worried voice.

Startled, Diana froze. Impossible. She'd only just gotten the warning telegram.

"Mr. Leeves is waiting in the Chinese parlor."

Diana relaxed and had to smile at her own foolish fancy. No one could get halfway across the country in less than six days, not unless they found some way to sprout wings and fly. "What does he want?"

"How should I know?" But Jane looked worried.

Diana kept the smile on her face, but she was remembering that her mother had been lured from the hotel by a message from Ed Leeves. What if that had been deliberate? What if Leeves was part of a conspiracy to frame Elmira Torrence for murder?

Big Ed was involved in just about every illegal activity in the Denver underworld, from policy shops that ran numbers and sold tickets in the Louisiana Lottery to the opium dens of Hop Alley. Diana had asked a few pointed questions about him while she was visiting newspaper offices, and she hadn't liked any of the answers.

Her throat suddenly as dry as her hands were clammy, Diana removed her hat and smoothed her hair. Whatever Leeves claimed to feel for her mother, he was a dangerous man, and she was frankly suspicious of his claim to be so fond of Elmira. Clearly he had no idea where her mother was hiding, nor did he know about Elmira's early morning visit. Indeed, it was possible Elmira Torrence was hiding from Ed Leeves as well as from the police.

Pasting on a new and even brighter smile, Diana entered the parlor. She found Leeves staring up at Elmira's portrait.

He glanced at her, a sour expression on his face, and made a point of taking his watch out of his pocket, opening it, and looking at the time. "I'm a busy man, Mrs. Spaulding, and I've been waiting for you for quite a long time."

"Had I but known you were coming, I'd have made arrangements to be here when you arrived."

Leeves clicked the watchcase shut and turned to face her head on. "I've been thinking about your mother's difficulties. I've come to the decision that I'm the best one to look after her interests while she's . . . away."

"Indeed?" Diana rang a small hand bell. A moment later Ning appeared. "Bring coffee, please, Ning." Leeves, she noted, had already helped himself to whiskey.

"I'm surprised your mother didn't take him with her." His nod indicated the boy. "She's got an unnatural affection for that little coolie."

Diana bit back a sharp comment. She knew already that long-time residents of Denver looked down on more recent immigrants. Their attitude galled her, especially when so many of the newcomers had not had much choice about settling in Colorado. They'd been employed in railroad construction and suddenly found themselves out of work when projects ended in Denver. That had happened first to a large group of Chinese laborers and some years later to Italian workers. To Diana's mind, those people deserved sympathy, not scorn, but by the standards of the charitable organizations hereabouts, neither group was "worthy" of help.

Leeves was watching her as he sipped at his whiskey. "I'm here to offer a solution to your problems, Mrs. Spaulding," he said at last. "I am sure you are anxious to return to your own home. All you have to do is leave me in charge of the hotel, and you can do so with a clear conscience."

Something moved behind the portrait. Eyes. For a moment Diana thought her mother might be spying on them. Then she realized it had to be Jane. The other woman must have moved at a good clip to get from the reception desk to Elmira's suite and down the hidden stairs so quickly.

"Mrs. Spaulding?"

"I'm afraid that won't be possible, Mr. Leeves. I came here to prove my mother innocent of the charges against her. I have not, as yet, succeeded."

At some point during her long, frustrating day, Diana's resolve had strengthened. She could not give up just because Elmira didn't want her help. Her father had been murdered.

The irony of her decision to stay was not lost on her. Her father had died a thoroughly corrupt and unlovable man. But he'd once had a spark of decency in him. He'd once loved his daughter.

To prove her mother innocent, and to avenge the loss of the father she remembered from all those years ago, Diana wanted his killer found and punished. She wanted justice. If that proved impossible to obtain then, at the least, she wanted the truth, all of it, no matter how painful.

"I don't think you understand me, Mrs. Spaulding." Black eyes boring into her, Leeves lowered his voice to an ominous whisper. "Stay in Denver or not, you cannot remain at the Elmira."

"It's my mother's place. In her absence—"

"In her absence, you have only two choices. I take over and the Elmira stays open. Or you stay on and the hotel is closed down by the local authorities, and you are arrested for operating a lewd house."

She stared at him, shocked in spite of the warnings she'd had about the way he did business. Suddenly she was very glad help was on the way, even if it would not arrive until Friday at the earliest.

Heart in her throat, she stalled. "I'll consider what you've said, Mr. Leeves. Thank you for your . . . interest."

The noncommittal reply earned her a sardonic lift of pale yellow-white eyebrows, but for the moment Leeves chose not to pursue the matter, or make further threats. He swallowed the rest of his whiskey in one gulp, set the glass down on a table with a thump, bowed slightly, and left the room.

Diana sat abruptly, her knees as wobbly as they'd been when she'd first heard about her father's murder. "Now what?" she whispered.

If Leeves was lying about sending that note to her mother, he could be the one who'd killed William Torrence. It would have been simple enough for him to plant the bloodstained glove when he'd called on Elmira the next day.

Ning brought her coffee and she sipped gratefully. "Fetch Miss Jane for me, will you, Ning? And then, as soon as I've talked to her, we'll have that reading lesson I promised you."

"I'm here," Jane said from the doorway. "I heard." Her eyes cut to the portrait. "Come back in ten minutes, Ning."

"Does Ed Leeves have the power to put the hotel out of business?" Diana asked as soon as the boy had gone. "Can he have me arrested?"

"Oh, yes." Jane looked wistfully at the empty whiskey glass. "He's the most powerful man in Denver. You won't stay in jail long, of course. Just pay the seventy-five dollar fine, and they'll let you out."

Diana choked on her coffee. Seventy-five dollars would be a small fortune to most people. Three months' wages or more. Jane spoke as if it were a pittance. "Perhaps I should let him take over."

"He'll make changes, and not for the better," Jane warned. "If the way he operates his other businesses is any indication, he'll take a bigger cut of what the girls bring in, and probably try to crowd in more girls too. And he'll do away with all of the little luxuries Elmira provided."

"I may not be able to stop him. What will you do if I can't?" Diana felt responsible for all the residents of the hotel, but Jane in particular concerned her. She was a cut above the others here, more refined. And she had, Diana thought, at least a chance of leading a respectable life.

"I've accumulated a nest egg. Still, I don't particularly want to leave. Not yet." Jane met Diana's gaze, but the light was wrong for

Diana to see beyond the spectacles. She had no idea how Jane really felt about her situation. Or if she had any prospects for becoming Mrs. Alan Kent.

"I need to get back to the desk," Jane said when Ning returned for his lesson. "I left Red Katie in charge, but Monday is one of our busiest days. She's needed to entertain our guests."

Reminded of what was going on in the other parlors on this floor, and in various bedrooms, Diana decided to use her mother's suite as a classroom.

Ning was a delight. The child had a natural aptitude for recognizing letters and remembering their sounds. "That my name," he said as soon as Diana wrote it on a blank sheet of paper.

"Yes, that's right. And by changing the first letter, you spell other words that rhyme with Ning. See? Ring. King. Sing." She inscribed each one as she sounded it out.

"Mrs. Elmira sing sometimes."

"She does?" Astonishment laced Diana's voice. "You've heard her?"

He nodded earnestly.

It seemed her mother had developed a soft spot for Ning, just as Diana had herself. "Did you see my mother the night my father died?"

She hadn't meant to ask that. The words just slipped out. But since they had, she waited eagerly for Ning's reply. He was clearly the most observant person on the premises.

"I not here then. I go home at night."

A small sigh escaped Diana. "Of course you do." So much for the hope he might have noticed something that would exonerate Elmira. Apparently Nellie was the only one who'd seen her that night.

"Do you live with your aunt?" Diana asked Ning.

He nodded. "She own laundry. Very fine business."

Relieved to discover that the aunt Jane had mentioned was not a prostitute, Diana coaxed Ning into telling her about his life in Hop Alley. For a short while, listening to his enthusiastic chatter, she was able to forget the dilemma that plagued her and simply enjoy a little boy's company.

The respite did not last. As soon as Diana had installed Ning at her mother's desk and set him to copying letters of the alphabet, her thoughts returned to the night of the murder. Nellie, she recalled, had described lace trimmed gloves—black silk with silver stripes and frothy black lace at the wrists. Curious, she went in search of them.

Elmira kept her gloves in a drawer in the wardrobe. Diana found three pairs, but none were lace-trimmed black silk. She supposed someone might have borrowed them. The girls working at the Elmira were hardly the most upstanding citizens in Denver. One of them might well have helped herself to Elmira's property in her absence.

But Diana had always had a lively imagination. Now it occurred to her that there could be a more sinister explanation for the disappearance of the gloves. After all, it had been Nellie, the only witness to Elmira's return to the hotel, who'd nearly been run down by a dog cart. Had the real murderer, anxious to ensure that Elmira continued to look guilty, removed the black gloves? And could that some person, she wondered, have also tried to do away with Big Nose Nellie?

The bright beams of Tuesday's full moon lit the parlor of Diana's mother's suite. When she opened the window, she also let in the raucous nighttime noises of Holladay Street. With bleak amusement, she concluded that this was quite probably the only room in the neighborhood with a raised sash. There wasn't much to see, and in any case the grillwork across the opening prevented her from leaning out, but just now she needed a breath of fresh air.

"I've just wasted another day," she said without turning. "This morning I finally tracked down Henry Burnett, the reporter, but he was no use at all."

He hadn't even bothered to take a look at her father's body. He'd relied for his information on the same source Diana had already consulted, good old Charlie, the assistant manager of the Windsor Hotel. Worse, Burnett adhered to the party line in his conclusions: Elmira had run away, therefore Elmira must be guilty.

"I spent the afternoon," she continued, "reading every word in every issue of the *Rocky Mountain News* from the week of my father's death, hoping there might be some clue contained in the events reported there."

The exercise had given her a blazing headache. Thank goodness she'd agreed to try one of Long Tall Linda's cures to alleviate the pain. She'd been leery at first of the mixture of sliced potatoes and coffee grounds, but desperate enough to take to her bed and allow the country-bred woman, who had a reputation for knowing useful home remedies, to place it on her forehead with a rag tied around it to keep it in place. She'd closed her eyes, breathed in the fragrance of coffee, and dozed for an hour. By the time she'd awakened, the headache had subsided.

Discarded newspapers still lay scattered about the suite, literally carpeting the parlor with loose sheets of newsprint. The *Rocky Mountain News* sold for five cents a copy. On weekdays there were ten pages, six-columns wide. The Sunday edition was longer and more inclusive, with features on society and entertainment and even a book review column. Diana supposed she'd hoped some line might leap out, providing just the solution she'd been looking for. No such luck.

She'd been briefly encouraged when she'd discovered lists of visitors to Denver, along with what hotel each had stayed in, but without a name for her mystery woman she had no way to link any of those people to her father. The information she sought remained elusive . . . as Matt Hastings had been of late. Until tonight, she hadn't seen or heard from him since her visit to his house on Saturday.

She turned from the window to hurl a blunt question in his direction. "Have you learned anything?"

"Gilbert is still trying to worm his way into the confidence of Miranda's servants. For some reason they are reluctant to speak ill of their employer."

With a sigh, Diana reached for the nearest paper. The least she could do was tidy up the room and offer Matt a place to sit down.

"A bribe might help," Matt said, "but given your financial difficulties . . . ."

Diana paused with the crumpled pages clutched to her bosom. He still thought her penniless and she couldn't think of any plausible explanation for the fact that she now had over five hundred dollars in her possession, thanks to the bills Elmira had flung at her. She supposed she could admit to the bank draft from Horatio Foxe. After all, she'd never actually said she had *no* money.

"About my finances—" she began.

"Diana," he said at the same time. "I've had an idea."

She yielded the floor, secretly relieved not to have to confess her deception just yet.

"You're not comfortable living here. I can tell that. Listening to . . . well, I don't need to spell it out. This is no place for a lady."

He was right. The first few nights she'd been too tired to pay much attention to what went on around her, but the longer she stayed at the Elmira the harder she found it to ignore exactly what kind of business was being transacted in her mother's "boarding house." She did not look forward to trying to get to sleep later. The Elmira was busiest, she'd been told, on Tuesday nights. That was when the big-money men came around. They never showed up on weekends. They were with their families then.

Had she really only arrived in Denver last Thursday?

"What do you suggest?" Diana asked. She had to admit her

will to remain at the Elmira had weakened considerably since her mother's visit, and she had been shaken by Leeves's threats.

"Move into my house. You'll have access to your prime suspect, Miranda, since she lives right next door. Furthermore, I can introduce you to people you could not possibly meet if you stay here. Your father's acquaintances. If anyone knows anything that can exonerate your mother, that's the way to discover it. We need to work together on this, Diana."

He didn't give her the opportunity to object, simply rushed on with the details of his plan. "We'll pretend you've just arrived in Denver and that we plan to marry. I've already found a suitable older woman to act as a chaperone. And Dorcas is back. With two respectable older women in residence, there will be no scandal attached to a widow and a bachelor living in the same house."

Diana didn't much care what Denver's whist-playing society matrons thought of her, but there was a more serious drawback to the plan. "I was about to accept a real proposal of marriage when I got word of Father's death."

Matt's face contorted in sudden anger. "Don't tell me the cad broke it off when he heard about the murder. If he cared for you at all, he should have come with you to Denver."

"I didn't tell him what had happened, only that I had to go away for a while on family business. I was in New York. He was in Maine, where he practices medicine. I didn't want to ask him to abandon his patients."

Matt was silent for a moment, then cleared his throat. "I see no problem, then, in pretending you plan to marry me. Your doctor is an entire continent away. He'll never know. There's no reason you need ever tell him anything about me."

"But if you and I are engaged—"

"An engagement of convenience. That's all it will be. A ploy to allow us to work together to discover the identity of your father's killer and bring him, or her, to justice."

Diana pondered Matt's suggestion. She didn't quite see why

they needed a false engagement in order for her to live as a guest in his house. She'd stayed at Ben's house in Bangor when she'd been in Maine. Maggie Northcote hadn't been much of a chaperone, but the proprieties had been observed. There had been no scandal—at least none that stemmed from sharing close quarters with an unmarried man.

"Why claim we're to marry?" she asked. "It seems an unnecessary lie. Besides, Miranda already knows when I arrived in Denver."

"And she'll want to find out what you've been up to. She can visit my bride-to-be. She can't come here to see you."

He hadn't answered her question, Diana thought, but she let the matter drop. She was more than ready to leave Holladay Street. She'd done all she could here, and there seemed little advantage in staying longer at the Elmira. The only thing holding her back was the sense of responsibility she felt towards her mother's employees.

"I'd like to close the Elmira," she said, "but I can't just toss the other residents out into the street."

"Is that all that's keeping you from agreeing to move in with me?"

"I guess it is," she admitted, although she still had reservations about passing herself off as his future bride.

"Send them all to Torrence. You know I own a dance hall there. They can have the rooms on the second floor."

"That's very generous of you, but are you sure you want to risk having them turn your dance hall in to a brothel?"

"What they do once they move in is their own business."

Diana stared at him. He was almost too anxious for her to move in with him. She wondered, as she watched him examine one of the framed fashion prints that decorated the walls, if she should be suspicious of his motives. He hadn't said he believed in her mother's innocence, or that he agreed with her that Miranda was the most likely suspect. Was something else going on here?

"Why are you willing to do so much for me? For them?"

"Because I care about you, Diana, and I don't want you to have to worry about these people." He took both her hands in his much bigger ones. "Let me ease the burden a bit. Send everyone but Jane to Torrence."

Diana frowned. "What's to become of Jane?"

His smile was gentle. "It had occurred to me that my fiancée should have a lady's maid."

A chuckle escaped her. "If you're not careful, you'll turn me into one of the less admirable characters in Miss Austen's novels." Or one of Mrs. Radcliffe's! "I'll feel quite hemmed in by society's restraints if you have your way."

"The strictures will not be so severe, I promise you."

Needing to put a little space between them, Diana stepped back and tugged free of his grip. "I'll talk to the boarders tomorrow. If they agree, then yes, I will leave the Elmira and accept your hospitality."

"And you'll tell them we intend to marry?" He saw her hesitation. "People will talk to you more easily if we pretend to be engaged, Diana. Especially Miranda."

"All right," she promised. "For now we'll let everyone think we're to wed. But the moment that lie no longer serves any useful purpose, we tell the truth."

"Of course," he agreed.

CHAPTER NINE

૭ઝଓ

The next day, Diana took the opportunity the morning meal provided to talk to everyone who worked at the Elmira Hotel. "I feel fairly certain now that my mother is not coming back," she said. "If she does, she'll be arrested. If she doesn't, someone else must take over here."

"You're selling out?" Red Katie slammed down her fork, making the sausage on her plate leap into the air. Her face turned very nearly the color of her hair and her eyes flashed with a mutinous gleam.

"I'm closing the hotel," Diana answered, "but any of you who want to can go to Mr. Hastings's place in Torrence. He's offered you free lodging until you get established there."

"Torrence?" Jane looked startled.

"A mining town?" Honeycomb sounded offended.

"Them miners got money," Long Tall Linda mused, her horsey face creased in thought.

"True enough," Maybelle agreed.

Diana took a deep breath and told them about Ed Leeves's threat. "He was *not* here on my mother's behalf. I am certain of that."

"Why should Matt Hastings do us any favors?" Maryam asked, fixing cold eyes first on Diana, then on Jane.

Diana hesitated. She didn't have a good answer for them, except the lie Matt wanted her to tell. If she was going to convince Miranda the engagement was real, she supposed this was as good a time as any to practice the role of bride-to-be. She could use the rehearsal. "Mr. Hastings has asked me to marry him."

That announcement caused even more of an uproar than her suggestion that they leave town. Congratulations seemed sincere. So did the quizzical look she got from Maryam. No one questioned her story outright, making her wonder if she was a better actress now than when she'd been with Todd's Touring Thespians. She'd only been on stage twice while Evan was a member of that company. Both times she'd been filling in for an ingenue so ill she couldn't rise from her sick bed. Both times she'd forgotten lines and missed cues. Evan had been furious with her.

"So. We're moving to Torrence." The professor polished off the last of his coffee and tipped back in his chair. "Does the town have a base ball team?"

"If it doesn't, you can start one," Red Katie told him.

And just that easily, the decision was made.

"Then the Elmira is closed," Diana said. "We'll spend the day packing and leave first thing tomorrow."

There were a dozen small tasks to be done before abandoning the building. The professor took on the job of boarding up windows. Jane handed out dust covers to put over the furniture.

When Jane headed for the Chinese parlor, Diana followed, hoping for the opportunity to speak to her in private. "If you'd care to stay here instead of going to Torrence," she said, "there is a position open in the Hastings house as my personal maid."

Jane's expression remained bland but her eyes snapped behind her spectacles. "I do not believe I'd care to be someone's servant." She shook out a dust cover with a snap of fabric and threw it over a chair.

"No, I didn't think you would." A number of aspects of Matt's plan seemed less reasonable by daylight. "Does the title of companion suit you any better? All it entails is accompanying me whenever I go out, along with the chaperone Matt has hired."

Jane sighed. "If you're determined to close the hotel, I don't suppose I have much choice. I have nowhere else to go."

"You could make the trip to Torrence with the others. Mr. Kent is there, I believe."

"Mr. Kent would not appreciate having me show up on his doorstep unannounced," Jane said. "I'll stay with you."

She flung the next dust cover with even more force. Diana decided it might be best to leave her alone for a bit. Whether it was because the Elmira was closing or because Alan Kent had disappointed her in some way, Jane was not happy.

Diana slipped out of the Chinese parlor and nearly collided with Maryam.

"Jane's to be your companion?" Maryam's sarcasm was as obvious as the fact that she'd been eavesdropping.

"Is there something wrong with that?"

Maryam shrugged and toyed with the pink ribbon that held her dark hair away from her face. "Just strikes me as peculiar, that's all."

"Why?"

"Maybe because Matt Hastings was talking to her last night, before he went in to visit you. Heads together, real intense. None of my business," Maryam added, "but I can't help but think maybe he's looking to have two women for the price of one." Sniggering, she sashayed off down the hall.

"That Maryam no like you." Ning spoke at her elbow, giving Diana a start. She had no idea where the boy had come from, but she wished he hadn't overheard a remark so obviously inappropriate for a child's ears.

He was correct about Maryam. But then, Maryam didn't seem to like anyone very much. Diana was inclined to attribute her malicious parting shot to jealousy. "Companion" was, after all, a decided step up from prostitute. Matt had probably just been making some innocuous remark to Jane. About the weather perhaps.

Ning tugged at her sleeve. "Where I go, Mrs. Diana? I come with you to Mr. Hastings?"

"No, Ning. For now I want you to stay with your aunt, but you'll still be working for me." Fishing into her pocket, she drew out an envelope in which she'd put most of the cash Elmira had tossed at her. "This is your pay, in advance. If you're as wise as I think you are, you'll make it your nest egg. Do you know what that means?"

Ning peered into the envelope. "I know." The money disappeared into the folds of his blue blouse.

"Do you also know where Mr. Hastings lives?"

He nodded.

"And are you familiar with the Windsor Hotel?"

Another nod.

"Mattie Silks says there's a Chinese boy working at the hotel. Do you know him?"

Ning scraped the floor with one toe, head bowed, and grudgingly admitted it. "Wen. My cousin."

"Excellent." At his frown, she chuckled. "Don't worry, Ning. I'm not planning to replace you. In fact, you have a very important role to play. Wen will be your contact, but you'll be the boss."

She reached once more into her pocket and this time retrieved a letter she had written early that morning.

"Take this to the Windsor Hotel and give it to the desk clerk. It is for a gentleman who will be arriving from the East in a day or two. It tells him to send word to me by way of the Chinese boy in the Windsor's bar. Make sure Wen knows how to reach you, so that you can come at once to Mr. Hastings's house."

She hesitated, tapping one finger thoughtfully against her lower lip. She hadn't told Matt what Horatio Foxe's last telegram had said and she didn't intend to. A day or two should be long enough to find opportunities to talk with Miranda and with some of her father's friends. After that, she'd face the music.

"It would be best if Mr. Hastings didn't know what you're really up to." She'd have enough explaining to do as it was. "If anyone asks, say you've come for your reading lesson. Do you understand?"

"Yes, Mrs. Diana. I understand good."

She watched him head out to run her errand, wishing she had even half his confidence. Moving into Matt's house might be a huge mistake, but belated second thoughts weren't enough to make her change her mind. Not at this late date.

She'd just have to hope that everything went according to plan when "the gentleman from the East" arrived at the Windsor.

ଞଠଔ

Thursday afternoon was the time most of the girls who plied their trade on Holladay Street had free. After sleeping till noon, some frequented the horse races at Overland Park. Others paraded uptown in tallyhos drawn by two horses, ostensibly to do their shopping but really to see and be seen.

On the twenty-sixth day of April, however, the activity started early. The Denver, South Park & Pacific Railroad ran two daily express trains that stopped in Torrence. The first left Denver at eight in the morning.

A platform wagon and two six-passenger hacks stood in front of the Elmira Hotel at seven, the first piled high with trunks and the others occupied by eight boarders, one piano player, a cook and a night maid.

"Ning, you young scalawag," Red Katie called out. "Come and give us a kiss goodbye." She lifted the brown veil she wore to ward off freckling and the boy, who had been watching from the shadow of the porch, darted forth and complied.

The sound of another vehicle approaching distracted Diana

from her farewells. She turned to see an open victoria turn onto Holladay Street and had no difficulty recognizing its sole passenger as Mattie Silks. The diamond-studded cross she wore around her neck winked bright in the morning sun.

Mattie remained ensconced on the plush upholstery until her driver came around to help her out of the four-wheeled vehicle, then descended to the street with as much dignity as any wealthy dowager.

In the harsh light of day, fine lines showed around her eyes and mouth, suggesting she was closer to forty than Diana had previously thought. More surprising still was how alert Mattie was for such an early hour. Her face had a fresh scrubbed look and her blue eyes sparkled with curiosity. It was possible, Diana supposed, given how little she knew about the personal habits of the many madams of Holladay Street, that some of them rose at dawn. And perhaps, like Jane, Mattie started the day with a bracing splash of cold water and a session of calisthenics.

"So it's true," Mattie said, coming to a halt at Diana's side and tilting her head back to peer into her face. "You're closing up shop and sending everyone away."

"I thought it best."

"A word of advice, Mrs. Spaulding. It is never a good idea to give up your independence completely. And marriage is not always the best bargain a woman can make."

Diana's hands clenched at her sides. "I hadn't realized my engagement to Matt Hastings had become general knowledge." She should have warned the girls not to gossip but it hadn't occurred to her that they would. Foolish of her.

"If I were you, I'd tell him you've changed your mind. Keep this place open. If you don't like living here, buy a little house of your own elsewhere."

"Is that what you do? Live somewhere else?"

"Just moved into a place over on Lawrence Street." Pride underscored every word. "It's in a fashionable residential district.

I've got posh neighbors now."

Diana couldn't help but share Mattie's pleasure in the accomplishment. "It is kind of you to offer advice, but there are other reasons for closing the Elmira."

"Threats, you mean?"

"So you know about my visit from Ed Leeves, too?" Why was she surprised? Holladay Street was worse than a small town. She could see Pearl Adams's house from where she stood. Pearl was watching them from the porch, still in her nightgown, a bright paisley shawl the only thing keeping her decent.

"I know," Mattie said, "and I can solve that little problem for you. Lease the Elmira to me. I'll pay you $120 a month. That's more than the going rate."

But Diana just shook her head. "The hotel isn't mine, either to sell or to lease."

"You can't believe your mother intends to return?"

"I don't know what my mother is up to." And that, at least, was the truth.

"Waste of a good real estate. Waste of good talent, too. Whyever did you insist Hastings pension off your mother's girls before you'd agree to marry him? You'd have done better to ask for jewelry."

That twist of the facts made Diana blink in surprise. But if Mattie didn't have all the details straight, Diana saw no reason to enlighten her. Let the denizens of Holladay Street believe what they liked.

Mattie was watching her, waiting for an answer. Diana permitted herself a small, secretive smile. "It seemed a good idea at the time."

"Mrs. Diana. They leave now."

"Coming, Ning."

"You sure he's not for sale?" Mattie asked, eyeing the boy with a predatory gaze.

"Very sure."

☙❧

Mrs. Ernestine Bowden, stout and white-haired, was the very model of a dignified elderly lady. She wore a plain, single-skirted brown velvet dress with a soft tulle handkerchief folded across the breast and lace ruffles at her wrists. On her head was a decorous white cap tied loosely under her chin with ribbons. She did not look up when Diana, Matt, and Jane entered Matt's sitting room. She did not appear to hear them, and from the way she squinted at her embroidery, Diana suspected she was half blind as well as somewhat deaf.

"Mrs. Bowden," Matt shouted, "may I present my fiancée, Diana Spaulding."

Mrs. Bowden didn't move.

He touched her sleeve and she jumped. "Oh, Mr. Hastings. I did not realize you'd returned. Good afternoon, sir." She peered nearsightedly around him at Diana and Jane. "And which one of these lovelies is your betrothed?"

Diana stepped forward to be presented.

Mrs. Bowden smiled politely as the introductions were made, but said nothing, making Diana wonder if she had all her wits about her. Matt repeated himself. Diana leaned forward to say how pleased she was to meet Mrs. Bowden and ask if she had lived in Denver long.

"Did you hear what I said?" she asked when Mrs. Bowden did not respond to conversational gambit.

"I like red," the old lady announced, and held up her embroidery hoop. Crimson silk threaded the needle with which she was cross-stitching a large flower.

Diana glanced at Jane, who shrugged.

"Deaf as a post, poor thing," Matt said.

"Does she at least understand why you hired her?"

"To keep you company."

This became only too clear when Mrs. Bowden insisted upon making her way up the stairs, in spite of painful arthritis, to "help" her new charge get settled in.

"You and Mrs. Bowden have adjacent bedrooms at the opposite end of the hall from mine." Matt showed Diana into a large, airy chamber. "Jane will sleep in your dressing room."

Diana made no objection once she saw that it was larger than the attic quarters Jane had occupied at the Elmira. She inspected the view from her windows next, pleased to discover that they overlooked her former home. In fact, if she wasn't mistaken, she was directly across from Miranda's bedroom. That view might prove useful, she thought, especially if Miranda were given to entertaining suspicious gentlemen.

She wondered where that thought had come from. Although Miranda had been her father's mistress before she'd become his wife, Diana had heard nothing to indicate that she'd taken a lover while he was still alive. Then again, she didn't suppose she would have. She hadn't been associating with society women on Holladay Street.

Although the suspicion was unsupported, it continued to nag at her as she, Jane, and Mrs. Bowden unpacked. If Miranda had taken a lover, that would have given her even more reason to get rid of her wealthy older husband.

Among the belongings Diana had brought to Matt's house was the list of questions she had made for herself on her first full day in Denver. Jane came across it while putting away Diana's clothing.

"Are you still trying to prove your mother's innocence?" she asked.

"I'm still hoping to prove someone else killed my father," Diana corrected her. She laid out her tortoiseshell comb and hair receiver on the dresser and reached into her gripsack for the hand mirror, brush, button hook, and shoehorn that completed the set.

"'What evidence is there against Mother aside from the glove?'" Jane read.

"None," Diana replied, "and the glove was planted. Remember what Nellie told us. Mother was wearing a different pair that night."

"She could have changed them."

"Gone prepared to get the first pair bloody? I don't think so. And if she had, she'd have tossed them away, or left them at the Windsor along with the knife."

Jane blanched at the mention of the murder weapon.

"I wonder why that was left behind?" Diana mused. "I never thought to ask about it. No one is claiming it belonged to Mother, so I suppose it must be a very ordinary type of knife, something anyone might carry for protection. In the heat of anger, it came out. Passionate hatred made the killer plunge it into Father more than once. That took strength . . . or very great anger."

"Stop!" Jane shuddered. "I don't want to hear about such things. I've had nightmares about it as it is, imagining the sensation of steel sinking into flesh, striking bone, pulling out with a little sucking sound and a great gush of blood."

Diana stared at her. "And I thought I had an overactive imagination! Don't dwell on it, Jane." She took the list of questions from the other woman's limp hand and glanced at it.

When and where did Mother threaten Father before witnesses and who were they? At the Windsor, according to Charlie, in a ballroom at Christmas time. But what she'd threatened was not murder. She'd vowed to make him pay for what he'd done to her. Elmira claimed she had been planning the worst kind of revenge on her former spouse—financial ruin. She'd wanted him alive so she could watch him suffer.

Who else had overheard? Miranda? Was that when she'd conceived the idea of framing Elmira for her own crime?

Did anyone see Mother at the Windsor that night? No.

Who saw Father at the Windsor before he was killed? No one had seen him enter the suite. That was an important point. That had to have been deliberate on his part. He'd been hiding something. Which brought Diana to *Why was he at the Windsor?* Answer: to meet someone, probably his mistress.

Who else besides Mother might have wanted to kill him?

She'd written only one name after that question: Miranda. But there were other possibilities. In all fairness, Diana knew she should consider them suspects. She located the stub of a pencil in a pocket and scribbled briefly.

Jane came up behind her and read over her shoulder. "Ed Leeves. Matt Hastings. Father's mistress." She pursed her lips. "No other suspects?"

"Not so far. And I still think Miranda is the most likely person to have killed him. I hope Matt's right, that her own curiosity will drive her to call on me here. I want very much to talk to her."

In the meantime, there was one other person Diana had been looking forward to seeing again. As soon as everything had been unpacked and put away, she found her way to Matt's kitchen.

Dorcas Johnson was just as Diana remembered her, a red-cheeked and robust individual of indeterminate age with bags under her eyes, wobbly double chins, and enormous dewlaps thickening her upper arms. She greeted Diana with a hug that almost smothered her against an ample bosom.

"You've grown, child! Let me look at you." She set Diana away from her and examined her thoroughly, a wide grin on her face. "Very nice. Now what's this I hear about you marrying Mr. Matt?"

Diana found she could not lie to Dorcas. At the first attempt, the old woman knew she was fibbing and promptly whisked her away into the private quarters she occupied as cook and housekeeper.

"No one here now but us chickens. Out with it."

Diana confessed everything.

"Can't say I approve," Dorcas said. "But then I haven't approved of much going on around here the last few years. I wouldn't work for her." She jerked her head in the general direction of Miranda's house. "But I wasn't about to follow your mama into sin and degradation neither."

"I'm glad you stayed close."

"You just want me to make you some of my blackberry buckle."

Diana's mouth watered at the thought. "Would you?"

"I'll think about it. I cook the meals here, but I'm not at anybody's beck and call. I'm too old for that nonsense. I don't wait on people and I don't do extras. You or your chaperone or your companion want anything more than three squares a day, unless I'm in a very good mood, you fix it yourselves. Even Mr. Matt understands that."

"Trained him well, did you? I seem to remember you tried to make Father fend for himself when it came to late night snacks. He threatened to fire you."

"I work hard," Dorcas grumbled. "I need my sleep. To bed at nine, like clockwork, that's me. And up with the roosters."

Diana remembered Dorcas's uncompromising stance on "extras" late that same night, after an evening out with Matt. He'd introduced her as his intended bride to dozens of people who'd known her father.

"Some warm milk?" Jane asked when Diana and Matt found her waiting up in the sitting room upon their return. "Long Tall Linda swears by it to help a body settle down to sleep."

"No need," Diana assured her. "And if you want some for yourself, you'll have to fix it. Mrs. Johnson went to bed hours ago." So, she was certain, had Mrs. Bowden, who had not accompanied them to the gathering at the St. James.

"Let me show you where everything is," Matt offered. "I often make a hot toddy for myself in the evening."

Jane sent Diana a doubtful look before going with him.

Diana climbed the stairs to her bedroom alone. She was exhausted and knew the next day would be just as busy. Unfortunately, she'd gained nothing but sore feet and the beginnings of another headache from tonight's venture into society. No one seemed to have liked her father, but neither had anyone she'd met displayed enough hatred to have killed him. Tomorrow she must speak with Miranda, she decided. Somehow, she had to get the woman to give herself away.

Yawning, Diana stepped into her room.

Something moved in the shadows, causing her to bite back a scream.

"Only me, Mrs. Diana."

"Ning! How did you get in here?" She hastened to light the lamp.

Grinning, Ning pointed to the open window. "Drainpipe outside."

There was so much pride in his voice that Diana couldn't bring herself to reprimand him for the risk he'd taken. "You could have come to the kitchen door. Dorcas would have let you in."

"Gentleman say not."

For a moment Diana couldn't breathe. "He's *here?* So soon?"

Ning nodded. "He send message. Not written down. Say you come first thing tomorrow to hotel." He gave her the room number. "He wait."

"Oh, Lord."

"You okay, Mrs. Diana?"

"Yes. Yes, of course, Ning. You've done a fine job, but you'd better go now, before anyone sees you here or hears us talking."

"You go first thing tomorrow?"

"Oh, yes, Ning. I go." But she doubted that her long-awaited reunion with Ben Northcote would go as smoothly as she'd hoped.

soc

You weren't supposed to get here so soon," Diana said the moment Ben opened the door to let her into his suite at the Windsor Hotel.

That's my Diana, Ben thought. *Tart and truthful.*

He stepped back to study her. To his mind she was perfection from her pert little nose to her trim ankles. A lock of her hair tumbled over her collar, having escaped the confines of the bun underneath her favorite green hat with its jaunty feather. Ben resisted an urge to tuck the curl back into place. If he touched her, he wouldn't want to let go, and if she hadn't wanted him to come to Denver, if what he'd heard last night turned out to be true and she was going to marry someone else . . . .

She was staring back at him as if she were trying to memorize his features. The look in her wide-spaced blue eyes gave him hope.

"You knew I'd follow you," he said, in the mildest voice he could manage.

"I hoped. But I appear to have some large and frightening skeletons in my closets."

Her voice, low and slightly husky, washed over him like warm rain. He'd missed her voice. He'd missed everything about her, from the way she folded her hands in her lap when she was trying to control her temper to the pencil stubs and little notebooks covered in green cloth that she habitually carried on her person.

"After all you've learned about me and my family," Ben said, "how could you think that anything your parents might have done could change the way I feel about you?" He held his hands up, palms out, to prevent her from answering. "If you compare me to Evan Spaulding, I *will* lose my temper."

"You're nothing like Evan. And I did write to you as soon as I could think clearly enough to compose a letter."

He'd have been happier if she'd turned to him full of confusion, needing him to take care of her, but then she would not have been the self-reliant, impulsive, passionate Diana he loved. She'd had to see for herself what was what and a delay would have been intolerable. In his mind he understood that, but his heart was another matter. He fished a telegram from his pocket and handed it to her.

"LETTER ARRIVED FOR YOU FROM DENVER. INTERESTING READING. MOTHER."

Diana groaned. "Maggie read it?"

"Apparently." He opened his arms, and she glided into his

embrace. A long, satisfying while later, they separated. He put a little distance between them. "We need to talk."

"You are a master of understatement," she said. Rather than try to straighten her hat, she removed it, and took off her gloves as well.

"Why don't you start by telling me why you agreed to marry another man?"

Her eyes twinkled. "*How* long have you been in town?"

"Long enough to hear gossip and to wonder, just for a moment, if you make a habit of moving into strange men's homes on short acquaintance."

She hit him on the upper arm with enough force to make him wince. He found the pain oddly reassuring.

"I've known Matt Hastings since I was a child."

"You aren't a child now, and neither is he."

"You're jealous." She sounded surprised, which sparked his anger as nothing else could have.

"Of course I'm jealous! I love you. You've just moved into another man's house, claiming to be his betrothed. How do you expect me to feel?"

"A little confidence in me would be nice!"

"Diana, I don't want to quarrel."

"Then don't!"

They glared at each other for a moment. Then they were kissing. When they separated this time, they were both breathing hard.

"I'm sorry, Ben. I should have written sooner." She reached up to straighten his silk neck scarf. "At first I didn't know what to say to you. Then, by the time I was here and could organize my thoughts . . . well, I did write."

"I wish you'd simply told me what had happened to begin with. I could have come West with you. Or taken the next train. You didn't have to be on your own for a week."

"Maybe I did. And in any case, I didn't want to force you to choose between me and Aaron."

He took both her hands in his and studied her face. She had very fair skin. He'd once compared her complexion to gardenia petals. "Diana, you are the most important person in my life. There are other doctors in Bangor. You know that. But there's only one woman I love and I've been worried sick about her."

"I love you, too, Ben." She sighed. "I had a letter all written, one in which I said I was on my way to Maine to marry you. And then I found out about my father's murder . . . and my mother."

"Foxe filled me in on some of the details."

"Which details? The information he's gotten from the newspaper here is biased. You would not believe what—"

"He told me your mother had disappeared."

"Well, yes."

"And that she had . . . ties with an underworld figure named Ed Leeves. He was concerned about you, Diana. As I am. Do you know where your mother is? If she'd turn herself in—"

"No!" She pulled away from him and began to prowl the confines of the room.

"No you don't know, or no she shouldn't surrender?"

"Both."

"So, you've seen her? Talked to her?" He couldn't say why he was so certain of that fact, but there was no question in his mind but that she had been in direct contact with Elmira Torrence.

"Yes. Once. She didn't kill my father, Ben. I'm sure of it."

He sighed. "So now you're trying to discover who did." It was not a question. "I was afraid of that."

"What else am I to do? Will you help me?"

"I'm here, aren't I?"

"When did you leave Maine?"

"It feels like weeks ago. I bearded Foxe in his den on Saturday morning." He'd been traveling almost constantly since then. He'd left New York that same evening and, after two nights and a day, had reached Chicago, 900 miles distant. He'd suffered through a twenty-four hour delay there, then covered the next legs, from

Chicago to Omaha and Omaha to Denver, on the fastest trains he could catch.

"That explains it. He warned me you were coming, but I assumed you'd been in touch with him by telegram and that he meant you were leaving on Sunday from Maine. I thought I'd have time to carry out a certain . . . plan before you arrived in Denver."

"A plan? I'm not sure I want to hear this."

She made herself comfortable, legs curled beneath her, in the room's one overstuffed chair, and started at the beginning. When she'd finished recounting everything she'd already written to him, she filled in the details of what had happened since.

Ben alternately clenched his jaw and prayed for patience as the story poured out. "Dangerously impetuous" did not even begin to describe Diana's actions.

"How does your engagement to Hastings help the cause?"

"It gets me close to my primary suspect, Miranda Torrence. I planned to move out of Matt's house as soon as you arrived, but since I only moved in yesterday, I'll have to continue the charade a bit longer."

"Isn't that a little unfair to your Mr. Hastings?" He couldn't quite keep the sardonic tone out of his voice.

"I've told you. The engagement isn't real. And it was his idea, a way for us to work together to find Father's killer."

"I don't like it, especially when Hastings himself is on your list of suspects."

"I can eliminate him easily enough. While I'm asking questions of and about Miranda, I can also find out more about Matt. Living in his house provides the perfect opportunity to snoop."

"Just as living in my house let you learn all about me?" He could feel his face stick in a scowl.

"This is not the same." Exasperation edged into her voice. "How many times do I have to tell you that I've already told Matt about you. The engagement is a fiction, Ben. You know it. I know it.

And he knows it."

"But everyone else thinks it is real. Even the gentlemen who gather in hotel bars at midnight to exchange the latest news of the day. You made a dashing couple at the St. James last night. And from the description, you wore the dark green silk." He had particularly fond memories of that dinner gown. "I don't like this, Diana, not one thing about it."

"The engagement will stand only a few more days. I promise."

Ben saw the way her jaw was set, took note of the determined gleam in her eyes, and accepted that he would not be able to dissuade her from her "plan." He resigned himself to letting her go her own way. He'd keep a watchful eye on her, though. He was not about to let her come to any harm.

"I'll say one thing, Diana. Being married to you is never going to be dull."

"What is that supposed to mean?"

"It was intended as a compliment."

Her blue eyes narrowed. "It didn't sound like one."

"It's the closest I can come at the moment." At a loss what else to do, he resorted to hauling her back into her arms.

To Ben's relief, Diana cooperated fully from the moment his lips settled on hers. Neither one tried to speak again until they emerged, breathless, from a long, passionate kiss. By then, the jacket of his dark gray cheviot suit was off, his vest was unbuttoned, and his hand-embroidered silk braces were hopelessly twisted. Her clothing was in similar disarray.

"Do you have any 'plan' for the next hour or so?" he asked in a husky voice.

She smiled sweetly up at him. "Nothing that can't wait."

CHAPTER TEN

ℬↃℭℛ

After wiling away an entire morning with Ben, Diana was more anxious than ever to make progress in finding her father's killer. As soon as she returned to Matt's house, she went into the back yard. As she'd hoped, Miranda's maid was once again outdoors, this time taking advantage of a stretch of good weather to launder and bleach silk hose.

Diana chose her location carefully, then leaned across the wall. "I am surprised she doesn't just send those out to be washed," she called.

Startled, the servant gave a squeak, then looked uncertain. She glanced towards the house but, seeing no sign of Miranda, sent Diana a tentative smile. "Costs money, missus. And she'd rather have black hands than yellow touching her personal stuff."

"Have you been with Mrs. Torrence long?" Diana asked as the young woman went back to sousing the silk up and down in a small tub.

"Two weeks," the maid said. "Seems longer. Haven't been out except to go to church on Sunday. She won't even let me take the evening off to go to Wednesday prayer service."

Diana's hopes plummeted at this confirmation of Matt's

information. A different girl, a redhead, had been employed by Miranda at the time of William Torrence's murder. "Who was here before you?" she asked. "Come to think of it, in a house this size, shouldn't there be two or three girls?"

There had been in her mother's day, she recalled. Two men and three girls had been needed to look after the needs of Mr. and Mrs. William Torrence and daughter.

"Don't know who was here or what happened to 'em." She wrung out each piece of hosiery before dropping everything into a second tub for rinsing. "Shouldn't be talkin' to you, missus. Can't afford to lose this job."

"Just a moment more of your time. Please." Diana abandoned her half-hearted efforts to trick information out of the maid. She preferred a direct approach in any case. "I need your help to find my father's killer. And from inside the house, no one can see me standing here."

The latter statement earned Diana a doubt-filled look.

"I lived there once. I know."

"I'm sorry your father got killed, missus, but Mrs. Torrence, she's a devil to work for. She won't like me talkin' to you."

"If she's such a devil, then you'd be better off in someone else's employ. It's my understanding that cooks and girls for private families are in great demand all over the state. I'll find you another job if she fires you. You have my word on it. What's your name?"

"Martha."

"Well, Martha, you can rest assured you won't have any difficulty getting another place. I might even hire you myself. Mr. Hastings thinks I need a lady's maid and at the moment all I have is a companion. And a chaperone."

She felt her lips twitch at the absurdity of that situation, then got herself under control. There was nothing remotely funny about murder.

"Now, Martha," she continued. "I know Mr. Hastings's man Gilbert has already bothered you about this, and talked to the others in the household, too, but it is terribly important that I learn as much as I can about my father's widow."

"Gilbert? He the one with the mutton chops?"

"That's right." Matt's manservant was inordinately proud of his whiskers.

Martha soused and squeezed, then spread the last pair of hose on the grass for the sun to whiten and dry. "Nobody's been asking questions, missus."

Diana swallowed her surprise and pressed doggedly on. "It wouldn't have seemed like an interrogation. No doubt he was more subtle than I am." And perhaps that was why Gilbert had failed to learn anything. "You can help me, Martha, if you will. Even if you weren't here when my father died, you must know something of Mrs. Torrence's habits. I will be blunt. Does she have a lover?"

Martha lifted the first tub and dumped the water into the nearest flower bed. "What goes on behind closed doors I can't say, but she's sure enough had gentlemen callers." The note of disapproval in her voice was so strong it almost qualified as moral outrage. Martha the devout church member was plainly in conflict with Martha the loyal servant. She and Dorcas would get along splendidly.

"What gentlemen?" Diana asked. "And do you remember when they called and how long they stayed?"

Picking up the second tub, Martha walked towards the brick wall, ostensibly to toss the contents onto a border of rosebushes. She stopped in front of Diana and met her eyes. "Your Mr. Hastings for one."

"He is her closest neighbor."

"*Real* close," Martha said. "He lets himself in the back way whenever he wants. You ask me, he'd been doin' that for some time before I came here."

Taken aback by Martha's certainty, Diana was momentarily at a loss for words. Miranda and . . . Matt?

Before she could reconcile herself to the idea of the two of them as lovers, Martha offered a second candidate. "Then there's the other one," she said. "Mr. Kent."

That suggestion wasn't much more palatable. Poor Jane!

"He works for the Torrence Mining Company," she reminded Martha. "His visits might be just business."

"Maybe so, but the other morning he was here at the crack of dawn, right off the train, and he went straight up to Mrs. Torrence's bedroom and shut the door." She gave a disapproving shake of her head.

"The day after I came to call?" Diana guessed.

"Musta been."

"Has he returned since?" She hesitated. "Has Mr. Hastings?"

"Both of 'em. Mr. Kent, he was back the next day. Saturday, that would be. And the next. Sunday. And Mr. Hastings, he came once, that I know about, the day after that."

"Monday?"

Martha nodded and dumped the last of the water.

And on Tuesday, Matt had proposed his "engagement of convenience." Diana rubbed her hands over her arms, suddenly chilled. She was very much afraid there was a connection between one event and the other.

"Thank you, Martha," she murmured. "You've been very helpful. If Mrs. Torrence causes you any difficulty, go to the Windsor Hotel and ask for Mr. Northcote. He'll see that you're taken care of."

Martha started to turn away, then glanced back over her shoulder at Diana. "Missus? That Gilbert? Wasn't just he was careful what he asked. He didn't come asking questions at all. He ain't been on this side of the wall since I come here."

Diana watched until Martha disappeared into the house. She tried to tell herself that Gilbert had done his investigating elsewhere, perhaps finding Miranda's bodyguard in some local saloon and questioning him there. But the more she thought about what Martha had told her, the more certain she became that Matt had lied to her.

Neither he nor his man had asked any questions of Miranda's servants since the murder. More damning still, he was apparently a regular visitor at the Torrence mansion, in spite of his rift with Diana's father. Or because of it? He had been having an affair with Miranda.

She studied the house, wondering if she should call on her stepmother. If Matt was counting on jealousy to bring the widow to his door, he'd obviously miscalculated, but perhaps there was more to it than that. What if Miranda and Matt had plotted together to kill William Torrence?

Diana frowned. That wouldn't explain Alan Kent.

Diana hated to believe Kent would abandon a good-hearted girl like Jane for a murdering hussy, but she knew it was entirely possible he had. Miranda was a wealthy widow now, a condition many men found most attractive. She remembered, too, that he and Jane had been quarreling when Diana interrupted them that first morning. And only yesterday, Jane had told her that Alan Kent wouldn't be happy if she, Jane, turned up in Torrence.

Perhaps, Diana thought, she should ask *Jane* what she knew.

But first she needed to find out what Matt was up to. He had left the house early. He'd told Diana he had business to attend to concerning a civil case. He'd said he expected to dine in town with his client. How long he'd be away she could not say, but she imagined that she had time to start her search for incriminating evidence. It was more imperative now than ever that she consider him a suspect. If he had been Miranda's lover, even if he'd since been replaced by Alan Kent, then he'd had as much reason as Miranda herself to get rid of William Torrence.

Two hours later, she'd gone through Matt's study and moved on to his bedroom. She'd found nothing significant. She hadn't expected to unearth a love letter inciting him to murder, but she'd hoped for something to tell her if he was friend or foe.

"Diana? What are you doing in here?"

She jumped at the sound of Matt's voice and whirled to face him. He lounged in the doorway, watching her through narrowed eyes.

"You need a woman's touch," she informed him. She'd planned for this eventuality and had her excuse ready. "You've let the place go shamefully since your mother died. Dust everywhere! And that marble-top wash-stand is in dire need of cleaning. A rag dipped in turpentine is best, since it will not only clean but disinfect as well. And do you know that there is an envelope in your handkerchief drawer—one your mother must have put there—that contains trimmings of rose geraniums and sweet clover? Sachets must occasionally be freshened."

"I had no idea you were so domestic." Matt sounded amused.

"Every woman is given instruction in making a home. It was part of the curriculum at the young ladies' seminary I was sent to in San Francisco. Do you know, for example, why the head of the bed should always face north?"

"No, but I'm sure you're going to tell me."

"It is necessary in order to preserve the harmonious circulation of the body's nervo-electric fluids."

"What on earth does that mean?"

"I have no idea." She forced a smile. "But I do know that iron or brass beds are more sanitary than wood and why feather beds, though soft and warm, are unwholesome. They retain the dampness of perspiration, which develops into the germs of disease. Besides, the odor can become very offensive. I was given an excellent piece of advice concerning feather beds—if you have one, put it in the garret, lock the door, and lose the key."

Matt came into the room and closed the door behind him. "I can see that I do need a woman's touch here. Perhaps we should consider making our engagement real."

She hoped he was joking. She feared that he was not. Reminding herself that Matt had been nothing but kind from the first and that her recent suspicions might well be unfounded, Diana made her voice gentle. "If I'd met you again before I knew Ben, we might have made a match of it. But I love him, Matt, and I imagine, knowing Ben, that he will turn up in Denver soon. He has . . . strong feelings for me, and a certain reluctance to leave me on my own."

Matt hesitated, then put one hand on each of her shoulders, his grip just a little too tight for comfort as he forced her to meet his eyes. "I have feelings for you, too, Diana. Strong feelings. Real feelings. I didn't intend to tell you. I thought, perhaps, if you stayed here awhile . . . ." His face flamed and he let the sentence trail off as his hands slid away.

Her heart went out to him. "I think of you as a friend, Matt, but I love Ben."

"No." He caught her forearm as she tried to walk past him. This time his grip was downright painful.

Diana didn't know what to say to him. She'd never suspected Matt contemplated making their engagement anything more than a ruse. Or that he might be jealous of Ben.

Abruptly, he released her. "Never mind how I feel about you. That isn't important. Or, at least, it isn't important now. What is, Diana, is your mother's safety."

The rapid shift of topic had her blinking in surprise.

"I'll be blunt. She will be caught, Diana. I have no doubt of it, and when she is, I have the means to save her from trial and execution. If you want to spare your mother's life, you will send your Mr. Northcote straight back to Maine when he arrives. I am sure you don't want to cause him unnecessary pain. I suggest a quick amputation rather than a lingering death from gangrene. That's a comparison I'm sure he'd appreciate, being a doctor."

The analogy made her shudder. "I can't let Ben think I've been unfaithful to him."

"You'll have to, if you want your mother freed. You see, I also have information that could hurt her case."

"What information?"

But he shook his head. "I think I'd best keep that quiet, even from you. Suffice it to say that I will turn over all I've discovered to the authorities unless I have a good reason to help Elmira. In other words, if you expect me to keep quiet, you'll do the same. And you'll convince everyone that you really are my fiancée. In a month or two, we'll marry."

"Are you *threatening* me?" She could hardly believe it. Nor could she entirely believe he had evidence against her mother, but she wasn't certain enough to call his bluff.

"I'm telling you the simple facts."

Stunned, Diana gaped at him. "How can you claim to have feelings for me and then use blackmail to try and make me stay here? That's not the act of a lover."

"It is the act of a practical man, and I think you are a practical woman. When Northcote gets here, we'll face him together, tell him he's been displaced in your affections. He'll leave and that will be the end of it."

"Only if he believes me."

"He'd *better* believe you."

There was something in his voice that frightened Diana. Matt was deadly serious.

Even if he was lying to her about having evidence of her mother's guilt, Diana could not help but believe that he was a threat to Ben.

The last thing she wanted to do was put the man she loved in danger.

❧❦

The Windsor Hotel had several bars. The one off the lobby was all but empty when Ben walked in. The Chinese boy in native costume, whose sole duty was to keep the marble floors free of cigar butts and quids, had nothing to do. His face took on an eager expression when Ben passed him, probably remembering the generous tip he'd gotten the night before.

Ben nodded to Wen but kept going. He'd already discovered which of the six bartenders was most inclined to gossip and headed straight for his station. "Evening, Harry," he greeted him.

"Mr. Northcote, isn't it?" Harry's whiskered face, dominated by large blue eyes, wore a friendly expression.

"That's right. A whiskey, if you please."

"Right you are." He bounced off, light on his feet for one so rotund, and was back a moment later with Ben's drink.

Only one other customer sat within earshot, a man in a red bow tie and a costly fedora the color of old ivory. A few minutes later, he finished his drink and left.

Harry watched him go, shaking his head in disapproval as he stared at the fellow's boots. "I never trust a man whose heels are run-over."

Ben chuckled appreciatively at the comment. It was easy to fall into casual conversation after that, small exchanges each time Harry came back Ben's way. In between, Ben worried about Diana. She was a terrible liar and a worse actress. He wanted her out of the Hastings house as soon as possible.

Earlier in the day, he had made a point of tracking down Matt Hastings so he could get a look at him. He hadn't been hard to find. Hastings was well known in Denver. Ben had been directed to a restaurant where the lawyer was dining with a client. He'd gotten close enough to their table to decide that Diana's benefactor had shifty eyes.

"You like base ball?" the bartender asked. "I can tell you where they play."

It took a moment for Ben to think what he meant. Although the local mills back home sponsored leagues, Ben had never attended a game.

"Our club belongs to the National Association of Base Ball

Players," Harry continued, a note of pride in his voice.

Ben pretended interest, but his patience was wearing thin. "Hear you had a murder here not too long ago," he said at the next opportunity.

"You heard right, friend. Fella stabbed to death in his room."

"Killed with a knife? Nasty."

But the barkeep shook his head. Lowering his voice to a conspiratorial whisper, he said, "Letter opener."

"What?"

"Letter opener. Brass. With the hotel's name on it. There's probably one just like it in your room."

"So someone just picked it up and stabbed him? Murder on impulse?"

"They say his ex-wife did him in."

"You don't sound like you believe it."

The bartender shrugged. "Plenty of other folks had as much reason to hate him. And I don't figure he'd have turned his back on Elmira."

"He was stabbed in the back?" Diana had said that the knife was sticking out of his chest when he was found.

"Looked to me like he got it first in the back, staggered away as the blade came free, then turned to take another blow or two from the front before he fell."

"You saw the body?"

"I saw it. Spit on it, too. That's how little I thought of Timberline Torrence."

"You sure *you* didn't kill him?"

Harry chuckled. "Not me. I'm a peaceable soul."

Ben took a long swallow of whiskey. "Who might have, if not the former wife?"

"Old enemies. Old rivals. Big Ed Leeves, for one. He's a friend of the ex-wife's, if you know what I mean. Then there's the new wife's old suitor." Another customer came in, and Harry went off to fill an order.

Ben didn't press for details right away, much as he wanted to. Wary of seeming too interested, he waited an hour before bringing the conversation back to the subject of Miranda Torrence and the man who'd been courting her before her marriage.

"Fella named Matt Hastings," Harry said. "Lawyer here in Denver. He used to be partners with Torrence in a mining venture. Mrs. Torrence was Miranda Chambers then. The way I heard it, she was going to marry Hastings, until he lost his fortune. Swindled by Torrence. Short time later, he lost Miss Chambers to the old man, too. Well, can't blame a girl for taking advantage of a situation. Old 'Timberline' Torrence had a lot of money and it's all hers now."

Well, well, thought Ben. What a coincidence.

He didn't believe in coincidences.

"Must have made her nervous."

"What?"

"Thinking he might replace her one day."

The bartender laughed but didn't comment. If Torrence had been keeping a mistress at the Windsor, his secret was still safe. No one on the staff would admit to a thing.

Ben sipped his drink and wondered about the identity of the "other woman." Maybe it wasn't loyalty to the dead man. Maybe the missing mistress was someone influential enough in Denver society, or wealthy enough, to buy the continued silence of the hotel's employees.

"How come folks here know so much about what went on in a little town way up in the mountains?" he asked after a sufficient interval had passed. "I never even heard of Torrence, Colorado before I arrived in Denver."

"Lots of folks came here from there. Just like folks from Leadville did after their big silver strikes. Got to spend the money somewhere," he added with a chuckle.

"So William Torrence might have had a lot of old enemies up to Torrence, as well as in Denver?" Ben hoped he didn't sound too eager for information.

Harry gave another shrug, then jerked his head towards a heavily-jowled gentleman drinking at the other end of the bar. "They're sure thick to the ground here. That there's Charlie Duncan. Assistant manager of this hotel. Once upon a time he worked for William Torrence. Didn't like him much, though I haven't heard him say so since the murder."

Charlie, the assistant manager. The man who'd given tours of the murder scene. Ben recognized him from Diana's description.

Another coincidence?

"Mr. Duncan," he called. "Buy you a drink?"

೮೨⧖

"You look restless," Jane said. "Let me make you some warm milk. It worked wonders for me last night."

Diana turned from the window. "Why are you so anxious to get warm milk down me?"

Matt had watched her like a hawk all through the evening meal and insisted on staying in afterward. They'd passed three interminable hours playing whist with Jane and Mrs. Bowden, until Diana's nerves were stretched to the breaking point.

When Jane wouldn't answer her question or meet her eyes, Diana was suddenly awash with dire suspicions. She sank into the bedroom chair, her hand over her mouth. Was it possible?

"You meant to drug me again," she whispered. "Oh, Jane . . . why?"

"It wasn't my idea," Jane protested. "Not this time."

"Then whose—?" The truth burst upon her with shattering clarity. "Matt."

"It isn't laudanum, either. It's something stronger. He wants you out cold tonight. He said he'd turn me into the street if I didn't get you to take the stuff."

"Why?"

"Why do you think? He doesn't want you to be able to fight him off."

"Did he arrange this on Tuesday, before he proposed to me?"

"How did you—? No. No, on Tuesday he just asked if I'd like a job. I told him no. I didn't know then that you meant to close the hotel."

The way Jane's face was working, Diana was afraid she was about to burst into tears. "It's all right, Jane." Enfolding the younger woman in her arms, Diana patted her on the back. "It's all right. You didn't go through with it."

"I almost did. I would have if you'd taken the milk last night. I told myself what he was up to wasn't so bad. He wants to marry you."

"He wants to force me into marriage against my will."

"Most women would think he's a good catch," Jane reminded her. "You could do worse."

"Not if he's a murderer."

With a gasp, Jane broke free, her eyes wide and startled. "You can't mean that!"

"He *was* one of my suspects. But if he killed my father, why does he want to marry me? Miranda's the one who inherited Father's money."

"Maybe Miranda found somebody she likes better," Jane whispered.

Once again Jane had dropped her gaze to the carpet, so that Diana could not see the expression on her face. She almost asked if Jane knew about Alan Kent's visits to the house next door, but she was still preoccupied by thoughts of Matt's perfidy. She shuddered at the knowledge that Matt wanted to marry her badly enough to try and trap her into wedding him.

"As soon as it is possible to do so without causing a fuss," she told Jane, "we are leaving this house."

"If you don't want a fuss, you'd better pretend to drink the warm milk."

Diana supposed she was right, but the more she thought about the narrow escape she'd had, the more nervous she became. As soon as Jane brought the milk, Diana dumped it into the chamberpot. Then she sent Jane off to bed in the adjoining room.

Once she was alone, she paced. As she went over everything she'd learned since coming to Denver, she became more and more concerned. She had been foolish not to leave here as soon as Matt threatened her. He couldn't have stopped her. It had been broad daylight, and Jane and Dorcas and Mrs. Bowden had been in the house.

Cursing her own stupidity, she stopped at the window, staring across at Miranda's dimly lit room. Her focus sharpened. The other woman appeared to be packing. Trunks and boxes were scattered everywhere.

So much for luring Miranda into visiting Matt's house.

Diana raised the sash and studied the drainpipe Ning had used. It would never hold her weight. A pity Ning wouldn't be back tonight, but he'd come for his lesson just as she'd been about to start searching Matt's study and she'd sent him away. She'd told him not to come back until tomorrow.

Tomorrow was entirely too far away.

She swung around to glare at the door. There was no lock. Clearly Matt's plan was to wait until she was asleep, creep into her bed, and compromise her. It sounded like something out of a novel, but that didn't mean it wouldn't work.

Diana had never cared for the role of helpless heroine tied to the railroad tracks. She seized a straight back chair, carried it to the door, and wedged it underneath the knob. It wouldn't stop anyone determined to break in, but she didn't think Matt wanted to call attention to himself. The revelation of a late night foray into her room would only work in his favor if it appeared she had invited him in.

An hour passed with no sound from the hall. Then she heard footsteps. The knob turned. The chair moved an inch and stopped.

CHAPTER ELEVEN

∞∞

Being polite to Matthew Hastings over breakfast on Saturday morning was one of the most difficult things Diana had ever done.

"I believe we can successfully challenge your father's will," he said as he spread marmalade on a slice of toasted bread.

"I beg your pardon."

"The Torrence fortune can be ours, Diana. I may not be much of a criminal lawyer, but I'm an excellent civil attorney."

"I don't want the money."

"Nonsense. You're entitled to it. And Miranda is not."

"She's his widow."

"There are several grounds on which we can challenge that. The ceremony in which they were wed was irregular, for one thing. And she deceived him before their marriage."

And after, Diana thought, but instead of saying so she bit into a tender slice of beefsteak. With her mouth full, she'd get herself into less trouble.

Matt continued to outline his plans, convincing her with every word he uttered that this was what he'd been after all along—the Torrence fortune. He was only interested in marrying her because his plans to wed Miranda had fallen through.

Diana kept her eyes on her plate. It seemed she'd been wrong about Miranda having the best motive for murder. Matt's desire for revenge and his obvious greed for wealth now made him her primary suspect.

She wished there had been something to find in the house, but she'd searched almost every nook and cranny and come up empty. If Matt had kept any kind of evidence, it was not in his home, and she couldn't think of any excuse to visit his office on Lawrence Street, let alone search the premises.

"I've sent Gilbert to the train station and the hotels to ask about your friend Mr. Northcote," Matt said. "We'll know when he turns up and act accordingly."

Diana silently cursed her host's efficiency. She had to get out of this house, but how? She didn't want to challenge Matt directly. If she did, she was afraid he'd somehow prevent her from leaving at all. A man who'd secretly feed opiates to a woman and then try to enter her room in the middle of the night to compromise her virtue, could not be trusted to behave like a gentleman. She was considering pleading a headache, which would at least give her privacy to think, when Gilbert unexpectedly returned.

"What are you doing here?" Matt snapped at him.

Gilbert went as stiff as his celluloid shirt front. "I thought you'd want to know. Mrs. Torrence took the express to the mountains this morning."

"Which Mrs. Torrence?" Diana asked.

"The one next door." Gilbert unbent slightly. "She had a great deal of luggage with her, and her maid. I don't think she's coming back for a while."

Matt's curses were not silent, but he recovered himself before he gave away any useful information. Belatedly remembering Diana's presence, he ushered the hapless Gilbert out of the dining room, leaving Diana alone with Jane and Mrs. Bowden.

"Do you think she's really deaf?" Diana asked, sliding her eyes towards the chaperone.

Jane managed a half smile. "I tested her myself. She's lucky if she catches one word in twenty."

"Good. We have to get out of here, Jane."

"I know. But where will we go?"

"To Torrence, after Miranda. And to tell the folks at Matt's dance hall that they're about to be evicted. I doubt he's going to be feeling generous once he discovers I've left him."

"Torrence? Are you sure that's a good idea?"

"No, but that's where Father's business interests were centered, and he had another large house there. I'd still like to talk to Miranda. And Alan Kent, too." Diana caught Jane's eye. "I think he might know more about Matt and Miranda than he's said."

The slight rise of color in Jane's face was all that gave her feelings away. "Shall I pack?" she asked.

"Yes, but don't let anyone see what you're doing. We'll have to time our departure so that there is no one to stop or delay us. Mrs. Bowden takes an afternoon nap. Gilbert will probably be sent back to the depot. That will only leave Matt to worry about."

"Dorcas?"

"She'll help if I ask her to. We need to be ready to set out at short notice. Surely Matt will leave at some point during the day."

Diana glanced again at Jane. Did she really trust the younger woman? Enough to tell her about Ben? The last thing she wanted was for Matt to find out that Ben was already in Denver. If Matt *had* killed her father, he'd have no qualms about committing another murder to secure the fortune he seemed so determined to acquire.

Since Matt Hastings was not rational on the subject of the Torrence inheritance, Diana had no idea to what lengths he'd go in order to achieve his goal. Force an unwilling woman into marriage, it seemed. As long as he needed her to get at her father's fortune, she should be safe from overt violence at his hands. Ben, on the other hand, might be in harm's way.

She pled a headache when Matt returned to the dining room.

"What a pity," he murmured. "Why don't you go lie down? I'll send up a soothing tisane."

Ten minutes later, the steaming drink had been delivered and duly consigned to the chamberpot. Then Diana put the chair back against the door and set about helping Jane pack. They were soon ready to go, but Matt was still in the house.

"We'll wait him out," Diana said with grim determination.

"Is Ning coming for a lesson?" Jane asked. "We could send him for the police."

"And tell them what? It would be our word against Matt's. 'Boarders' against a wealthy, respected attorney."

When Ning arrived, she could sent a message to Ben instead, but he was the last person who should ride to her rescue. The attempt would likely get him killed.

In the end it didn't make any difference whether she decided to put Ning at risk as a messenger or not. Matt greeted the boy at the door and sent him away, telling him "Mrs. Diana" was resting and couldn't be disturbed.

❧❦

Ready?" Charlie asked, grinning from ear to ear.

Ben didn't deign to reply, but he went out of the hotel in the other man's company and climbed into the closed cab Charlie had arranged for. This was probably not a good idea, Ben thought, but he had come up with nothing better since the previous evening.

Ning would keep an eye on Diana until nightfall. Ben had sent the boy off to Matt Hastings's house only a half hour earlier, after a long session with the lad at the hotel. Ning was an observant child. Between them, and with the aid of the Pinkerton men Ben had hired, they'd make sure nothing untoward happened to Diana.

Ben checked his pocket watch. Three o'clock. By now Ning would have told Diana she had bodyguards waiting out on Broadway. If she needed help, all she had to do was open a window and yell.

"Absolute discretion guaranteed," Charlie promised when the driver let them out in Denver's Chinatown a short time later.

In spite of his guide's reassurances, Ben's misgivings increased as he took in his surroundings. "If you're here to hit the pipe, I want no part of it."

"No. No. Only a fool thinks he can indulge himself with opium and not develop an insatiable craving for the drug."

But the sweet scent of the poppy hung in the air, along with the smell emanating from a nearby Chinese laundry.

"This is just a way to reach Holladay Street without anyone getting a look at you," Charlie insisted. "You did say you didn't want to be seen."

From what Charlie had told him, there were a good many Denver citizens, as well as visitors to the city, who'd rather chance being taken in a raid on an opium den than be observed entering a whorehouse. It seemed a trifling distinction to Ben, but he was willing to pretend he shared the sentiment if it got him the information he needed.

Without another word he followed Charlie into a nondescript building and up several steps. They proceeded along a dimly lit hallway until they reached a locked door at the back.

"Who?" asked a muffled voice on the far side when Charlie knocked.

"Pearl," said Charlie. He winked at Ben. "If I wanted to smoke, I'd have said *en she quay.* That means opium smoker in Chinese."

"If you say so."

The sound of a bolt being drawn back riveted Ben's attention to the door, which creaked slowly open to reveal an elderly Chinese gentleman in colorful flowing robes. He was standing on a wide landing, guarding stairs that clearly led into the basement.

"Pay the man," Charlie said.

Ben obligingly deposited five dollars on the outstretched palm, thinking as he did so that the fellow had a rather large, pale hand for an oriental. He did not have time to consider the matter further, however, since Charlie was tugging at his sleeve.

They descended a half dozen steps by the light of a lantern hung from the ceiling and came to another, smaller landing at the turning. A door opened off it, the solid wooden surface broken only by a wicket. At the sound of their footsteps, someone opened it.

"How many?"

Charlie ignored the quavering voice and kept going down. Ben followed, though he cast one glance back over his shoulder. As a physician, he'd studied opium addiction. He had a fair idea what was inside that room.

There would be a plentiful supply of little lamps, pipes, and the black, tarry-looking substance that was opium. The smokers would recline on raised platforms, since the drug took away the will to do anything but sleep and take more opium. Even those who were new to the habit felt the compulsion to smoke at least once a day. True opium addicts were a pitiful sight, with sallow complexions and over-bright eyes dotted with tiny pupils. They were often emaciated, as well, since one of the first symptoms was a loss of interest in food.

The stairs ended abruptly and Ben found himself in a basement, from which a tunnel led underground to the lower level of a parlor house on Holladay Street. He knew it was a high-class place even before they encountered a Negro porter in livery because there was a furnace in the basement. He'd heard such innovations were available but this was the first time he had seen one.

The porter collected their entry fee, then escorted them upstairs and into one of the parlors. The walls were decorated with flocked wallpaper, gold on red in a pattern of flowering tulips enclosed by diamonds, and every few feet a large mirror had been hung. The glass reflected a bevy of young women wearing the high-waisted muslin gowns in fashion some eighty years earlier.

Easier to dispense with, Ben supposed. And certainly more

revealing than more recent styles with hoop skirts and bustles.

A thin, waiflike girl leaped up at the sight of them, dislodging the poodle that had its head on her lap. "Charlie!" she cried. "Did you bring me a present?"

"Would I dare come without one?" he asked, embracing her. When he let her go, he produced a gold ring with what appeared to be a toothpick sticking out of it. On the other end of the toothpick was a small clamp designed to hold a cigarette.

Delighted, the young woman slid the ring onto her finger and gave Charlie a smacking kiss on the cheek.

A demure young brunette, also accompanied by a white poodle, approached Ben. "This is my place," she said, "and I don't know you."

"I brought him, Pearl. He's okay."

Swallowing his surprise that the madam of what Charlie had called "the richest and most exclusive brothel in Denver" was so young, Ben made a polite bow over her hand, brushing his lips across the back of it. "I hope you'll let me stay. I have a most particular reason for wanting to meet you."

Her delicately plucked brows lifted in unison. "To meet *me,* sir?"

He nodded gravely but said no more. He didn't want Charlie knowing any more of his business than necessary, especially since Charlie had once worked for William Torrence. In spite of his obvious dislike of the dead man, he might still have some loyalty to Torrence's widow. Let everyone think he'd come to the parlor house for the usual reason. Time enough to tell Pearl the truth when they were alone in her bedchamber.

But Pearl was not so easily won over, and she had responsibilities. He had to content himself with chatting with her, on and off, for half an hour, while Charlie disported himself in one of the upstairs rooms with his light o' love.

Ben did not give his name. No one expected him to. But in the course of conversation he did reveal he was a physician. He was sipping his second whiskey when he noticed that Pearl, who had been summoned away by one of her girls, was standing in the archway between parlors, watching him with a considering expression on her beautiful face.

He thought at first that someone must have discovered who he was and what he wanted, but quickly dismissed that idea. The only people in Denver who even knew his name, besides Diana and Ning, were Charlie, the desk clerk at the Windsor, and Harry the bartender. No one could possibly connect Ben Northcote from Maine with William Torrence of Colorado.

A moment later, Pearl approached him. There was something tentative in her manner that had not been present earlier. "Are you a good doctor?" she asked abruptly.

"I like to think so."

"And doctors keep confidences, is that right?"

He nodded and took a stab at guessing the problem. "One of your girls is sick?" He hoped she wasn't about to ask him to perform an abortion. He preferred not to engage in criminal activities if he could help it.

"Keep your voice down," she snapped. Seizing his hand, she led him from the room, climbing the stairs to the third floor.

In a small upper room, separate from the others in use, a woman dressed in a loose robe sat at a small table, her face buried in her arms. She was sobbing piteously.

"That's Gwen," Pearl said. "Help her and the night's on the house."

A short time later, Ben was shown into Pearl Adams's private boudoir on the second floor of the parlor house. It was dominated by a brass bedstead covered with a Prince Albert canopy of primrose brocade. The white satin bedspread was embroidered in violets.

"Well?" his hostess demanded. "Is she diseased?"

Ben fought the urge to laugh. The subject was not cause for

amusement among women who depended upon keeping their bodies healthy and attractive in order to earn a living. That "rich and exclusive" clientele would avoid Pearl's place like the plague if it got out that one of her girls had the clap or "old ral," as syphilis was popularly called. An infectious disease like measles or smallpox would hardly be welcome either.

"She has a bad case of barber-itch," he said, settling himself on the satin-covered loveseat by the window. He wasn't planning to leave for some time.

"Never heard of it."

"It is generally a problem for men, but this girl apparently shaves her legs and underarms."

"Most prostitutes do." A wry chuckle burst from Pearl's lips. "One of the things that distinguishes those in our trade from real ladies, along with wearing cosmetics and riding astride."

"Be that as it may, people who shave with a dull razor risk this sort of reaction." He could understand why Pearl had thought it was more serious. What began as pale yellow pimples soon burst and formed hard brown crusts which, in turn, fell off to reveal purplish pimples that took a long time to disappear. The condition could be obstinate, sometimes lasting months. In the meantime the appearance of the skin would tend to discourage potential customers.

"It's not contagious?"

"No. And the treatment is simple enough. I've told her to stop shaving entirely until she's healed, then make sure she uses only a clean, sharp blade. Avoiding exposure to excessive heat and practicing temperance in eating and drinking will speed healing. I recommend a cool, light diet."

"I'll see she gets it," Pearl promised.

"Good. Now, about my payment. I want information, not services."

Suspicious again, Pearl leaned back against an Empire dressing table and crossed her arms beneath her bosom. "What kind of information?"

He let the moment stretch. The only sound in the room was the ticking of the miniature French clock on the mantel. Expensive, he noted, as were all the room's furnishings. Even the perfume stand on the dressing table was made of gold and crystal.

His attention seemed to make Pearl nervous. She crossed to the bed, reached into the night stand drawer, and brought out two items, a small revolver and a prayer book. "Protection for both body and soul," she quipped. "What do you want to know?"

"A simple question to start. You deal with a high-class clientele. How did a fellow like Charlie get in?"

He could see she fought a smile. "This is Saturday night, doctor. All the richest men are at home, pretending to be respectable."

"So you lower your standards?"

She bristled at the implied insult. "Charlie and I go way back. I knew him when I lived in Torrence. It's a little mining town up in the mountains. You've probably never heard of it."

"On the contrary. The name is very familiar." He tracked her movements with his eyes as she moved about the room, now toying with the long strand of pearls wound around her neck, now straightening one of the sketches of flowers that decorated the walls. "In fact, that's why I wanted to talk to you, Pearl. Last night Charlie let it slip that William Torrence provided the money to open this place."

"Damn that Charlie! No one's supposed to know that."

"But Charlie does."

"He *was* the only one. Now he's gone and blabbed to you." Her voice conveyed her disgust with the hopeless Charlie. "I suppose he was drunk."

"Was Torrence one of your rich and exclusive customers?"

"He never came here."

"Just gave you money to set up in business?"

"I earned it." She sounded defensive.

"How?"

Pearl came close, circling him. "I'm beginning to regret asking you to look at that rash. Sure you won't take something else in trade?"

"I was prepared to pay you for information, Pearl. I still am."

"How much?" She ran a finger along the rim of his ear and looked disappointed when Ben didn't react.

"A hundred dollars."

Involuntarily, her eyes widened. Ben was certain she'd earned as much from a single customer before now, but it was an extraordinary sum to pay just to talk. "All right." She left him alone and went to perch on the edge of the bed. "Why not? Timberline Torrence is past caring. A couple of years back, he paid me to move from Torrence to Leadville."

"Leadville?" He'd expected her to say Denver. "Why?"

"I was supposed to keep a real close eye on a fella, if you know what I mean. Report back to Mr. Torrence on everything he did."

"This 'fella' have a name?"

"Evan Spaulding."

Silently, Ben digested that. "Who was he?"

"Somebody who made an enemy of William Torrence. After I got to know him, Evan boasted to me that he'd gotten money out of Mr. Torrence to start his own acting company."

"He was an actor, then?"

"At first. Actor-manager, he called himself. But he wasn't much good at the managing part. By the time I got to Leadville, he was already fighting with the members of his company. A short time later, it folded. He didn't have an act on his own, and he thought vaudeville and burlesque were beneath him, so even though there were plenty of theaters and concert halls in town, he ended up taking a job at the Texas House. That's a gambling hall. A dozen faro tables available twenty-four hours a day."

"Not a bad way to make money."

"Not at all. Most faro banks range in amount from five hundred to two thousand, and that's when the dealers limit single card bets to twenty-five dollars. At the Texas House the proprietors are always willing to take the limit off for the real high-rollers. One fella I know of bet ten thousand dollars on the turn of a card." Her eyes glittered at the memory. "When things get that serious, the floor manager takes over the dealer's box. I heard tell that one floor manager won more than *eighty thousand* for the house during the first few months he was working at the Texas House. Faro banks don't always earn that much, but the ones in Leadville probably average a thousand dollars in profit a month."

"So, did Spaulding make enough to reorganize his troupe?" It wasn't easy pretending he didn't already know what had happened to Diana's late husband, but Ben persevered.

"Not a chance. The damned fool gambled away most of his money." She gave a delicate, ladylike snort. "I found out later he'd nearly lost it all even before he got to Leadville. Charlie told me that. You see, doctor, Mr. Torrence sent Charlie to Denver, to keep an eye on Evan until he left for Leadville. Once he got there, I took over."

"Why all this interest in an actor?" Ben asked.

"You don't ask someone like Mr. Torrence for reasons."

"What happened to Spaulding?"

"Cheated at cards. Got caught. Another fella shot him." She shrugged. "It was no surprise. He may have been a charmer but he was never an honest man."

"So, Spaulding ended up dead. You came here and invested your . . . earnings. And Charlie got a pretty good job at the Windsor."

"That's about the size of it." The caution was back in her voice.

"And then Torrence was killed at the Windsor. There are rumors going around that he was using that suite for assignations. Were you the woman he met there?"

Pearl leapt off the bed, reaching for her revolver. "Get out."

"I'm not accusing you of murder. I only want to know what Torrence's mistress saw that night."

"Nothing. She saw nothing."

"How do you know?"

She just glared at him.

"A hundred dollars an answer, Pearl. If the replies are honest."

Avarice warred with caution in her eyes. Slowly she lowered the gun. "Ask."

"What can you tell me about the woman he was meeting in that room?"

A small chuckle escaped her. "Cleverly phrased, doctor. You don't want to spend more than you have to."

"I can be generous, if I'm satisfied with your answers."

She returned the revolver to the night stand and once again sat on the bed, but this time she curled her legs beneath her, tailor-fashion, and kept her hands loosely clasped in her lap. "I supplied William Torrence with girls. He liked variety, he liked luxury, and he liked secrecy. That night, he sent word that the girl wasn't to show up until after midnight. I figured he was expecting one of his spies to make a report earlier in the evening and didn't want to chance anyone seeing who came to his suite."

"Spies?"

A hint of sarcasm edged her tone of voice. "What? So much interest in Mr. Torrence and you don't know about the spies?" When he made no reply, she grinned. "Torrence and his former wife spied on each other. It was almost a game with them, each one vying to learn the other's secrets."

"All right. He was meeting a spy. So you think. What did your girl see when she arrived?"

"A dead man. She got out fast. She didn't see anyone else around."

And she'd have had no reason to murder Torrence.

Neither would she have been a threat to Miranda. Torrence wouldn't have been likely to get another divorce just to marry one of Pearl's girls. The second Mrs. Torrence might have resented knowing her husband used prostitutes, but that was a situation many wives faced. Most of them learned to live with it, or filed for divorce themselves. Given what Diana had told him about Miranda, it seemed unlikely to Ben that she'd have been provoked to violence.

So who *had* killed Torrence? Ben was no closer to an answer than he had been before he'd left the hotel.

He returned to his room at the Windsor in a morose frame of mind. His efforts were getting him nowhere, and he'd be surprised if Diana had made any progress, either. First thing tomorrow, he decided, he'd go to Matt Hastings's house and get her out of there. They'd continue to look for Torrence's killer, or they'd return to the East, but whatever they did, they'd do it together.

He opened the door and stepped into light and warmth. He frowned. He hadn't left the lamps burning.

The sound of feminine voices wafted out from his bedroom into the parlor of the suite. One of them was familiar.

"Diana?"

She came out in a rush and flew straight into his arms. He caught only the briefest glimpse of the other woman, bespectacled and timid-looking, before Diana crashed into his chest, all but knocking the wind out of him.

Diana hugged him tightly and inhaled deeply, expecting the reassuring scent of Ivory soap that always clung to him. Instead she got a strong whiff of heliotrope.

She lifted her head and sniffed. "You smell—"

"Like the inside of a whorehouse. Yes, I know."

His candor deflated her irritation before it had a proper chance to grow into anger. She swallowed hard. "Which one?"

"The madam's name is Pearl."

Jane gave a little squeak of surprise.

Diana studied the dark gray wool cheviot in front of her nose. The jacket of his single-breasted sack suit was soft to the touch.

Reassuring. "So, these pale blonde hairs are . . . ?"

"Poodle." The word flowed over her in his resonant baritone, warming and comforting. "Hard to avoid them. There must be a dozen white dogs in that house."

Her fingers closed on his lapels. "Ben, why did you go there?"

"Why do you think?" Jane asked, *sotto voce.*

Diana ignored both the question and the tug on her sleeve. She had no doubts about Ben's fidelity. If he'd been with a prostitute earlier, there had been a reason for it other than sexual congress.

He was staring at her, and at the pile of luggage in the bedroom beyond. "You have more to explain than I do, Diana."

The ominous undercurrent that had insinuated itself into that deep rumble of a voice warned her to tread carefully. "I thought it best to move out of Matt's house." They'd left as soon as he was asleep, sure of their escape because Matt's supper had contained a liberal dose of the opiate Matt had given Jane for Diana's warm milk.

Waiting for more information, Ben eyed Diana warily. When she didn't add anything to that first statement, he asked, "Where is Ning?"

"I sent him home to his aunt after he and the detective you hired escorted us here." She paused. "Thank you."

He ran long, flexible fingers through his gently-waving, jet-black mane and sighed. "You're keeping something back, Diana. Out with it."

"I'm more interested in hearing about your adventures."

"I'm sure you are." His mustache twitched as his firm lips twisted into a small, ironic smile. He covered it with the hand he lifted to smooth an already perfectly groomed short beard. Their eyes met. Diana saw no censure in his gaze, only concern for her. She stared into the dark brown depths, delighting as she always did in the unexpected flecks of amber she found there. She loved Ben's eyes.

She loved everything about him, even his stubbornness.

She dropped her gaze and lifted one hand to toy with the silk shield bow he wore with his turn-down collar. She didn't want to confess all, but there wasn't really any way around it now. Trust worked both ways. There were times, she was sure, when total honesty was not the best policy, but for here, for now, she and Ben needed to pool information. Neither pride nor embarrassment must be allowed to stand in the way.

"I suppose it's useless asking you to promise not to be angry?"

"With you or with Hastings?"

She winced. "I want you to hear me out and then stay right here to tell me all you've learned since we last met. And tomorrow I want you to go with us to Torrence."

"Us?"

Belatedly, Diana realized that she'd never introduced Jane to Ben. She remedied that situation, then said, "We have to catch a train at eight in the morning. It's important, Ben."

His dark brows lifted, but he nodded. "All right. We'll all go. Now tell me why. No editing," he added before she could even draw breath to begin. "I want to know everything, Diana. And in turn, I'll hold nothing back from you. Agreed?"

"Agreed."

And so she began.

He kept his temper, but barely.

"I've warned Ning to stay away from Matt," she concluded.

"A piece of advice I wish you'd followed yourself."

"Ben, we're here. We're safe. Now, what did you find out from Pearl?"

"That your father paid her to keep an eye on you and Evan, particularly Evan, when you were in Leadville. And that the mystery woman in your father's suite was one of Pearl's girls. She arrived after he was already dead."

Diana was glad she was already sitting down. Jane, who had been standing by the window, sank into the nearest chair, eyes wide.

"Did she see anyone?" Diana asked.

"Apparently not."

"I want to talk to her."

"That's not possible. She was shaken up by her experience. And afraid the police might blame her. She told Pearl what happened, then took off."

"Maybe she lied. Maybe she *did* kill him."

"Why would she? She barely knew him. According to Pearl, she was looking forward to the evening. Pearl said your father had a reputation for being generous with . . . ladies who pleased him."

"Then who did kill him?" Her frustration was almost palpable. She'd been wrong about the suite. It had not been window-dressing to impress a mistress. At the same time, she'd been right in believing there had been a mystery woman. Diana didn't know what to think about Ben's discovery.

"Pearl suggested Torrence might have been meeting someone earlier," he added. "To use her word, a spy in his employ. It seems your father liked to keep tabs on people. These last few years, he's paid more than one person to report back to him about your mother's activities."

"I don't like the sound of that," Diana said.

"No," Ben agreed. "For one thing, it may have given your mother yet another reason to want him dead."

CHAPTER TWELVE

ഇരുജ

Two daily Express Trains equipped with Pullman Palace Sleepers, Horton Reclining Chair Cars, Elegant Regular Coaches, Modern Open Observation Cars, Westinghouse Air Brakes, and running over Steel Rails, Iron Bridges and Rock Ballast," Ben Northcote read, "insure the highest type of rapid, safe, and luxurious railway travel."

He squinted at the small print on the railroad schedule as the badly misnamed "express" train left Union Depot for the morning run. "Looks like we'll be travelling all day," he remarked. Arrival time in Torrence, after many stops, was listed at six in the evening.

"And once again you'll have to miss church," Diana said with a faint smile.

On Sundays patients who lived in rural areas visited Ben's surgery. He rarely had an opportunity to attend services at home. Diana was coming to learn him well, he thought. Most of the time he didn't mind missing church, but just now he'd been thinking that a few prayers might help.

The train moved southward, slowly gaining speed as it crossed the bed of Cherry Creek on a long bridge and left the more populated sections of Denver behind.

"I hadn't realized Torrence and Leadville were so close together," Ben said, resuming his study of the timetable, "or that either was quite so far from Denver." According to the schedule, an additional hour and a half on this same line would bring them to the latter city.

Diana took the form printed up by the Denver, South Park & Pacific Railroad for the benefit of passengers and flipped it over to reveal a map showing the connections. She pushed her veil away from her face so she could see better and spread the page out across the light gray flannel skirt of her traveling suit and the darker gray wool of his trousers. "Our route will take us south for more than 130 miles, as far as Buena Vista, before turning north again to reach Torrence."

Ben frowned. "Seems roundabout."

"The mountains are in the way." Diana tapped the sketched-in elevations with one gloved finger. "There's a line to Leadville that cuts across to the west. Here. We could catch a train there for Torrence, but we'd have a long wait for the connection."

"Was there train service from Denver to Leadville three years ago?"

She frowned. "As I recall, this line was not yet open. But it may have been that Evan wanted to have our own buggy for transportation after we arrived. I cannot remember why we ended up traveling west from Fairplay along the post road. It was rated for travel 'by hack and saddle,' as they say. The mails go by hack only in the summer months, or when the road is not obstructed, and by saddle animals in winter or when the road is bad."

"No six-horse Concord coaches with Sir Jehu sitting in his box?"

"Not many. The route over the pass is direct but hazardous." She gave him an odd look. "What were you quoting?"

"*Crofutt's Grip-Sack Guide of Colorado.* I purchased a copy when I first arrived in Denver, though I haven't had a chance to do more than glance at it." He grinned as he said it, but the humor abruptly faded as he recalled more of the details of her ordeal in the mountains. She and Evan had been caught in an early snow squall and nearly perished going over Mosquito Pass. "If you were travelling all that distance, weather aside, why on earth choose an open buggy?"

Diana looked down at her hands, tightly folded in her lap, then glanced out the window as they passed a cluster of machine and repair shops belonging to the Rio Grande company.

"Diana?"

"Evan thought it *looked* well. And he had it in his head that we could travel from Denver to Leadville in a single day. I tried to tell him that we'd drive half the first day before we'd even reach the point where the mountains began, but he'd taken bad advice from someone and was convinced I was wrong. By that time things were so bad between us that I gave in without a fuss. I assumed we'd stop for the night in one of the towns along the way. We did, but Evan wasn't happy about it."

"I wonder who Evan's source of information was."

"Charlie?"

As they'd agreed, he'd told her everything he'd learned from the bartender at the Windsor, from Charlie, and from Pearl, but they had not had much time last night to speculate about what any of it meant. By the time they'd shared a late supper in his suite, Diana had been hard put to stay awake. She hadn't slept a wink, she said, under Matt Hastings roof. She and Jane had retired to Ben's bedroom, leaving him to toss and turn on the hard, too-short sofa in the sitting room.

"Perhaps we should have confronted him before we left the hotel," Diana said.

"We know where to find him when we get back."

She nodded. "And to be truthful, I'm relieved to get out of that place. Your suite was almost identical to the one Father died in. It made me uneasy."

"More so than being at Hastings's place?"

"You promised not to—"

"I know. I'm sorry." He meant the apology, but his blood boiled every time he thought about Matt Hastings and his plans for Diana.

"I still don't understand why Father wanted such a close watch kept on Evan," Diana said, after a moment.

"Perhaps he was concerned about his daughter's welfare."

"I doubt it."

"You said he asked Col. Arkins to keep your connection to Evan out of the Leadville newspapers."

"That was to protect *his* reputation, not to give me privacy. He never contacted me afterward, or offered to help me, and if Pearl was still in Leadville, he must have known I was destitute."

"According to Pearl, Evan borrowed money from him."

"Borrowed?" she repeated, sounding doubtful.

"You think he extorted it?" Ben saw no reason not to be blunt. When Pearl had told him that Evan had boasted of "getting money out of Mr. Torrence," the first thing he'd thought of himself was blackmail.

"I can't imagine what he knew that Father would have paid to keep secret, but yes, I do think that. Nothing else makes sense. Father certainly wouldn't have given him that much money just because he was married to me."

He took her hand in his and felt the tension beneath the soft kid of her glove. She'd been hurt, first by her father's rejection, then by Evan's disloyalty. He wanted to keep her safe, but here they were, headed straight into trouble.

And straight into one of the most magnificent landscapes in the country. He nudged Diana and nodded towards the vista beyond her window. Pike's Peak lay directly ahead of the train. To the right, beyond the Platte River, was a wide strip of rolling prairie leading up to the base of the mountains. From a previous visit, he knew they were still at least fifteen miles away. Distances were deceiving.

"You climbed that," she said, remembering that he'd boasted of the accomplishment early in their acquaintance. "Voluntarily."

"You grew up in these mountains. How can you fear them?"

"*Because* I grew up in these mountains." She looked at the height again and shuddered. "I hope you don't expect me to enjoy the same sports you do."

"Women do climb."

"I know, but I don't intend to be one of them. You may go off on a spree without me if it involves mountains."

He gave her a hard look. "Can you tolerate this trip to Torrence?"

"Tolerate. I don't anticipate taking any pleasure in it. And I will have my eyes closed part of the time. I prefer not to look out at the view when the train is perched on narrow-gauge track laid only inches away from the edge of a bottomless gorge."

Neither of them spoke again until after the stop at Littleton, a town of a few hundred inhabitants with a post office, stores, and hotels. Ten miles south of Denver, it boasted a station of the Denver & Rio Grande on one side of the Platte and a station for the South Park division of the Union Pacific railway on the other. Some Denver businessmen had homes here, Ben had heard, from a talkative Harry the bartender, and rode the train into the city each day for a fifty-five cent fare.

After Littleton, the bluffs and ravines to their left seemed to gradually close in as they rolled through numerous cuts and crossed a canal that supplied part of Denver's water supply. At some points, the grade was so steep and the gorge so deep that the mountains seemed to tower overhead while the train perched on a narrow strip of rail. Ben watched the scenery, picking out pine, spruce, and cedar on the slopes, and the beginnings of summer's ferns and flowers.

At his side, Diana's eyes stayed squeezed shut. He'd have thought she slept if it hadn't been for the death grip she kept on his hand.

It was when he was still in college, Ben recalled, that he'd first visited Colorado. He and some friends had spent the summer travelling. Climbing Pike's Peak had been just one of many western adventures.

How strange to think that he'd been so near to Diana back then and never realized. She'd have been a young girl still living with her parents in Denver. If he'd chanced to meet her, would anything have changed? Might he somehow have spared her all she'd endured with Evan Spaulding?

He felt his lips curve into a wry smile at the fanciful thought. Diana wouldn't have become the woman she was now, the woman he loved, without the hardships she'd faced and overcome. It was doubtless a very good thing people could not go back in time and change the course of events. Good or bad, life dealt each of them a hand. It was how an individual played it that made all the difference.

"Mother said I had reason to want revenge," Diana murmured, cutting short Ben's philosophical musings.

He opened his mouth to ask what she thought that meant, but a small sound from Jane stopped him. He'd almost forgotten the other woman was with them. She was the sort who could sit quietly in a corner and blend into the woodwork. Now, however, her face was a mask of astonishment.

"You talked to Elmira? When? Why didn't you tell me?"

"I thought it best if no one knew," Diana said in an apologetic voice. She risked a peek out the window, apparently saw no drop-offs to alarm her, and visibly relaxed. Quickly and concisely, she recapped the highlights of Elmira's early morning visit for Jane's benefit. Ben listened with particular attention to the comments Diana's mother had made about Evan.

"So she knew something," he said when Diana had finished.

"But Mother wasn't there when they met. Father was already married to Miranda. She probably didn't know any more than she said. But what did she *mean?*"

"I'm not so sure she doesn't know more. Remember what Pearl told me about your parents spying on each other?" He turned to Jane. "Did Elmira ever talk about that? Do you know who reported to her on Torrence's activities?"

"I don't know a thing about it." Jane was so insistent in her denial that Ben took a harder look at her. He'd always thought there was a great deal of truth in Shakespeare's line about the lady protesting too much, and there was a haunted expression on Jane's pale face,.

Diana did not seem to share his suspicions. "Mother kept a great deal to herself, Ben."

"Then how can you be so sure she didn't kill your father?" Jane asked.

"Because she was lured out of the Elmira with a note." Diana frowned. "I'm still not certain where Ed Leeves fits into this. I can't think of any reason why he'd want to frame Mother for murder."

"He tried to take over the hotel," Jane reminded her.

Diana just shook her head, unconvinced.

Each lost in individual thoughts, they rode in silence as far as Plum—twenty-four miles from Denver, according to *Crofutt's Guide.* When the train resumed its journey, they headed southeast, up Plum Creek. It was rough country, with no cultivation that Ben could see. The land appeared to be used for stock-raising.

Some considerable time passed before Diana roused herself from further closed-eyed musings and spoke. "Keep a lookout for Castle Rock," she said. "It's one of the sights to see in Colorado." Her voice sounded strained, as if it took tremendous effort to focus her mind on the scenery. "It's a huge, castellated rock that projects out into the valley westward, as if it had been put there to bar further progress."

Once Castle Rock had passed out of sight, Diana fell silent once more. There was an air of listlessness about her that worried Ben. He couldn't blame her for being discouraged, and he understood her trepidation about venturing up into the mountains, but she was ordinarily such an energetic person, so full of optimism and enthusiasm, even if she did tend to be a bit too impulsive. It broke his heart to see her like this.

"Let's reconsider what Elmira said about Evan," he suggested. If he could not distract her from her worries, at least he could help her reason out some of the answers she sought. "What did you think when she told you he'd met with your father?"

Diana blinked at him, and it was a moment before she answered. "That Evan had tried for a reconciliation, hoping to see me put back in Father's will, and that he failed so utterly that he never even mentioned their meeting to me. He never did like to admit to failure."

Ben wondered where her thoughts had been, but he had her attention now. That was the important thing. "How did you think he got the money for the move to Leadville?"

"I thought he won it at cards. That's what he told me. And sometimes he was lucky." She closed her eyes a moment. "And sometimes he was not. He did cheat. Pearl was right about that. It was only chance that someone didn't shoot him for it sooner."

Jane made a small sound of distress. Sympathy, Ben assumed. He ignored her, keeping all his attention fixed on Diana. "What happened to the man who shot him?"

"He took off. As far as I know, he was never caught."

"There was no suggestion of premeditated murder?"

Color leeched from Diana's already pale face. "I was told Evan was shot in a quarrel over a poker game in the casino where he'd been working as a faro dealer. The other players said he was cheating, but the killer was never questioned. No one even knew his name."

"Blackmail is rarely a one-time demand," Ben said softly.

Both Diana and Jane looked appalled.

"You think Father had him killed?" Diana's voice was flat. "That he was afraid Evan would demand more money?"

"It's a possibility. Some of the things we've learned about your father indicate he wasn't above using underhanded means to achieve his ends. He hired someone to lie about your mother in court. Is it so hard to believe he'd hire someone to get rid of a man he perceived to be a threat?"

"But what threat? Ben, I can't think of a single thing Evan could have known that would make Father give him a large sum of money. And if he didn't extort that first payment, then the rest of this speculation is absurd." She managed a faint smile. "If *I'd* come up with this theory, you'd accuse me of letting my imagination run away with me."

"I might. On the other hand, that active imagination of yours is right more often than I like to admit."

₨⇒℞

Bits and pieces of Diana's early life had been coming back to her throughout the journey from Denver to Torrence. By the time the train reached Buena Vista, the county seat, she was flooded with memories.

"We used to come here to shop," she murmured. "Before we moved to Denver."

The town was much as she remembered it, with its impressive courthouse, its churches, and stores of all kinds. There was even a cosy little opera house. And there were at least three hotels—the Lake, the Park, and the El Paso.

"There are hot springs west of here," she said to Ben. She grinned at a stray memory. "Some folks come all the way from Denver to visit them. Eleven dollar fare. Mother thought that an extraordinary amount to pay for such foolishness."

They were soon moving again, through the forest of small pine and cedar trees that surrounded Buena Vista, and on into rough broken country covered with scrub-pines and more cedars. Directly west was Mt. Yale, piercing the clouds, and on the opposite side ahead, Mt. Harvard.

Torrence was only a few miles away.

The flashes of memory increased in volume. Diana recalled a cottonwood tree from which her father had hung a swing one summer. And there had been a trumpet vine winding around the door of one of the shacks they'd lived in before William Torrence found the Timberline Mine, although she wasn't certain where that had been. Fairplay, perhaps? Or Oro City?

She wondered what her life would have been like if her father had never struck it rich.

"Why is she so nervous?" Ben asked in a voice low enough that Jane, the subject of his question, could not hear him.

Jerked back to the present, Diana stared at the younger woman. Jane's hands twisted together in her lap, and she was alternately pursing and licking her lips.

"I assume it has to do with Alan," Diana whispered back. She hadn't yet shared with Ben her suspicion that Alan had abandoned Jane for the wealthier, prettier Miranda. She hadn't wanted to speak of that possibility in front of Jane, since she still had not questioned the younger woman about her beau. "I'll tell you later."

Ben gave Diana an odd look, but didn't press for details. Instead he asked about their destination.

"I'll be honest with you," Diana said, "Torrence is not a very hospitable place. It sits on a barren hilltop 9800 feet above sea level. Gales blow in, one after another, from the Continental Divide, making it necessary to brace all the houses on that side. In summer, there are violent thunderstorms, and winters are even fiercer. That's why we usually moved into Denver in late fall, even before Father struck it rich. The one time we stayed all year, I saw for myself just how deep a snowdrift could get. The house was covered to the second floor and we had to use the upstairs windows as doors."

"Is Torrence as large as Leadville?" Ben asked.

"No, but I'm not sure of the population. What does *Crofutt* say? It was published in 1885 and is probably more accurate than my memory."

"About five hundred." He glanced at the entry again. "'Chaffee County. On the Denver & Rio Grande railway between Buena Vista and Leadville. A post office, several stores, a good depot building, one smelter, one stamp mill, the Grand Hotel, and a score of private residences. Two churches. Fare from Denver, $12.50.'" He turned to look at her. "How long did you live in Torrence."

"Less than three years after Father founded the place. Then he moved us into the house in Denver. We'd been in the area before that, of course. For as long as I can remember. But we were dirt poor until I was nine, and we moved around a lot."

"That's when he found a vein of silver? When you were nine?"

She nodded. "In 1873. He noticed a flow of blossom rock on a high hill near the Continental Divide. When he took a load of the ore to the smelting works in Argo, on the outskirts of Denver, he had hopes, but I don't think even he expected it to assay so high in silver. He took six thousand dollars worth of ore out of the Timberline Mine that year, all from the first twenty feet of his shaft. The following year, he organized the town, and by 1875 it had sixty houses. He used to brag about that."

He'd also, she recalled, boasted of how his mine had produced seventy thousand dollars in silver in 1876, the year they'd moved to Denver. Diana hadn't been back to Torrence since.

The train slowed, pulling in at their destination, and for a moment she had a clear view of the town cemetery.

"Is your father buried there?" Ben asked, noting the direction of her gaze.

"I'm ashamed to admit that I don't know. I never thought to ask." She'd had little experience paying her respects to the dead. The only cemetery she'd ever visited had been the one in Leadville, and then only once. Evan had been buried without ceremony in a grave marked with a wooden cross. She'd had to grit her teeth and accept charity to be able to afford to give him even that much.

"Where do we go?" Jane asked as the train groaned and came to a halt at the station.

"To the dance hall Matt Hastings owns. The others arrived three days ago. They could be set up in business already, or still be settling in. Either way, we need to warn them they're about to be evicted."

"I thought you came here to talk to Miranda." Jane gathered up hatboxes, bags, and gripsacks, and Diana and Ben did the same.

"I did, but no one's going to throw her out of my father's house. She'll be there when I get around to her." Diana had a great many more questions for her father's widow now than she'd had when they'd left Denver. She still intended to find out what Miranda knew about William Torrence's murder, but she also wanted to know if Torrence's wife had been at that mysterious meeting with Evan.

Diana made her way along the aisle in the direction of the exit with Jane in the lead and almost ran into the other woman when she stopped short instead of stepping down onto the platform. "That's the headquarters of the Torrence Mining Company," she whispered, staring at a building a little way down the dusty street. "Alan works there."

"Do you want to stop and let him know you've arrived?" Diana nudged her forward.

Jane shook her head. "He's going to be angry with me."

"Why should he be?" Ben asked, bringing up the rear.

But Jane just kept shaking her head. She seemed almost afraid of Alan Kent.

Once again, Diana was reminded of her own relationship with Evan Spaulding. He could be charming one minute, brutal the next. If Alan Kent was cut from the same mold, Jane would be well rid of him. Perhaps Alan's pursuit of the rich widow Torrence would turn out to be a blessing in disguise.

She forebore comment. Jane would undoubtedly ignore any advice Diana tried to give her. Diana had experience there, too. She'd listened to no one when she'd decided she was in love with Evan. She'd married him in spite of all the warnings. And she'd lived to regret that hasty decision.

Once they were off the train, Diana took a moment to study her surroundings. The place still had the same bleak, windblown look she remembered.

"I wonder why Miranda decided to come back here," Ben said. "From what you've told me about her, this doesn't appear to be an environment she'd care for."

"At first I wondered if she'd heard about Matt's generosity and thought Mother might turn up here, too, but then I remembered that the one time I met her, Miranda seemed afraid of her."

"Then maybe she's here because she thinks this is the one place that's safe," Ben suggested.

Whatever her reasons, Miranda had arrived just twenty-four hours earlier. By now she knew, if she hadn't before, that the former residents of the Elmira Hotel were also in town. In a place this size, it wouldn't take long before she also heard that Diana, Jane, and a tall, dark stranger had arrived on today's train.

Diana had sent a telegram ahead to announce their impending arrival. Ben watched her search the platform for a familiar face, but plainly she saw no one she knew. A perplexed expression crossed her face as she glanced back at him.

"I wonder where everyone is? I expected at least a few of the girls to meet us. There isn't all that much to do in Torrence. The train coming in should have counted as fine entertainment."

"Maybe they've already set up in business." Jane had to shout to be heard above the noise of the train steaming out of the station.

Ben didn't see any reason for concern. Almost the entire town was visible from where they stood. They wouldn't need an escort to find their way to the Alhambra, the dance hall Matt Hastings owned. In fact, since he could recognize vaguely Moorish-looking designs on a sign swinging in the breeze a hundred yards away, he'd wager his hat, if he had one, on that weathered old building being their destination.

At that moment a man opened its door, stepped out into the dusty street, and started their way. His size, his battered physiognomy, and Diana's sigh of relief all confirmed his identity. This must be "the professor."

Ben watched his approach through narrowed eyes. Something wasn't right. He could see it in the way the fellow moved. He kept glancing behind him, and from side to side, as he advanced towards them, and he was sweating profusely, even though there was a distinct chill in the mountain air.

On the surface there didn't seem to be anything to fear. Several of the good citizens of Torrence were visible, going about their daily business: a shopkeeper closing up for the evening; a woman with a child hurrying towards home; an older boy rolling a hoop along the wooden sidewalk and earning himself a ripe curse from the old prospector he nearly sideswiped.

Ben moved in front of Diana without consciously thinking about it and took up a protective stance. The professor skidded to a halt when he was still a few feet away and gave Ben a suspicious look. "Who are you?"

Jane pushed to the forefront. "This is Diana's real fiancée, Professor. Doctor Benjamin Northcote. I'm afraid we've brought bad news. The invitation to use the dance hall is about to be rescinded."

"Doctor? There's a piece of luck."

"What's happened?" Diana eluded Ben's grasp and slipped in front of him, reaching out to clasp the professor's arm.

"It's Big Nose Nellie, " he said, patting Diana's hand. "She's been shot."

Ben saw Diana go rigid and heard her horrified gasp. He stepped up behind her, settling both hands on her shoulders, and met the professor's eyes. "How bad?"

"Flesh wound, but . . . well, we don't think it was an accident." He sent a nervous glance over one shoulder. "We'd best get back inside."

Feeling hideously exposed, and next to useless as a bodyguard, Ben accompanied Diana, Jane, and the professor down the wide, unpaved street. Buildings on either side provided far too many places for a gunman to hide.

"What happened?" Diana demanded. "When?"

"I wasn't with them," the professor said, obviously relieved to have someone else take charge. "I was working on the place here, fixing things up for us. The girls got done cleaning and went out to explore the town, such as it is. On their way back from the mercantile, someone started shooting at them."

"You're certain they were the targets? It couldn't have been stray gunfire?" Even in Ben's own, supposedly civilized, eastern city, there were occasional incidents of that type. Some drunken fool decided to shoot up the town, or kill a cheating spouse, and innocent bystanders got in the way of a bullet. As one of the city coroners, he'd seen more than his share of the dire results.

"No one saw who fired the gun," the professor said, "but the bullets were aimed at the girls. Several struck the ground just ahead of them, raising puffs of dust, and then the one hit Nellie's nose."

"Her . . . nose?" Diana's steps faltered. For a moment Ben thought she was about to faint or have hysterics. Then he realized she was trying not to laugh. "I'm sorry. You'll see when you meet her."

"Was there much damage?" Jane asked. She, too, was fighting a smile.

"She thinks there was. That's why I'm glad he's a doctor. Maybe he can quiet her down. Didn't help that Maryam told her she'd have to change her moniker to 'No-Nose Nellie.'"

Within minutes of entering the Alhambra, Ben understood the reason for Diana's reaction.

"Bled like a pig," said the plump brunette Diana had addressed as Maryam.

With gentle fingers, Ben examined the damage. "Nothing's broken. You were lucky, Nellie."

"Lucky? This here's my trademark!"

"And it will heal just fine." He applied a bit of sticking plaster to the nick she'd sustained. It was already beginning to scab over.

"I've had a terrible shock," Nellie maintained. "I need bed rest and pampering."

The others hooted, but Ben nodded solemnly. "An excellent idea. There is only one problem. You're all moving out of here tonight."

A chorus of protests greeted his announcement, but when Diana had explained, the objections vanished. "There's only one place to go," she told them when she'd finished. "The Grand Hotel."

"And who's going to pay for that?" Maryam demanded.

"I am," Ben said. Before taking a look at Nellie, he'd dispatched the professor to secure rooms for them, a mission it had taken the other man only a short time to accomplish. He'd returned and given Ben a thumb's up while Diana was still explaining Matt Hastings's perfidy.

The move took only a short time to accomplish. They settled Nellie first, in a black-walnut bed of the finest quality. Eyes wide, she surveyed her surroundings. "My stars! Ain't it grand!"

Ben tried to see the room as she did, but the furnishings seemed ordinary to him. There was a bureau with diminutive drawers with pendulous handles like bell pulls and a black walnut washstand to match the two beds in the room. It held an enormous water-pitcher and basin and the hotel provided scented soap and hand towels. Nothing special there.

"Lie back, now," he told his patient, "and try to get some sleep. You've had a rough day."

"Fine advice from a doctor!" she exclaimed, glaring at him. "I always sleep sitting up."

"Why?" he asked in astonishment, exchanging a puzzled glance with Diana.

"To prevent tuberculosis, of course. What do they teach you in those doctor schools?"

"Obviously not enough." Ben forced a smile. It wouldn't do her any harm to sleep upright. Unfortunately, it wouldn't do her any good, either.

He shooed Diana and Jane out of the room ahead of him, leaving Nellie alone to recuperate.

They gathered below, in a large parlor on the first floor. It was dominated by a square rosewood piano. Steel engravings of Landseer's "Deer Stalking in the Highlands" and "Bringing Home the Buck" decorated one wall.

"We need to talk about what happened," Ben said. "Whether it was a deliberate attempt to harm any of you or not, it should be reported to the sheriff."

"Of course it was deliberate," Maryam snapped. "Katie'll tell you."

Diana caught Ben's arm and he fell silent. She was right. She knew these people and he did not. They'd answer her questions more easily, and in greater detail, than they'd respond to his.

"Where is Katie?" she asked.

A redhead rushed in, out of breath and apologetic. "Sorry. Have you seen the outhouse? It's a wonder. Furnished with soft wrappings from peach crates instead of catalog pages. And it's surrounded by larkspur trained onto lattice work."

"Have a seat, Katie. We were about to discuss those gunshots." Diana gestured towards the only open space, an end of the horsehair sofa.

Katie wrinkled her nose. "No, thanks. I hate horsehair. Slippery stuff. And once you do get a good seat, you get stabbed in the rump for your trouble." She settled her back against the doorframe instead.

Ben had to agree with her assessment. He'd never understood why the upholstery was so popular. There were always hairs poking upright, sharp as porcupine quills. He'd supposed women had some protection, what with all the skirts and crinolines, but Katie and the others seemed to prefer thin fabrics. He could understand how that would present a problem for them.

Diana rapped on a marble table top for attention. "Who was with Nellie when she was hit?" she asked when they quieted down.

It was the redhead who answered. "I was. And Chastity."

A dark-eyed, full-figured young woman, who sat tailor-fashion on the Brussels carpet in front of the horsehair sofa, waggled her fingers at them but said nothing. For a moment, she reminded Ben of Pearl Adams, but the resemblance was only superficial. Pearl was much more delicate and refined.

"Alright, Katie," Diana said. "What happened?"

"We just went for a walk. Didn't hurt no one." Her lips formed into a pout. "We went to the mercantile and bought penny candy."

"That old woman didn't like it," Chastity piped up.

Katie chucked. "Turns out she was a minister's wife."

"Scandalized, she was." Chastity ventured a tentative smile.

"Somehow I don't think she's the one who shot at you." Diana tapped one finger against her chin as she thought over what they'd said.

Ben could tell she didn't like it that Nellie'd had another close call, but there didn't seem to be any connection to the incident in Denver.

"No one saw anything," the professor said. "No one knows anything to tell the sheriff. No sense in bothering him."

The others seemed in agreement on that. None of them trusted the law.

"Did anyone try to keep you from moving into the Alhambra?" Diana asked.

Maryam snorted, but it was the professor who answered first. "The place had been closed up for years."

"I heard Matt Hastings shut it down and left Torrence for good the same week Timberline Torrence married Miranda."

"That was four years ago," Diana said in amazement.

"Looked like it had been that long," the professor said. "We spent most of our time just trying to make it habitable." He shrugged. "We didn't have a chance to make any enemies."

"Well," Diana said, "I don't suppose there's much point to sending for the sheriff tonight. But since we don't know who fired those shots, we would all do well to stay in this evening."

"Too late," Maryam said with a sardonic smile. "Jane's already flown the coop."

"I'm sure she's only gone to visit Mr. Kent. He'll look out for her." The look Diana gave the cold-eyed brunette would have silenced most people, but Maryam seemed to delight in causing dissension.

"Will he? I'm thinking she's in for a surprise."

"What do you mean, Maryam?"

"Only what everyone knows—Alan Kent's got his sights set on the widow Torrence." With that she picked up a stereoptican and pretended great interest in the selection of scenes available. "Oooh, Ausable Chasm!"

A few of the girls gathered around her, wanting a look, although this was a pastime better suited to a sunny afternoon. The professor, after a glance at Diana to make sure she was through with her "meeting," took a seat at the piano and began to play "Sylvan Echoes."

Diana looked at Ben. "And the evening's entertainment begins."

"Not quite the usual, I trust?"

She grinned at him. "Not with three or four women to a room."

He choked on a laugh and, realizing how her words might have been interpreted, Diana's face flamed.

"Dreadful man!" She smacked him, hard, on his upper arm, but there was love in her eyes as she gazed up at him.

"I don't suppose I could persuade you to leave Torrence on the early morning train?" he asked.

"Not even if everyone came with us. There are answers here. I'm certain of it."

"And if whoever shot at Nellie tries for you?"

She pursed her lips. "It must have been an accident. Some hothead shooting in the air. Because if he'd meant to kill Nellie, surely she'd be dead."

"You think it was an accident, not a warning?"

Just the hint of a smile played around her mouth. "Well, if it was the latter, then that means someone thinks I'm getting close to the truth. And since Matt Hastings is still in Denver, that only leaves Miranda."

"She could be dangerous, Diana."

"If she killed my father, then I cannot let fear for my own safety keep me from discovering evidence of it. Indeed, if she attacks me, wouldn't that prove I've been right about her all along?"

"Diana—"

But she wasn't listening. "Tomorrow we will visit my dear stepmother, just as I planned."

"You think she killed your father and yet you walk into her parlor? Does the expression 'lamb to slaughter' mean anything to you?"

"I'll have you with me for protection. If it becomes necessary, you can overpower her."

He winced at this display of overconfidence. He didn't have a clue why anyone would have tried to harm Nellie, but if it had been Miranda or one of her henchmen who'd shot at that young woman, then they weren't just dealing with someone who'd seized a knife in a fit of passion and killed a cheating spouse.

"We'll make a production of the visit," he said. "Rent a buggy from the livery stable. Make sure as many people as possible see us arrive there. But there is nothing more frightening than a woman with a gun, especially if she's scared, too. There's no way to predict what she'll do if you come right out and accuse her of murder."

"I only want to ask her a few questions," Diana insisted. "That's all I've ever wanted from her. But this time I don't intend to leave the house until I have answers."

The stubborn tilt of her jaw warned him it was useless to argue. Short of binding and gagging her, stuffing her in a trunk, and loading it onto the train in the morning, the only thing he could do was go along with her plan and hope her confidence in him was not misplaced.

CHAPTER THIRTEEN

⚡✦⚡

Diana and Ben went together to the house in which she'd lived for almost three years. The front hall was as she remembered it, furnished with a handsome French plate mirror flanked by an inexpensive blue and white Japanese umbrella jar and an oak hat stand. A large photograph of the mountains hung in a plain wood frame on the wall. What was different, as in the Denver house, was the pervasive smell of frangipani. It overpowered the more delicate scent from a vase holding a cluster of evergreen cuttings.

Elmira's salon, now Miranda's, consisted of two rooms thrown into one by means of an arch. In Elmira's time, there had been so many doilies and antimacassars scattered about that the crocheted pieces were the first thing to catch the eye. Now there were distractions everywhere, from the design of hearts woven into the border of the large rug to an imported French candelabra.

The arch was defined by a frieze of plaques against a background of pale green crêpe drapery, while the rooms themselves had been hung with pictures from baseboard to ceiling. In one corner stood a terra cotta bust of Miranda, arranged so that it was reflected in the Venetian mirror.

Miranda herself sat enthroned in the midst of all this clutter, a vision in lavender framed by the French blue brocade of her chair. A bell pull was near at hand, as if she expected trouble. Diana imagined that her henchman waited in the basement kitchen, near an annunciator just like the one in the Denver house, where arrows indicated the source of any given bell.

When Martha showed them in, Miranda did not get up to greet them, but she looked resigned to dealing with Diana again. "Did you follow me here?"

"Not really," Diana said. "May I present my future husband, Dr. Benjamin Northcote."

That did startle the other woman. "I thought you were going to marry Matt Hastings."

"So did he, apparently." Without being invited, Diana perched on the end of a matching sofa and inclined her upper body towards Miranda so that she could watch the other woman's face. "Matt isn't the man I thought he was, Miranda. I think you came to see the same thing."

"I don't know what you're talking about."

"Don't you? Matt was nothing to you?"

"That's right. A neighbor. Unimportant. Your father thought him beneath notice."

"My father cheated him. He came close to ruining Matt financially."

"That's no concern of mine."

Diana could feel her temper building, but Ben's hand on her shoulder stopped her from hasty words she'd later regret.

"Mrs. Torrence," he said in that remarkable voice of his. "Mrs. Spaulding has a natural desire to know what really happened to her father. She does not believe her mother killed him. What harm in letting her ask a few questions?"

Miranda wavered, plainly charmed. Diana said nothing, but her teeth were clenched so tightly that her jaw ached.

"She has been wondering," Ben continued, "if there might be some link between Mr. Torrence's murder and the death of her husband back in '85. Mr. Spaulding died shortly after a meeting with your husband, Mrs. Torrence. Shortly after receiving a rather large sum of money from him."

"I know nothing about that." The denial came quickly, but it was plain Miranda was intrigued by this news.

"The two deaths may be unconnected, but there are certain . . . circumstances that lead us to believe otherwise."

The wariness came back into Miranda's eyes. Diana wasn't surprised. Why should her stepmother trust her? And Miranda had doubtless encountered more than her share of charming men before, most of them duplicitous.

"I am no threat to you, Miranda," Diana said, pleased to find her voice even again. "To convince you of that, I'm willing to sign a paper saying I'll never make any claim to Torrence money. Getting it away from you was Matt's plan, not mine."

"What do you want in return?"

"Your cooperation. Let me go through Father's papers in this house and in the house in Denver. There may be some record of the money he gave Evan, my late husband. And there may be some clue the police overlooked in finding his killer."

"The police never asked to see anything," Miranda informed them. "They are certain Elmira killed him." When Diana bristled, she held up a hand, forestalling a diatribe against the local constabulary. "Never mind. I can see you believe in her innocence. You'll forgive me if I don't share your opinion."

"It seems to me you had more reason to kill him than my mother did." The words were out before Diana could stop them. She hadn't mean to blurt an accusation, but there was something about Miranda that eroded her self-control.

Miranda shot angrily to her feet. "How dare you!"

Diana gave the gown Miranda wore a pointed look. "You should be in mourning black. Most widows wait at least two years before switching to half-mourning, but apparently you did not think it necessary." She didn't herself, but she wasn't about to tell Miranda that. "You weren't faithful to him. He may have been about to replace you."

"Diana—"

She waved off Ben's protest. Tact was not going to get them anywhere with a woman like this one. "You're the one who ended up with all his money, Miranda. What better motive for murder?"

"I put up with him for four years. I earned every penny! And no, I don't regret his passing. But I didn't kill him. I can prove it if I have to, but until someone in authority asks me where I was and who I was with that night, I've no intention of explaining myself." Fists clenched at her sides, Miranda glared down at the still-seated Diana.

The strident voice grated on Diana's nerves, but to her dismay she realized she believed Miranda's heated denial. She rose slowly, accepting Ben's hand to help her to her feet and to lend moral support. "Let me try to find out who did kill him, then."

Miranda drew in one deep breath, then another. She looked at Ben, then back to Diana. "You're going to marry him?"

"When things are settled here, we'll go back East. You'll never see me again."

"I want that paper signed first."

"Agreed."

It took only a few minutes to write the document. Once Diana had signed it, with Ben and Martha acting as witnesses, Miranda retired to her bedchamber and left them to their search. Her two bodyguards, the man and the boy, lurked in the background but did not interfere.

They found nothing in Torrence's study or his bedroom, which was separate from Miranda's. If William Torrence had kept any documentation of his payment to Evan, it appeared that he'd long since destroyed it. "I suppose it was hopeless from the start," Diana said.

"We haven't looked downstairs."

"I don't think my father spent much time in the kitchen."

"Let's be thorough," Ben said, and started down a flight of back stairs so narrow that his elbows brushed the walls on either side.

Hampered by her wide skirts, Diana followed more slowly, fearful of losing her balance. The kitchen was much as she remembered it. There was no cook in sight, but Miranda's maid was just taking the teakettle off the stove.

"Did you want to talk to the old man?" Martha asked.

"What old man?" Ben asked.

"Name's Morris," Martha said, jerking her head towards a closed door. "He lives here year round. Takes care of the place. Leastways he used to, before he got so sick."

Diana's pulse rate quickened. She'd remembered Morris during the trip from New York to Denver, but she hadn't thought of him since. He'd always been the self-effacing sort, there when one of the Torrences had an odd job to be done but keeping to himself when he wasn't needed. "He worked for my father for years," she said aloud.

Ben crossed the kitchen and rapped on the door Martha had indicated.

A quavering voice bade them enter.

Leander Morris sat in a rocker, bundled in blankets. Blind eyes, deeply sunken, stared at them out of a wrinkled face the color of lead. Violet circles bordered his nose. After one good look at him, Ben leaned close to Diana's ear. "He has a face struck with death. I'm going back to the buggy for my medical bag."

Left alone with the infirm old man, Diana approached him slowly. She remembered him as a ruddy-faced, healthy individual who'd sometimes given her horehound drops. The change in him saddened her. "Mr. Morris," she said softly. "It's Diana. Diana Torrence."

He gave a start before reaching out with one gnarled hand to clasp her fingers. "Come closer," he rasped. "I don't see so well anymore. Little Diana. Well, well. Torrence's girl?"

"Yes."

"And you're here in Torrence again. Well, well."

"Mr. Morris, I need your help."

"Well, well. Came back after all. Good. Good." He patted the back of her hand. His skin felt dry and thin as parchment.

She tried again. "Did my father tell you I was married?"

Blue lips twisted into a parody of a smile. "Told me when you were in the family way, too. What was it? Boy or girl? He was hoping for a boy."

She stared at him in shock and tried to pull free of his grip but it was surprisingly strong. "I never had a child."

"Lost it, eh? Too bad. He was going to raise it right, he said."

"He . . . my father was going to raise . . . my child?" Eyes wide, a feeling of panic sweeping through her, she turned with relief at the sound of Ben's return.

"Mr. Morris," Ben said. "I'm Dr. Northcote. Is it all right with you if I listen to your heart?" He already had his stethoscope out.

Diana's thoughts were racing. Why would her father think she'd been with child? And why would he talk to Morris about it? About raising his grandchild? Had he expected her to die in childbirth?

She tried to dismiss an obvious answer but it would not be ignored. Bracing one hand on the wall for support, Diana fought to quell a rising nausea.

Evan had told him she was going to have a child. That was the only explanation. He'd lied to her father. And then he'd sold that imaginary child to William Torrence. That was how he'd gotten the money to start his own acting company—not blackmail; just another confidence game.

Ben had finished his examination of Mr. Morris. "I have a powder that may give you some relief," he said, fishing once more in his black doctor's satchel.

"Mr. Morris, did my father say anything more about Evan Spaulding?" Diana asked.

"Who?" He blinked several times and looked confused. "Who

are you again? Do I know you?"

"I'm Diana, Mr. Morris. William Torrence's little girl."

"She went away," he said. "He said she died."

And try as she might, Diana could elicit no more usef[ul] information from the old man. His mind, so clear only a fe[w] minutes earlier, had clouded. He couldn't remember who she wa[s] let alone what her father might have said or done.

"What was that all about?" Ben asked, when they were bac[k] outside.

She told him her conclusions as they drove away from th[e] Torrence house. When she'd finished, Ben gave a low whistle.

"It makes sense, in a perverted kind of way. And it gives you[r] father a reason to have kept track of you and Evan."

"He must have found out fairly soon that there was no chil[d.] Maybe even before we left Denver."

"Do you think Charlie was told to give Evan bad travel advice[?]" He turned the horse towards the cemetery they'd seen from th[e] train, the next stop on the agenda they'd worked out.

"I wouldn't put it past Father."

"Would you put anything past him? Could he have sen[t] someone to kill Evan?"

The idea of her father as a murderer did not send Diana int[o] heated denials the way the same accusation against her moth[er] had. "I don't want to believe that," she whispered.

"He might have thought he'd get you back if your husband wa[s] dead."

"He didn't want me back. He wanted a new child to raise 'right[.'] That's why he gave Evan money. He thought he was buying m[y] baby."

"After he paid Evan, he must have returned to Torrence an[d] sent Charlie to Denver to spy on you. When he found out fro[m] Charlie that you were going to Leadville, he recruited Pearl."

"She'd have found it easy enough to get information about me[."] Diana pondered the issue for a moment as they followed a windin[g] road past one of Torrence's two churches. "It would have been simple to bribe our landlady. She was a money-grubbing old besom."

"I wonder," Ben mused, "if she's still in Leadville."

"What does it matter? It's plain now what happened. Father found out he'd been lied to. I think you're right. Father might well have hired someone to shoot Evan. That must be what Mother meant when she said I had reason to want revenge."

Ben pulled up at the gate to the town cemetery. It was situated away from the windswept summit on which the rest of Torrence had been built. The monuments and markers were further sheltered by aspens and evergreens. They sat in silence, staring at the graves. Sounds from the town were but a muted whisper behind them.

"It's larger than I would have expected," Ben remarked, assessing the number of graves.

With a sigh, Diana hopped down. "We'll have to hunt for Father's marker." How hard could it be? It was probably the largest and most ostentatious one.

"Diptheria epidemic," Ben said, pausing to read an inscription. "From the look of things, it wiped out half the population back in '79."

"I was away at school then." Neither of her parents had bothered to write and tell her of the devastation.

She stopped at the sight of a familiar name on one tombstone, that of a childhood friend. Emily Pargeter had been dead all these years and Diana had never known a thing about it.

She recognized another name, then two more. By the time she found the ornate little obelisk with "William Torrence" carved on it, she felt numbed by the enormity of the losses. Whole families had been wiped out.

For a long moment, Diana stood at graveside reading the flowery inscription Miranda had chosen and staring at her father's final resting place.

Then she kicked the marble monument hard enough to bruise

her toes.

The Grand Hotel in Torrence, Colorado was anything but grand. It barely had sufficient space for them all. Diana was sharing the largest of the rooms, one of two with two beds, with Jane, Red Katie, and Long Tall Linda, while Ben occupied a closet-sized space at the other end of the same floor. The hostelry did, however, serve excellent food.

When he helped Diana back into the buggy at the cemetery, Ben suggested they return there and have a bite to eat rather than immediately continue on to the next item on Diana's agenda.

"You've done enough for one day," he said. "And we've already missed the noon meal."

"I wanted to talk to Alan Kent," she objected.

"What do you think he can tell you?"

"If I knew that, I wouldn't have to ask. Besides, even if he knows nothing about Father's murder, I intend to give him a piece of my mind about his treatment of poor Jane. She came back to the hotel last night in tears."

"Why?"

"She wouldn't say, but I imagine he told her he was through with her."

"You think he admitted he'd been carrying on with Miranda?"

"I don't know if he went that far, but it doesn't matter. He hurt her, Ben, and someone should take him to task for it."

They were already back in the center of town. Ben returned the buggy to the livery stable and escorted Diana into the headquarters of the Torrence Mining Company, which was right across the street.

"You can ask Kent questions about your father or you can berate him for breaking Jane's heart," Ben said in a whisper as they climbed the stairs to the second floor office, "but it you try to do both at once you'll only muddy the waters."

"What if the two are connected?" She whispered back. "I've been thinking. If Miranda did kill Father, who better than Alan Kent to have helped her? Through Jane, he had access to the Elmira Hotel. He could have planted that glove."

Ben had to admit that the second Mrs. Torrence had plenty of reasons to kill her husband. Jealousy. Revenge. Avarice. Any one alone would have been sufficient to drive her to murder. But they had no evidence. "You need proof, Diana."

"And that's what we're going to get." She opened a glass-fronted door without knocking and entered Kent's office. "Hello, Mr. Kent."

Kent was tall, with strawberry blond hair, sharp features, and thin lips. Ben wondered what Miranda Torrence saw in him. It certainly wasn't a pleasant personality. He sprang to his feet at the sight of Diana, cursed fluently, and ordered her off the premises.

"Not until you've answered a few questions."

"I don't work for you, Mrs. Spaulding."

"Thank goodness!"

"You're trespassing. If you don't leave, I'll have the law on you."

"What are you afraid of, Kent?" Ben asked, making his voice as reasonable as he could. He'd taken an instant, unreasoning dislike to the man and was finding it hard to stand still for his belligerent attitude towards Diana.

"Afraid? What's that supposed to mean?"

Ben continued to stare at him. He'd been told he could look intimidating when he tried. As if in proof of it, sweat beaded on Kent's forehead.

"I don't have to talk to you people." He fumbled in his desk drawer and came up with a gun, but his hand shook as he lifted it.

Ben grabbed Diana and started to back away. He'd have felt less nervous if the man showed an ease with the weapon. Nervous people tended to shoot themselves, and others, by accident. "You don't need that, Kent. We're leaving."

Still armed, he followed them until they'd retreated into the street. "And don't come back!" he shouted, slamming the door.

"That's not the behavior of an innocent man," Diana declared.

"Nor is it enough to accuse him of murder." Ben steered her towards the hotel. "Even suspecting him of planting that glove is a stretch. You said he was at the Elmira the night your father was killed, but he wasn't there the next day. When did he get the glove to plant it?"

"But *someone* put that glove in Mother's rooms, and he's the one with a connection to Miranda."

They walked the rest of the way to the hotel in silence and by mutual agreement went directly to the dining room. Maryam was the only one there, apparently enjoying her late and solitary meal. She made a point of ignoring Diana.

Ben pulled out a chair at one of the small tables, but Diana ignored it. She stared at the other woman. "Someone with access to the Elmira Hotel planted the glove in Mother's suite. Pearl said Father had a spy there. If Miranda knew who she was, and if she was willing to pay that person enough, the spy might have planted the glove."

Ben followed her gaze to Maryam. "You think she's the one?"

"That would explain how she knew about Kent and Miranda. It isn't common knowledge. I'm sure of that. I didn't suspect a thing until I talked to Miranda's maid."

"Jane may have—"

"I don't think Jane suspected a thing before we came to Torrence, but even if she did, she'd never have confided in Maryam."

Revitalized by a new sense of purpose, Diana stalked across the dining room towards the woman in pink. "I know what you did," she cried. "You framed my mother for murder!"

"You're daft." Maryam came up out of her chair in a rush and tried to get out of Diana's way. Cornered, she backed into an Eastlake sideboard hard enough to make the china rattle. "Why would I go and do a crazy thing like that?"

"For money. Cold, hard cash. You were a spy, Maryam. You

took my father's money. You met with him the night he died. Maybe you were even there when he was killed. How much did Miranda pay you to help cover up her crime?"

The pink-clad prostitute goggled at her. And then, to Ben's astonishment, she gave a snort of laughter. Either she was a very good actress, or her reaction was genuine. "Clutching at straws, that's what you're doing! Accuse just anyone and see what they'll do. Well maybe some folks cower and confess with that sort of treatment, but not me. The minute we get back to Denver, I'm looking for another place to work. A girl's got to have some pride!"

With that, she pushed past Diana and flounced out of the room.

Diana sent a sheepish glance in Ben's direction. "Well," she said, "if I were as devious as Maryam thinks I am, I'd have to account myself a rousing success. I certainly got a reaction!"

❧❧❧

Early the next morning, Diana heard Long Tall Linda get up, dress, and slip out of the room. Then Jane arose, noisily following her rigid routine of a cold splash and calisthenics. Diana watched the process through slitted eyes, feeling not the slightest urge to rise from the bed, let alone participate.

She had been up late into the night, making plans to move everyone back into the Elmira. After the others had retired, she and Ben had spent another hour discussing her father's murder. They'd gone round and round and were not one bit further ahead. The only decision they'd made was to accept a dinner invitation from the owner of the mercantile, who claimed he'd been a good friend of her father's.

Diana still liked Miranda as a suspect, but unless they could figure out how the merry widow had been able to plant that bloodstained glove in Elmira's suite, she despaired of ever proving Miranda's guilt. Accusing each of the other girls in turn did not seem like a viable plan. Besides, when she'd first questioned them, back in Denver, they'd all denied knowing anything about the glove. Diana had believed them. She still did.

When Jane had dressed and left the room, Katie opened one eye. "Thank the Lord that's over with!"

"Don't you believe in healthful exercise?"

"I get plenty of exercise at night. No need to exert myself first thing in the morning." She grinned, unrepentant.

Very faintly, Diana heard the sound of voices from the next room, occupied by Maybelle and Chastity. She wondered if Jane had stopped in to see if anyone else was ready for breakfast.

Bright sunshine flooded in through the sheer curtains hung over floor to ceiling windows, picking out the flowers on the carpet and the bright-colored squares on the quilt Diana still had pulled up to her chin. "It's not exactly the crack of dawn."

"Close enough. It's not noon yet, is it?"

One on each side, they rolled out of bed. Diana dressed rapidly, pulling on her comfortable old blue standby, and turned to find Katie wearing only lace-trimmed drawers and a cambric corset cover. She held a strand of her fiery red hair in front of her eyes, frowning at it.

"What's wrong?"

"I need to dye my hair again. It's getting dull." Catching Diana's involuntary reaction, she chuckled. "I like bright colors."

"What color was your hair before you dyed it?"

"Oh, it was red, but a very ordinary shade. Like a carrot. I wanted something people would remember."

Curious in spite of herself, Diana studied Katie's bountiful curls. "What do you use?"

"Alkanet boiled in baking soda water. Then, after my hair dries, I do a second wash with lemon juice and vinegar."

Diana was at a loss for words. One ingredient alone should have been sufficient to change the color, but she supposed the combination accounted for that unique shade of red.

Leaving her to it, Diana went out into the corridor and rapped on the door opposite, the room assigned to Honeycomb, Big Nose Nellie, Strawberry Sue, and Maryam. When no one answered Diana's knock, she started to go on down the stairs to the hotel dining room. She changed her mind at the last minute and turned the knob instead. She told herself that she had no particular reason to be worried about Nellie, but the young woman had experienced two close calls in the course of a week. Better safe than sorry.

A bulge showed beneath the covers of the far bed. One of the girls sleeping in. But an uneasy feeling crept over Diana, a premonition she could not ignore. She remembered what Nellie had said—she always slept sitting up.

She'd just see who it was, Diana decided, and go away again if it was one of the other girls. Feeling slightly foolish, she crept up to the side of the bed and tweaked the sheet away from the sleeper's face.

Nellie.

Her heart in her throat, Diana reached out and touched the young woman on her shoulder. Nellie's eyes fluttered open, but she didn't seem to recognize Diana.

"Go 'way." Her voice was slurred, and the way she inhaled and exhaled sounded odd, as if she couldn't quite catch her breath.

Alarmed, Diana seized Nellie's wrist and felt for the pulse. It was rapid and irregular. Diana started for the door at a fast clip, intent on fetching Ben, but before she'd gotten halfway across the room, Nellie moaned.

"Gonna be sick," she whispered. "Help me."

Diana handed her the chamber pot just in time.

"Feel giddy," Nellie murmured after she'd emptied her stomach. "Sleepy, too."

Nellie's pulse had slowed, but Diana wasn't sure that was a good sign. The other woman's breathing wasn't so fast now, either, but it was noisy in a way that wasn't right.

"Hang on," Diana told her. "I'm going for help."

First she tried Ben's room at the far end of the hall, but it was empty. Then she bolted down the stairs to the dining room, where everyone had gathered except Katie and Nellie. Diana caught Ben's eye and jerked her head towards the second floor. A moment later he was racing up the stairs beside her. She was breathless by the time they got back to Nellie's room.

"What's wrong with her, Ben?" Even from the doorway, Diana could see that Nellie looked worse than she had a few minutes earlier. She seemed to be in a stupor.

He checked her pulse, looked at her eyes, then glanced around, checking the top of the night stand, the floor, and finally the bed itself. He found what he was looking for under Nellie's pillow.

"Laudanum. She's taken an overdose."

For a moment Diana was too stunned to move or speak, but the sound of footsteps on the stairs finally spurred her into action. She stepped all the way into the room and closed the door behind her, shutting out curious onlookers. "What can I do to help?"

"We've got to induce vomiting. That she's already been sick is a good sign."

The door opened and closed. "Laudanum poisoning?" Long Tall Linda asked.

"Yes."

"I have mustard seed."

Ben glanced at Diana, a question in his eyes.

"Long Tall Linda has some experience with home remedies," Diana said.

"Get the mustard seed. Diana, I need warm water. Lots of it. And a feather to use to tickle her throat. Then go to my room for my bag. I have sulphate of zinc," he said to Long Tall Linda.

Diana did as she was told and helped where she could over the next half hour as they worked to empty Nellie's stomach of the poison.

"We aren't out of the woods yet," Ben said when he'd checked her heart rate yet again. "Now we need a strong stimulant. Coffee will do. Or brandy. And I want you to pour cold water over her head and the back of her neck."

"My ma always said to whip the skin with small cords or rods," Long Tall Linda offered. "Palms of the hands and soles of the feet."

"I don't think we need to go that far," Ben said, "but I'll keep it in mind."

In another hour, Nellie was sleeping normally, and there was time at last to think about what had happened.

"You knew it was laudanum poisoning," Ben said, turning to Long Tall Linda with a suspicious look on his face. "How?"

"Made sense."

"Why? Was she addicted to the stuff?"

"Not so you'd notice, but we all keep some around. There are times you need it to sleep."

"That doesn't explain why she'd be taking it at mid-morning," Diana said, "or why she'd take too much."

Long Tall Linda shrugged. "She never did have a lick of sense. Poor cow. She's sure had a run of bad luck lately."

It was more than bad luck, Diana thought. A silent exchange of glances told her Ben thought so, too. This was the third attempt to harm Nellie. Any one of them might have killed her.

Diana stayed with Nellie all that day, as did Jane. When at last Nellie awoke, much improved and even hungry, the first thing Diana asked her was why she'd taken the laudanum.

"But I didn't," Nellie objected. "The only thing I took was my tonic."

Diana retrieved the bottle Ben had found. "Is this it?"

Nellie nodded. "Revitalizing tonic. Good for what ails you."

Diana looked at the bottle. It was clearly marked as containing laudanum. "You don't know how to read, do you?"

"What's that got to do with anything?"

"Do you?"

"No." Nellie sulked. "Never went to school."

"If you'd like, I'll see that you are taught, but that's not the most important thing right now. Someone substituted a bottle of laudanum for your tonic. What would have been a normal dose of one was a dangerous amount of the other. That's what made you sick. Can you think how that could happen?"

Nellie shrugged. "Someone playing a joke?"

"A dangerous one. Is there any reason any of the others would want to hurt you?"

"You mean kill me?" As that idea sunk in, Nellie had the good sense to be scared.

"I think so."

"You're upsetting her for no reason," Jane interrupted. "Laudanum's not something anyone would use if they wanted her dead. They'd give her rat poison. Or Oil of Tansy. Always plenty of that around a whorehouse."

Tears rolled slowly down Nellie's cheeks. "What did I do to make someone hate me so much?"

"It has to be something you know without realizing its importance. It could be tied to my Father's death. If someone thinks you noticed more that night than you've said—"

"But I didn't see nothing!" Nellie wailed.

"No one coming out of my mother's suite? No one going in?"

"I wasn't anywhere *near* her rooms! Honest!"

"Nothing suspicious that night at all?"

"I'd tell you if there was. The only reason I remembered about the gloves was because I had a hankering to own a pair like that myself. I don't remember nothing else. Honest." Tears continued to stream down her face as an edge of hysteria came into her voice.

"All right, Nellie. All right. I believe you."

"I believe you, too," Jane said. "You didn't see anything." She turned to Diana. "You're making too much of this. She accidentally got hold of the wrong bottle. That's all it was."

"Maybe. Maybe not. But let's make sure everyone we can think of knows Nellie is no threat. That's the only way to be sure there won't be a fourth attempt to silence her."

CHAPTER FOURTEEN

ഇരൢ

Hugh Crymble," the sheriff of Chaffee County said a few hours later, holding out a hand to Ben. He was a big, burly man in his early forties, hardened by years of mining in the mountains. Ben had already asked a few questions about him. Crymble was honest as the day was long, but he lived in Buena Vista. He took a personal interest in law and order in Torrence only when it was brought to his attention. Ben had sent him a telegram.

They shook, and Ben introduced himself, then took a chair at Crymble's table in the saloon. The place smelled of sawdust and spilled whiskey, tobacco smoke and the contents of the spittoons.

"What can I do for you, Dr. Northcote?"

"Someone took a shot at a young woman named Nellie DuBois yesterday afternoon, Sheriff. And this morning she got an accidental overdose of laudanum that almost killed her."

"What's your interest in this Miss DuBois?"

"She's the friend of a friend of mine."

"That so?" said the sheriff.

Ben didn't know whether to try to clarify the situation, or let him think Diana was one of Big Nose Nellie's professional colleagues. It shouldn't matter, but he had a feeling it might.

"My friend is a young woman who lived here in Torrence for a few years, after her father founded the town."

"That so?" He took a swallow of his beer and contemplated Ben.

"Did you know William Torrence?"

There was caution now in the sheriff's eyes. He nodded. "Important man in these parts. Not well liked, though. Wasn't surprised to hear he got himself killed."

"Funny," Ben drawled, deliberately using more colloquial speech than usual. "That's what folks say about the murder of his daughter's husband, too. Fella named Spaulding. Happened a couple of years ago in Leadville."

"Not my county," Crymble said, but from the expression on Crymble's face, Ben thought that he recognized the name.

Since it was obvious the sheriff wasn't going to volunteer any information, Ben decided to take a risk. He'd helped out on criminal investigations often enough back home, being one of Bangor's coroners. He had some idea how the law worked, even in what easterners thought of as the Wild West. "Let me tell you a little story," he said.

By the time Ben was through, Crymble had finished his beer and was staring into the dregs. "Bad business all around," he said. "Don't see how any of it's connected to Miss Nellie's troubles though."

"Maybe it's not, but it looks to me as if you've got three unsolved crimes—the shot at Nellie was a crime even if the laudanum turns out to have been an accident—and in each case the criminal got away without being identified."

"Coincidence, Doc."

"Is there a lot of unsolved crime in these parts?"

"In fact, there isn't. And murder?" He shook his head. "We do our best to solve murders, even if we don't always get the killer to trial. Let me tell *you* a little story, if you've time. And if you're willing to buy the next round."

Ben was.

"Had a murder a few miles from here just last month, at Granite. Some of the section hands that work for the Denver and Rio Grande and the Midland were in a saloon and a row broke out. Whites against dagos. Got nasty."

"I can imagine."

"Maybe you can, maybe you can't." The sheriff paused to take a long swallow of his beer. "The fight was broken up. Six dagos were ejected and quiet was restored. Then, around midnight, a fella named Casey left the saloon to go home. A friend warned him not to go out alone. Said the Italians were treacherous, and that they wanted revenge because their saloon was burned down last year. Casey ignored him. His body was found the next morning behind the freight house, about forty yards from the saloon. There was a trail of blood to show where he'd been dragged for about twenty-five feet after being stabbed in the windpipe. The murder took place within six feet of the tracks and the bunk car the dagos were in."

"Let me guess—you arrested an Italian section hand."

Crymble tapped his forehead. "There's a brain in here, Doc." He chuckled. "I'm smarter than I look. I had the whole of the dago quarters corralled and the boss called the roll-call and one dago was missing. Fella named Guiseppe Zolanso."

"Case solved?"

"Maybe. Some say his five friends helped him kill Casey. Guess we'll find out at the trial. Meanwhile I had to keep the good people of Granite from setting explosives under the bunk car and blowing up all the dagos in one blast."

Unsure what the point of the story had been, Ben sipped his beer and studied Crymble's amiable face. He was not reassured. True, this Zolanso probably had killed Casey. But the presumption of guilt based on his disappearance and the fact that he'd quarreled with Casey earlier were disconcertingly similar to the police reasoning that had declared Elmira Torrence guilty of her former husband's murder.

"Evan Spaulding was gunned to death in plain sight of other gamblers, Crymble. No one came up with a name for the killer."

The sheriff shrugged. "We get drifters through our towns and cities every day, Dr. Northcote. A lot of them with shady pasts. Folks don't ask too many questions of strangers. Not healthy."

"Funny thing about unanswered questions, Sheriff. They tend to fester and smell after a while."

"Lake County's out of my jurisdiction. I don't go sticking my nose into another sheriff's business without a good reason."

When Ben bought another round, the sheriff gave him the names of sheriff and coroner and city marshall of Leadville. He already knew what *Crofutt's Guide,* published in the same year as Evan's murder, had said about the place: "No city in America is better governed; none where life and property are more secure."

"You should visit Leadville before you throw stones, Northcote," Crymble said. "No problem finding lodging. At last count there were over a dozen hotels."

"And how many gambling dens?"

Crymble considered him seriously. "Twenty or more. Maybe thirty houses of prostitution. At least eighty saloons." A glint came into his eyes. "One of Leadville's parlor houses is famous all over Colorado—the Red Light Hall on State Street. Run by a fella name of Charles Cole. It's strictly a temperance house, but he claims his girls are the roundest, rosiest, and most beautiful in town."

"Ever hear of a Leadville prostitute named Pearl Adams?"

The sheriff shook his head. "But these girls change their names all the time. Last I heard, Leadville had Mollies, Minnies, Carries, even a Frankie. Oh, and there was a Sallie Purple." He chuckled.

"Dressed all in purple?" Ben thought of Miranda Torrence, but quickly dismissed the idea that she might once have had another identity. Matt Hastings had known her as Miranda Chambers and had been planning to marry her, or so the Denver gossips said.

"Dyed her hair that color," Crymble explained, further

eliminating Miranda. "All her hair, if you know what I mean. Don't remember a Pearl, though."

Now that Ben thought about it, he wasn't even sure Pearl had worked in a parlor house in Leadville. She'd said she'd gone there to spy on Evan. Would she have been more likely to encounter him if she was performing in one of the dance halls or working as a dealer? He knew some females dealt faro, especially in the more exclusive gambling halls.

Cursing himself for not thinking to ask more questions when he'd been with Pearl, Ben tried to get more specific information out of the sheriff, but either Crymble didn't know or he wasn't saying. By the time Ben paid for a their last round of drinks, the sheriff was more interested in talking about his wife and children than he was in discussing crime.

He'd also, Ben realized, wormed a remarkable amount of information out of Ben about himself, Diana, and Elmira Torrence.

"She's wanted for murder, you know," Crymble said. "Your Mrs. Spaulding should have reported her reappearance to the police in Denver."

"And say what? That she was gone again? Diana has no idea where her mother is hiding out."

Crymble started to speak, then closed his mouth with a snap as the door of the saloon opened to admit a newcomer. Instantly on alert, Ben turned to look.

Unlike saloons in other parts of the West, Colorado's did not have swinging doors. It was too cold. The winds in Torrence, in particular, argued against using any door that did not close properly.

Alan Kent let this one slam behind him as he stormed into the saloon and marched towards their table. "Sheriff, arrest this man." Kent's eyes were bright with anger.

"On what charge, Mr. Kent?"

"He's a mac."

"A what?" Ben asked, genuinely confused.

"A pimp. He's got a half dozen whores from Denver over at the hotel and plans to set up shop here."

"The young ladies have conducted no business since arriving in Torrence, Mr. Kent." They'd been behaving with remarkable circumspection, simply getting settled and furnishing their new quarters and making plans. That the plans had originally included operating a parlor house in the old Alhambra dance hall wasn't something Ben felt he needed to share.

"If that's the case," the sheriff said, "he'll have some . . . licenses to purchase. But I don't see where the crime is, Mr. Kent. Or why you should be worrying about it."

"I represent Mrs. Torrence."

"Which Mrs. Torrence?" Crymble asked.

Ben might have thought it an innocent question had he not caught the sheriff's eye. Crymble didn't care for Alan Kent, and he was amused by this bumbling effort to make trouble for Elmira's girls.

"I want them out of town."

"It's a free country, Mr. Kent. And so far the only crime committed has been against the young ladies. Someone took pot shots at a couple of them yesterday afternoon and injured one. You wouldn't know anything about that, would you?"

Kent paled, then glared. "I am a respectable citizen, Sheriff. And a voter. You'd best remember that when the next election rolls around."

"I'm quaking in my boots," the sheriff assured him, "but it's time for me to be on my way. This isn't the only town in my county, you know. Good day to you, gentlemen."

"I believe I have other matters to attend to, as well," Ben said, standing. "Unless Mr. Kent has something else he'd like to say to me?"

The younger man glowered, but stepped away. He was shorter and less well-muscled than Ben and sure to lose at fisticuffs. But as Ben left the saloon in the sheriff's company, the hairs on the back of his neck prickled with the force of Kent's glare.

"I'd watch your back if I were you," Crymble said.

"Does Kent have a history of violence?"

"Far as I know, he's as mild-mannered as they come, but he was Torrence's clerk. He knows everybody Torrence did."

Ben took a wild stab. "Someone like a gunslinger Torrence might have hired, say, back in '85?"

"Don't think Kent was here then. Seems to me I remember hearing he's only been around a bit more than a year. But you never know." The sheriff shrugged and headed for the livery stable where he'd left his horse.

Ben started to return to the hotel, then changed his mind. He caught up with Crymble in front of the feed store. "If I went to Leadville, who should I talk to, the sheriff or the city marshall? Which of them do you trust?"

Crymble stopped dead a few feet away from the livery stable, drawing stares from a pair of calico-clad women on the opposite side of the street. "You go and get yourself into trouble, Dr. Northcote, I won't be happy."

He seemed to have forgotten he was the one who'd suggested Ben visit Leadville. "Then help me out," Ben said.

Crymble contemplated the saloon they'd just left. Kent had emerged to glower at them. "Tell you what, Dr. Northcote. Next time I go to Lake County, I'll check on a few things. But don't get your hopes up. Old Timberline Torrence was a sneaky bastard. He was real good at covering his tracks."

&)&

You don't need to come with me," Ben said for the hundredth time. "I'll be back around ten tomorrow morning."

Since they were already at the Torrence depot, waiting for the 6:00 P.M. arrival of the express from Denver, a train that continued on to Leadville, the point was moot. Her gripsack sat next to his on the platform. "My former landlady may not talk to you unless

I'm there."

"I'll bribe her."

Diana kept her smile in place, but not without effort. She wasn't letting him go alone, and that was that. Much as she wished she never had to set foot in Leadville again, if Ben intended to visit the place, she would be his shadow.

"You won't recognize the folks I knew when I lived there." Diana wasn't sure she would, either, if any of them were even around after all this time. She hadn't met all that many people, only a few faro dealers and an actress or two. She'd sewn costumes to earn enough to buy bread and milk and eggs.

"This is probably a waste of time," he said. "No sense both of us going."

Diana agreed with the first part. If anyone had possessed information about Evan's death, information they'd been willing to share, they'd have done so at the time. "Shall I stay here and be a target, then?" she asked.

The pulse in his neck throbbed. "You'll be in no danger if you avoid confrontations."

"I'm not about to hide under a bed while you're gone."

He gave her a hard look. "Does that mean you think everything that happened to Nellie was due to sheer bad luck?"

"No, but no one's tried to hurt *me.*"

"What about Alan Kent?"

"He's all bluster."

"He had a gun."

"So do most people around here."

"Did you, when you lived here?"

"I didn't have a gun of my own, but I was taught how to shoot. I can hit what I aim at with both a pistol and a rifle." Granted, the idea had been to shoot four-legged predators and occasionally bag something they could put in the cookpot, but the same principles applied to shooting a man.

"Somehow, that fails to reassure me," Ben muttered as a distant whistle heralded the arrival of the train. "All right. We'll go together. We should reach Leadville around eight. We'll go to your old lodgings first. Maybe you can stay there while I visit the Texas House. A gambling hell is no fit place for a lady."

"I won't be the only woman there," she reminded him. "There are always a few female faro dealers. I grant you it's not the most reputable place I've ever been in, but it isn't a den of iniquity, either. As long as it's clear I'm with you there will be no problems." She hoped she sounded more confident than she felt because she wasn't about to let Ben go wandering into that place on his own.

"Perhaps I *should* reconsider," Ben said. "After all, not many people who were there when Evan was shot will still be around."

"Folks don't stay put long as a rule," she agreed, "and they tell me Leadville's grown almost as fast as Denver. But the owner of the Texas House is likely the same." And he'd say what he'd said before, that the killer was an unknown card player. After all this time, it seemed even less likely anyone would be able to provide a name or description. Diana didn't count on the city marshall to be of any use to them, either.

As the train steamed and screeched to a stop at the depot, Diana suddenly remembered Col. Arkins. The newspaper publisher might be wrong about her mother, but he had a nose for a story. Had he suspected a connection between Evan Spaulding and William Torrence, other than Diana herself? He'd raised the subject of the murder when she'd visited him. But if he'd had any proof, any name, any lead to the unknown gunman, surely he'd already have published the story. That meant, she surmised, that there was nothing to be found in Leadville.

"This trip *is* a waste of time," she said aloud.

But Ben wasn't listening. He was staring at a clean-shaven, stoop-shouldered man who'd just gotten off the train. "Damnation," he muttered.

When Diana saw who it was, she silently echoed the curse.

Ben watched Matt Hastings approach, fighting an urge to knock him flat. He'd like to teach the rounder a lesson he'd never forget for what he'd tried to do to Diana. Her hand on his arm was all that kept him in check.

When she stepped in front of him, determined to fight her own battles, Ben balled his hands into fists. He was prepared to let her take the first shot. She had earned the right. But if she needed him, he'd be there beside her in a heartbeat.

"Trouble folks?"

Ben turned slowly to see Sheriff Crymble descending from train to platform.

"Delay departure for a minute or two, will you Pat?" Crymble said to the conductor.

"We'll be late getting to Leadville, Sheriff," the conductor argued.

"Then you'll just have to make shorter stops in Granite, Twin Lakes, and Malta, won't you?" When Crymble had gotten a reluctant nod of agreement, he turned his full attention to the three people on the platform. "You planning to go to Leadville, Dr. Northcote? Ma'am?"

"We've changed our minds," Diana said hastily. Responding to the badge prominently displayed on Crymble's chest, she introduced herself.

"Timberline Torrence's girl," the sheriff said, looking her over. "All growed up. You won't remember me, I don't suppose. But I met you once when you were just a little bit of a thing. Your daddy and I had mining in common."

"This isn't the time for reminiscences, Crymble," Hastings interrupted. "I've just arrived, and you're obviously on your way somewhere."

"Boarded the train at the last stop, Buena Vista. That's where I live, Mrs. Spaulding. My wife wasn't pleased about my having to be gone overnight, but I explained I had a little business in

Leadville." Crymble gave Ben a pointed look. "Looking into a matter a fella told me about earlier today. Case of murder."

Hastings didn't seem concerned by this revelation, or even curious. "You're Northcote, I presume," he said to Ben. "Are you taking this train, too."

"Not a chance." Ben picked up his gripsack and Diana's tweed bag.

"I don't want to hear about any brawls when I get back," Crymble warned. "You talk this out like gentlemen, you hear me?"

"I hear you, Sheriff." Whether Ben would heed the advice was another matter entirely. "And I'm sure Mr. Hastings does, too. Oh, and Sheriff? If for any reason Mrs. Spaulding and I aren't here when you get back, I'd advise questioning Mr. Hastings very closely about our whereabouts."

"You've made your point, Northcote," Hastings said. He straightened his collar and picked up his carpetbag.

Crymble reboarded the train. As it left the depot, Hastings turned to Diana and noisily cleared his throat. "I thought you might come here," he said. "Have you talked to Miranda yet?" His Adam's apple bobbed nervously as he waited for her response.

Body tensed as if for a fight, Diana spat it out. "Yesterday."

"Then you know that neither of us could have killed your father."

She blinked at him in confusion and cut her eyes to Ben, silently asking if he knew what Hastings was talking about.

Ben was equally puzzled, and didn't trust Hastings as far as he could throw him, but if the lawyer had information, Ben was willing to hear it. He could thrash the fellow later.

"Why don't we take this somewhere private," he suggested.

෨෬

At the Grand Hotel they claimed what the proprietor called the salesman's room. Thick blue and gold carpeting muffled their footsteps as they entered, but nothing could dispel the tension in the air. Diana and Matt settled into two deep leather armchairs arranged catercorner to each other near the unlit woodstove. Ben remained standing.

"All right, Hastings," he said. "Out with it. We have Miranda's side of the story. Let's see how well yours agrees with it."

Diana started at Ben's outright lie, but Matt didn't notice. He leapt to the conclusion that Miranda had told them more than she actually had.

"I hardly know where to start."

Unsympathetic, Ben made an impatient gesture. "At the beginning?"

Matt cleared his throat. "It began five years ago. I met a young woman named Miranda Chambers and fell in love with her. We were going to be married. Then she met your father, Diana, and decided that being very very rich was a better deal."

"It must have been difficult living right next door." To her own surprise, Diana felt a twinge of sympathy for him.

"No more so than after your father cheated me, then dissolved our partnership. And very convenient when Miranda found out he had a mistress. She decided taking up with me again would be the perfect revenge."

"Is that *all* she wanted? An affair? Or did she want you to kill her husband?"

"She may have wished he were dead, but you know perfectly well that neither of us killed him. We were together the night he died. In his house. In Miranda's bed. The servants—even the redheaded maid—will verify the truth of that if Miranda tells them it's okay to answer your questions. The redhead is in service with a family on Lawrence Street now."

"There are still some details I'm unclear on," Diana said, hiding her surprise at his revelations. "If you and Miranda were so . . . close, why did you help me when I turned up on your doorstep?"

He gave a wry laugh. "Didn't you think it odd that I waylaid you at the exact moment you were standing on the sidewalk in front of my place, wondering where to go next? Miranda telephoned me the instant you ran out of her house. She was hysterical. When she shouted, 'Why didn't you warn me his daughter might show up?' I realized you must have returned. I looked out the window and there you were."

She'd obligingly told him what was going on and how much she knew, Diana recalled, and she'd never had a suspicion then that he wasn't acting out of the goodness of his heart.

Matt dragged agitated fingers through his dull brown hair, leaving it standing on end. "I'm not proud of the way I deceived you, Diana. But I loved her. I never stopped loving her. Not until *after* you arrived in Denver."

"Oh, please! You aren't going to swear you switched your undying devotion to me, I hope?"

"Nothing so noble. I planned on making Miranda my wife as soon as a suitable period of mourning for Torrence had passed. But shortly after you entered the picture, we quarreled. She told me she'd decided years ago that I wasn't good enough to marry and that she hadn't changed her mind since. And she told me she had a new lover." By the look on his face, she'd made a few comparisons that had not flattered Matt.

His bitterness was justified, Diana thought, but it did not explain why he'd tried to force *her* into marriage.

Ben must have been thinking the same thing. "What happened with Miranda is no excuse for what you tried to do to Diana," he snapped.

"I meant her no harm." He kept his gaze on Diana. "Remember? When you first arrived, I tried to convince you not to go to the Elmira Hotel." Matt leaned forward to take her hand. "I admired you when you were younger. I wanted to protect you. You were a complication, but I had only your best interests at heart."

"But you *did* take me to the Elmira." She tugged free of his grip. "And once I was settled there, you reported to Miranda."

His hands closed into fists on the arms of the chair, and he cleared his throat several times before speaking. "I won't lie to you any more. At that point I'd have done almost anything for her. She was afraid you'd take her to court over the inheritance, no matter what you'd said. I went back to her house that first night you were in town, prepared to hold her hand and tell her not to fret. I assured her that if you did sue, I'd represent her in court, and that we'd win. Then we'd be free to marry, I said. When I left her, I thought our future together was a certainty, but the very next time I saw her—" His voice broke and it was a moment before he could continue.

"Her new lover had convinced her you were no threat to the inheritance, so she gave me my walking papers. I think I went a bit mad when I realized how she'd used me." He made a sound that was half bitter laugh, half sob. "That's what drove me over the edge, Diana. I wanted to hurt her, and the only way to make a woman like her suffer is to take away what she values most—her fortune. That's when I decided to marry you. Together we could challenge Torrence's will. She'd pay for using me by losing everything."

"You were greedy, not deranged." Ben's voice was a low growl of suppressed rage.

Matt gripped the arms of his chair so tightly that his knuckles went white. Once again he avoided looking at Ben and kept his focus on Diana. "I wronged you. I am sorry. But you must believe me. I never meant you any harm."

Ben came up behind Diana's chair and placed his hands on her shoulders. He said nothing, but she could imagine the look he was giving Matt.

Diana regarded her former neighbor with less outrage, but she did not entirely believe his protestations, either. She could forgive him some of his deceptions. Thwarted love could drive someone to desperate measures. Indeed, Diana now suspected that at least part of his motivation had been to make the other woman jealous.

But there had been more than mere deception in Matt's actions. Even setting aside that he'd tried to drug her, there had been the threats he'd made against her mother and Ben. Remembering, she hardened her heart.

"I told you from the first that I was going to marry Ben. You had no business trying to force me into marrying you."

Ben spoke before Matt could respond. "You tried to drug her. You meant to rape her."

"No!" Matt's face flushed.

Ben took a threatening step around Diana's chair. "We know you intended to make Diana pliant with opiates, Hastings. Jane didn't administer the drug. Instead she told Diana everything."

"I would never have taken advantage of her, not even when she was drugged. I . . . I meant to let her *think* I had, but—"

He shrank back in the chair, eyes wide, when he saw Ben's doubled fists. Beads of sweat popped out on his forehead and the smell of fear permeated the small space between them. "I wasn't in my right mind, I tell you!"

"You knew exactly what you were doing."

"Damn it, man, you can't hang a man for poor judgment!"

"No, only for murder. Seems to me you had plenty of reason to kill William Torrence."

Taken aback, Matt just stared at them.

Diana looked up at Ben, then back at Matt. "If Miranda verifies his story, they both have an alibi for the night of Father's murder. I expect she will. It fits in with what she hinted at."

"Hinted?" Matt looked appalled. "You mean you didn't already know that—" He'd scrambled halfway out of his chair before a threatening gesture from Ben caused him to subside.

"They could both be lying. They would, if they were in it together."

But she shook her head. Much as she'd like to accept Ben's interpretation, Diana found she believed Matt. He was dishonest and conniving, and clearly lacked a conscience, but she did not think he had murdered her father.

"We'll talk to her again," she said, "but first I have another question for our *friend* here." She fixed Matt with a withering glare. "You made a threat against my mother. You said you had proof she killed my father, proof you'd take to the police if I didn't cooperate. What proof?"

He squirmed and wouldn't meet her eyes. "Not proof, precisely. A theory. I know the murder weapon was a knife. The police would have a stronger case if they could link the knife to your mother."

Diana exchanged a look with Ben. Plainly Matt did not know that her father had been stabbed with a hotel letter opener.

"Your parents owned a pair of decorative knives," Matt continued. "Do you remember them, Diana? They were a gift from that English nabob they entertained on his visit to Denver. After the divorce, one of the knives disappeared. Torrence always said Elmira stole it, but he never charged her with theft. Miranda showed me the case once, with the empty place. She said that she'd heard Elmira had offered to give it back to him anytime he wanted it—blade first."

"That doesn't mean she used it to stab him," Diana objected.

"Is it at the Elmira Hotel?"

"I haven't seen it."

"Then it's possible the police will be interested in my information."

Ben glowered at him. "The killer didn't use a knife on Torrence. According to the hotel bartender, the murder weapon was one of the brass letter openers the hotel puts in every suite."

Matt cleared his throat. "That doesn't alter the fact that neither Miranda nor I went anywhere near the Windsor that night."

Diana sighed and glanced at Ben. "I believe him."

"I am inclined to myself." He didn't sound pleased.

"Let's go and see if we can find Miranda at home," Diana suggested.

This time they walked. Nothing was very far from anything

else in Torrence, although most of the going was rough and uphill.

Martha answered the door. "You can't come in," she said.

"Yes, we can." Diana gently pushed past her.

Ben took her arm to usher her into the parlor while Matt trailed behind. The reason for Martha's reluctance was immediately obvious. Miranda already had company. Alan Kent was with her. In fact, he was on one knee on the tiger skin in front of the hearth, clearly about to propose.

"Sorry to interrupt this touching moment," Diana said, "but unless you want to find yourself charged with my father's murder, Miranda, I suggest you take a moment to confirm Matt's story."

Alan Kent scrambled to his feet, irate, but Miranda seemed unruffled by their sudden appearance. "What story?" she asked.

"Oh, no. You tell us. It's obvious there's bad blood between the two of you now. You need to agree if I'm to believe you."

"What is she talking about?" Kent demanded.

Miranda ignored him. She toyed with the Turkish designs embroidered on the thick satin mantel scarf, a faint sneer on her face. "I couldn't have killed William, Diana. I never left the house that night. I never even left my bed."

"Can you prove it?"

"You know I can or you wouldn't be here with him." The look she turned on Matt was venomous. He glared back. "All he wanted was the money, not me."

"That's not true. I loved you. I . . . I still do!"

"Too late," Kent snarled. "She's mine now."

"Has she given you an answer?" Diana inquired.

"She will." He went back down on one knee. "Marry me, Miranda. Send this boor away."

The glance she spared Alan Kent was full of disdain. "Why should I marry anyone? I have money now. I don't need a husband."

"She never had any intention of sharing," Matt said.

Kent surged to his feet, fists raised. "Damn you, Hastings! This is all your fault."

Matt looked equally ready to fight. "I don't see it that way, Kent."

Ben got a firm grip on Diana's arm and tugged her out of the parlor. Leaving Miranda and her two erstwhile suitors to sort out their own affairs, they returned to the street.

Diana exhaled slowly. "How strange. Aside from a mild curiosity, I find I don't much care what happens to any of them."

"It occurs to me," Ben said thoughtfully, "that only two of them have been cleared of suspicion."

Her stride didn't falter but his suggestion surprised her. "You think Alan Kent might have murdered my father? Why?"

"In order to marry a rich widow."

"But he didn't take up with her until after Father's death."

"Are you sure of that?"

"No, I suppose I'm not. In fact, now that I think about it, I know nothing about Alan Kent beyond his name and the fact that he worked for my father."

"Perhaps," Ben suggested, "we should endeavor to discover a bit more."

CHAPTER FIFTEEN

೫ೲ೪

By noon the following day, Ben and Diana had talked to numerous employees of the Timberline Mine and the Torrence Mining Company and paid a second visit to Mr. Morris. No one had been able to supply answers to questions about Alan Kent, William Torrence, or Evan Spaulding. The old man didn't even remember who Diana was, and he fell asleep twice while they were with him. The second time, he lay so quiet and still that she was sure he'd stopped breathing and was glad Ben was with her to listen for his heart.

"What now?" Ben asked, after they left Miranda's house without ever catching a glimpse of Torrence's widow.

Diana let the cool mountain air ruffle her hair and feather across her face, enjoying both sensations while she thought about that question. "I suppose we could try to talk to Alan Kent again."

He hadn't been in his office when they'd called there earlier. Martha had told them he'd been in a rage when he'd left Miranda's house the previous evening, and that Miranda had locked herself in her bedroom after their quarrel. No one seemed to know what had become of Matt Hastings. Diana assumed he'd spent the night at his deserted dance hall.

"Let's have something to eat first," Ben suggested, as they walked back to the hotel. "Food aids thinking. Besides, little as you ate for breakfast, your stomach will be growling any moment now."

"That's not a very kind or gentlemanly thing to say."

"No, but it's true." He grinned at her, unrepentant, and for one giddy moment the rest of the world faded away.

A strident voice calling her name intruded on the idyll.

"Sheriff wants to talk to you!" Maryam bellowed from the front of the hotel. She seemed to take pleasure in the startled stares from passers-by.

"He got back quickly," Ben said.

"He only planned to stay in Leadville overnight." Diana increased her pace.

She was puffing a little from too-tight corseting by the time she entered the hotel dining room. Most of their party were already there having a light luncheon.

The sheriff looked up from a steaming plate full of oysters and waved them over. Diana ignored the little gurgle of hunger the delicious smells in the dining room provoked. The yeasty aroma of freshly baked bread was the least of them.

"Well," she asked. "What did you find out?"

He eyed her, then glanced behind her at Ben. "Nothing to prove your theory. Didn't suppose I would."

"Did you talk to my former landlady?"

"Indeed I did. Interesting woman. I didn't realize you'd lived in a room above a tobacco shop, Mrs. Spaulding."

"What difference does that make?" Genuinely puzzled, Diana sat in the chair Ben pulled out for her.

"Ever hear of cigar girls?"

Diana's eyes widened, and she felt heat climb into her face. "There was no brothel on the premises, not when I lived there."

"Perhaps her girls weren't old enough then."

"What girls?"

"Her daughters, Mrs. Spaulding. They're thirteen and fifteen now, and the oldest has been a prostitute for at least two years."

"She had no daughters. She didn't even like children. Are you sure we're talking about the same person?" The woman Diana remembered had seemed old as the hills, but Diana was well aware that women who lived a hard life often looked decades older than they really were.

"Maybe she adopted the girls. It's been known to happen. Times are hard. Women do what they can to survive. In any case, there's no doubt she was your landlady. She remembered you, and your husband, and a very refined and polite brunette who came asking about you about a month before your husband was killed. Said the brunette wore heliotrope perfume, whatever that is."

"Pearl," Diana said.

"Sounds like it." Ben glanced at the sheriff. "I don't suppose she had a white poodle with her?"

Crymble shook his head, concentrating on polishing off the oysters. They were nothing but a tasty memory before he spoke again. "The brunette wanted to know if Mrs. Spaulding was increasing."

When the sheriff had gone Ben ordered plain steak and potatoes and Diana the same. They sat facing each other across a small table, pondering what to do next.

"There's no proof of anything and probably never will be," Diana concluded, "but it makes sense to me that my father had a hand in Evan's death. He'd have been furious when he found out he'd been tricked." She gave a strangled laugh. "I almost wish he'd just challenged Evan to a duel and shot him outright. Hiring someone to kill for him makes it worse somehow."

Ben's hand covered hers. "If that *is* what happened, there's nothing to be done about it now. And I can't see how it could have any connection to Torrence's murder. You're the only one who'd have wanted revenge for what happened to Evan, and you were still in New York City when your father died."

She sighed, staring at the wall behind his head without really seeing the blue and white striped wallpaper. "What if there is someone else? Another woman, perhaps? Someone who thought she was in love with him?" There had always been other women.

"Not Pearl?"

She smiled at that. "I can't imagine Pearl cared what happened to Evan. Not if she took money to spy on him."

He turned her hand over in his and traced the lines on her palm. The contact made her shiver with pleasure but his words just as quickly pulled her thoughts away from feasting on sensual delights and back to the contemplation of the dilemma at hand.

"Even if someone did want revenge for Evan's murder," Ben mused, "how could she, or he, discover that your father was responsible? We only stumbled on the connection. We haven't found any solid proof that our conclusions are correct. It's all speculation."

"Charlie knew enough to allow us to put the pieces together once he told you," Diana reminded him. "Maybe he told someone else as much."

Ben considered that as their meal was placed before them. He cut a strip of the steak into smaller bits and ate two of them before he spoke. "Did Evan have any family?"

The question took her aback. "I don't think so. He never mentioned any."

Suddenly the meal tasted like cardboard. The pool of gravy on her potatoes looked even more unappetizing. How could she have been so self-centered? Of course he must have had family. Everyone had someone. And she'd made no effort at all to find them after he died.

Diana rose from the table, her meal forgotten. Evan had kept a great many things from her. Why not kith and kin?

"Where are you going?" Ben asked, catching her hand.

"The depot. The Western Union office. The quickest way to

get answers about Evan's family is to send a telegram to the editor of the local newspaper and ask."

"You know the town?"

"I know where he was born. It's a little place called Whitehead, Illinois."

"Witted?" he echoed, pronouncing it as she had. "As in slow-witted?"

She smiled and spelled it. *"Whittud* is how the natives pronounce it."

"Ah, I see. We've towns like that back home. Folks put the accent on the first syllable in places like Madrid and Vienna. And Calais comes out Callus."

A chuckle escaped Diana, surprising her. She hadn't laughed enough lately.

"Eat first," Ben suggested. "The matter has waited this long. A quarter of an hour more won't make any difference."

A glance at her plate had Diana's appetite returning. As she dug into the meal, her resolve strengthened. Surely they would be able to clear up this one small mystery. She had begun to despair of ever solving the larger ones, but now her confidence returned. She would not give up. She would find Evan's family. And then, somehow, she would discover who had killed her father.

෨෦ର

Diana and Ben spent the evening, as they'd promised, with the owner of the mercantile and his family.

"Your father's friends were very pleasant company," Ben said, as they walked back to the hotel.

"But singularly unhelpful in solving his murder." They'd *liked* Will Torrence.

"No one is all good or all bad. You've said yourself that Torrence was a different man before money corrupted him."

Diana thought about that for a moment before she replied. "I think it's the hypocrisy that bothers me most. Father was so self-righteous when he disowned me for daring to marry an actor. Compared to William Torrence, Evan was a paragon of virtue."

Ben grimaced at her exaggeration and appeared to be about to make some remark when Jane stepped out of the hotel to intercept them. "Ed Leeves is here," she warned them. "He arrived on the 6:00 PM train from Denver."

When Diana walked into the hotel parlor, Leeves came to his feet in a rush, assuming a wide stance that put her in mind of the drawings of gunslingers on penny dreadfuls. Thankfully, there were no six guns slung from his hips. He was dressed much as he had been when they'd first met, in those boots with the two-inch heels and a suit and necktie that would have been right at home in the business district of Manhattan.

"Where is she?" he demanded.

"Who?"

"Don't play dumb with me, girl. I want your mother."

"I have no idea where she is." She felt Ben come up behind her and saw that the professor had taken up a position on the opposite side of the room, ready to step in to protect her if the need arose. She couldn't see any of the girls, but she had a feeling they were close at hand.

"Impossible," Leeves insisted. "I know you've talked to her."

"Yes. Once. In Denver. As far as I know, she's still there. And if she'd wanted to see you, Mr. Leeves, she'd have managed it on her own by now."

"Damned stubborn female," he muttered.

Diana wasn't certain if he referred to her or to her mother.

"Why is it so important that you find her?" She couldn't figure him out, and didn't dare trust the instinct that was telling her he meant her mother no harm. After all, it had been a note from Leeves that had lured Elmira out of the hotel just when William Torrence was being murdered.

"I've a better question," Ben said. "How did you know Diana

had talked to her mother? She didn't tell anyone about Elmira's late night visit until after we were on the train coming here, and even then she only told me."

"And Jane," Diana said.

"I have my sources," Leeves said.

"What sources?"

"Me," Maryam said, stepping into the room in a flurry of pink ruffles. "He's got me."

"I thought you said you weren't a spy," Diana said.

"Not for William Torrence."

"How did you know about Elmira?" Ben asked.

"Jane told me. She told all of us when you first got here. Wanted to make sure we knew Elmira was still around. Told us to keep an eye out for her. So I sent Big Ed a telegram."

Sparing one fulminating glare for the traitor in their midst, Diana turned her attention back to Ed Leeves. "Do you really think Mother will come here? After all, Miranda is in Torrence."

Miranda is in Torrence.

Diana turned away from the others to stare out a window at the empty street. Was it possible? Would Elmira come to Torrence in order to confront Miranda? Diana didn't like her father's second wife, but Matt had convinced her beyond all doubt that Miranda was not responsible for William Torrence's death, and that *she* believed Elmira was. A meeting between the two women was *not* a good idea.

Ben was still arguing with Big Ed. "How could Elmira get here without someone seeing her? Recognizing her? There are only two trains a day. Their arrival draws what passes for a crowd in Torrence. Children. Old men. Prostitutes hoping for custom. Businessmen expecting something in the mail pouch."

"She rides, doesn't she?" Leeves shot back. "And there's a stagecoach. How difficult is it for a woman to hide her identity behind a veil? For that matter, she might dress up as a man." He gave a short bark of admiring laughter. "By God, she could pull it off."

"What do you want with my mother?" Diana demanded. There had been admiration in his voice just now but he still hadn't explained his interest to her satisfaction.

"Damned if I know," Leeves muttered. "But I can't just let her disappear like this. You tell her that, Diana." He seized her shoulders and put his face so close to hers that she could see that there were small flecks of color in what she'd thought were coal black eyes. "When she contacts you, tell her that."

He flew backwards before he could say another word. Ben had seized one arm, the professor the other. While Diana watched, too disconcerted by Leeves's vehemence to form a coherent sentence, they hauled him out of the room.

"You really have no idea where she is?" Maryam had arranged herself on the piano bench and was idly picking out a tune.

"No, I don't. She didn't want me to know. She'd finished with all of us, I think, especially Ed Leeves."

"He won't give up," Maryam predicted. "He doesn't like losing."

Diana was afraid Maryam might be right.

Leaving the other woman to her music, Diana headed for her room. She'd just started up the stairs when the proprietor of the hotel hailed her.

"Mrs. Spaulding. There you are. A letter came for you on the express from Denver." He handed it up to her with a little bow.

"Thank you, Mr. Perrin." Still on the third step, she stared at the envelope, curious but not alarmed. If Leeves had found out where they were, others could too.

There was no return address, but as she ran a finger under the flap, she considered the possibilities: Col. Arkins? Pearl? Charlie? Dorcas? None of them seemed likely. Ning might have tried to reach her this way, but he hadn't yet learned to write more than his own name. And if Horatio Foxe had followed her to Colorado, he'd have gotten on the train himself rather than send a letter from Denver.

Inside the envelope was a sheet of familiar cream-colored stationary. Diana's hand shook slightly as she unfolded it, and she was suddenly very glad Mr. Perrin had waited to deliver her mail until Ed Leeves had been forcibly evicted from the hotel.

The letter began "Dear Daughter."

❧❧

"Mr. Leeves and I have something to say to each other," Ben told the professor. "In private."

They'd released Big Ed as soon as they were out in the street. He showed no sign of wanting to return to the hotel. Tension radiated from him in palpable waves, but he had himself under control.

Once he was left alone with the other man, Ben got a firm grip on his temper. If there was anything to be learned from Leeves, Ben intended to discover it without resorting to fisticuffs. Since he'd refrained from pommeling Hastings, he had no doubt he could manage to control himself with Leeves.

"You had no call to threaten Mrs. Spaulding," he said in a deceptively mild voice. "She doesn't know where her mother is."

"Damn it, what ails the woman?"

"Diana—"

"Not Mrs. Spaulding. Elmira." With a snort of disgust, Leeves started towards the saloon, kicking small rocks out of his way as he went.

Reluctant sympathy chipped away at Ben's fury. Leeves was as frustrated as Ben had been when he'd gotten Diana's telegram, and for similar reasons. Leeves had romantic feelings for Elmira Torrence. He'd expected her to turn to him for help, not go off on her own.

They entered the saloon together and settled in at the same table Ben had previously shared with Sheriff Crymble. "Elmira told Diana that you sent her a note asking her to meet you somewhere," Ben said when they'd been served. "She didn't say where. Elmira apparently went. You didn't show. That's why she has no alibi for the time of Torrence's murder. Why didn't you meet her that night as you'd arranged?"

"I never sent her any note. I never send anybody notes." He looked ready to chew nails. "I told Elmira that."

"She didn't believe you."

"She thinks I had something to do with framing her for murder." He cursed colorfully, fell silent for a moment, then added, "Hell, for all I know, she thinks I killed him!"

Ben silently acknowledged that he could understand the urge to kill a man who'd hurt the woman he loved. But Leeves would never have planted that glove, implicating Elmira. Unless he'd had other plans all along and the feelings he professed for Elmira were a ruse.

"Why did you try to take over the hotel after Elmira disappeared? That didn't sit well with Mrs. Spaulding."

"Sometimes, my reputation as a . . . businessman puts me at a disadvantage." His smile was grim.

Ben waited.

Leeves shrugged. "Let me buy you another drink, Northcote. We'll talk about Torrence women."

₧₨

"Has Mr. Leeves left town?" Diana asked when she came down to a late breakfast the next morning.

"On the morning train," Red Katie mumbled, her attention more on her food than on the subject of who went where. "The professor saw him go."

Diana shot a questioning glance Ben's way. "Did you convince him I don't know where Mother is?"

"I think I did, but it occurs to me that he might not really have her best interests at heart."

"You don't think he loves her?"

"I think he might have quarreled with Torrence over your father's past treatment of Elmira. If Leeves lost his temper, I could see him turning violent."

"I have trouble imagining such a scene. It's not that I don't think Leeves capable of killing. I do. But I rather think he'd use a gun. Or his bare hands." She had no better idea, however, and finished her breakfast in glum silence.

Shortly thereafter, a telegram arrived for her, the answer to her query to the Whitehead *Sun*. "Oh, my," she said as she read the lengthy missive.

"What is it?" Ben asked.

"Evan did have family. Does have family." She could hardly take it in. That he'd concealed a mother and two siblings from her seemed as much a betrayal as his constant unfaithfulness. He'd led her to believe there was no one. "I didn't even try to find relatives to notify when he died. His poor mother!"

Ben took the cable from her limp grasp and read its contents for himself. "Someone at the newspaper must have known Spaulding personally or they wouldn't have made the connection. According to this, his mother remarried. The brother and sister don't have the same last name."

"And it says she died only a few months after Evan did. Did she ever learn what happened to her first born child? Oh, Ben. How terrible for her either way."

He read the cable again. "Her children left town right afterward. I wonder why?"

"What do you mean?"

"I mean I find it suspicious that Evan turns out to have a half-brother and we're looking for someone who might have wanted to avenge Evan's death by killing your father."

What Ben was suggesting made a terrible kind of sense. According to the telegram, Lawrence Markham was twenty-four.

"Alan Kent," she whispered.

"Alan Kent," he agreed. "He's only been here a year. He's about the right age."

"And there was something about him the first time I met him," Diana recalled, "that reminded me of Evan. Not any particular feature. Just an . . . attitude. But he was with Jane the night Father died. They were at the Elmira all evening."

"He might have persuaded her to lie for him. Which one do you want to talk to first? Alan Kent or Jane?"

"Kent," she said without hesitation.

But that proved easier said than done. Alan Kent had also left Torrence on the morning train. It wasn't a business trip. He'd packed his belongings and taken everything with him.

Miranda assumed it was because she'd rejected him.

Diana wasn't so sure.

Late that afternoon, she gathered everyone in her party together and announced that she and Ben were heading back to Denver on the next express, which would travel through the night and deliver them to their destination at mid-morning. "I suggest we all go."

"May as well," Red Katie said. "We aren't making any money here."

"Thanks to your friend Mr. Kent," Maryam said, glowering at Jane.

"He was just doing what his boss told him to."

"Boss *lady*," Maryam taunted her. "And we know why, too."

Jane looked blank. "What are you going on about now?"

Diana tried to stop Maryam from blurting it out, but she was too late.

"Your gentleman caller's been calling on Miranda Torrence, that's what. Why else do you think he told you to stay away from him while you're in Torrence? He's not going to marry you when he can have a rich widow instead."

"That's enough," Ben said, in a quiet, authoritative voice that made Maryam's mouth snap shut. "I don't think Alan Kent is going to be marrying anyone. In fact, he may have been the one behind all Elmira's troubles."

"We're going back to Denver to talk to Charlie Duncan at the Windsor Hotel, and to Pearl Adams." Diana glanced at Ben. At his nod, she gave them a short version of the story they'd pieced together. "So, it looks as if Alan Kent may really be Lawrence Markham, and that he had a reason to kill my father. If Charlie confirms that he shared his speculations with Kent, then we'll have the connection we've been looking for."

For a long moment, no one spoke. Then Nellie's eyes grew big and she gave an excited squeal. "Oh, that's it, then. That's what I knew!"

"What is, Nellie?"

"I saw Mr. Kent that night. He came in right before Elmira returned." Her gleeful expression faded into puzzlement. "But that can't be right. Jane was with him. Wouldn't she know if he'd just murdered someone?"

All eyes turned to Jane. Pale with shock, she looked from face to face, as if seeking another explanation. "I don't understand," she stammered. "You can't be serious. Alan didn't kill Mr. Torrence."

"You said you spent the evening with Alan Kent at the Elmira, Jane. If Nellie is remembering right, then you lied about that. Did you go out with him instead? And more importantly, did you stay with him the whole time?"

Jane sniffed, trying to hold back tears, but it was no use. She buried her face in her hands and sobbed. Several minutes passed before she had control of herself and could be questioned.

"Just tell us the truth, Jane," Diana said. "It will all work out if you just don't lie to us anymore."

Jane clasped Diana's hand and, with obvious effort, met her concerned and sympathetic gaze. "I did lie," she whispered, "but even if I'd told the truth, I couldn't have told you anything that would have helped you exonerate Elmira."

"Why did you lie?"

"Because I was afraid you would think I killed your father."

Diana gaped at her. Jane nodded. She took another moment to

gather herself. Then, finally, eyes averted, she began to speak again, so low that Diana had to strain to catch her words.

"Alan escorted me to the Windsor Hotel that evening to meet with your father. He'd sent for me, you see—Mr. Torrence. He paid me to spy on Elmira. That's how Alan and I met. Your father hired me to bring him information. But I wasn't really spying on your mother. Once I met her, got to know her, I confessed everything. After that I was really working for Elmira."

Diana had been told that her parents spied on each other, but she still had difficulty accepting the idea. All else aside, it seemed such a petty thing to do.

"Why don't you tell us what happened that night," Ben said, in his best coaxing voice.

Jane sent him a grateful, if watery, smile and complied. "We went to the Windsor, to the suite where Mr. Torrence died. Alan and I came in through the back so that no one would see us. Mr. Torrence was very particular about secrecy. He paid the hotel staff well not to be anywhere where they might see anything."

"Was Father alone?"

"He was when we left, but he was expecting someone. His mistress, we thought."

"But Father was already dead when she got there," Diana murmured. "Tell me honestly, Jane. Were you and Alan Kent together every moment?"

Jane closed her eyes briefly. "When we left, I went ahead to make sure the coast was clear," she whispered. "But no more than a minute or two passed before Alan caught up with me. I'm certain of it."

"It doesn't take long to stab someone," Ben said.

"But there was no blood on him. And there *was* on Elmira's glove." Jane began to sob again. "It *must* have been Elmira who came in and killed him. It *couldn't* have been Alan."

"There's only one way to find out," Diana said. "We'll have to track down Alan Kent."

CHAPTER SIXTEEN

ഇഐ

The train arrived in Denver on schedule. By ten Thursday morning, Diana, Ben, and Jane were at the Windsor Hotel. The others had gone back to the Elmira on Diana's assurances that they would be allowed to stay there. That much, at least, had come out of the evening Ben had spent with Ed Leeves in the saloon in Torrence. Leeves had promised to leave Elmira's girls alone.

Diana and Jane returned to Ben's suite while he made inquiries about Charlie the assistant manager. They found everything exactly as they had left it, and yet nothing seemed the same. A few days ago, Diana had trusted the quiet, unassuming young woman at her side. Now she wasn't so sure, and she was reluctant to take any risks with her mother's safety.

On the other hand, even if Jane had divided loyalties and might be tempted to warn Alan Kent, she wasn't likely to do Elmira any physical harm. "I need to send a message to Ning," Diana told her. "Can you find Wen and bring him here?"

"Of course," Jane said instantly. She seemed glad of something to do. She didn't even ask why.

As soon as she was gone, Diana took out the letter she'd received from her mother. It was brief and to the point. It ordered Diana to stop meddling. That was advice Diana had no intention of following, not with so many questions unresolved.

Fortunately, the short note also contained a clue to Elmira's present whereabouts. Diana lifted the paper to her nose and once again caught the faint scent of bleach.

Ning would be able to confirm her guess. He'd probably known all along that Elmira Torrence was hiding out in his aunt's laundry in Hop Alley. With luck, she'd still be there.

ℰℭ

Ben found Charlie Duncan easily enough. Everyone in the hotel knew where he was. Unfortunately, he wouldn't be answering any questions. He'd been dead long enough for rigor mortis to have passed off by the time Ben got a look at him.

"Dr. Northcote, is it? What's your interest in this?" Denver's coroner didn't look pleased to have a visiting colleague interrupt his work.

"This man was a potential witness in a murder case," Ben said. "His sudden death is very convenient for someone."

Raised eyebrows and a skeptical demeanor greeted this announcement. Before the coroner could go on the defensive, however, Ben took steps to help him save face.

"I see you've not begun the autopsy. If you wouldn't mind my observing, it would ease my mind about the circumstances of his death. And perhaps keep certain . . . concerned parties from needing an exhumation order at a later date?" He toyed with mentioning Ed Leeves, but concluded that might hurt rather than help his case.

"What murder did he witness?" the coroner asked.

"He knew more than he said about William Torrence's death. Someone may have wanted to make sure he kept silent."

With a grudging nod, the coroner agreed to Ben's request, proving himself an honest man after all.

Ben didn't know what he expected to find. Perhaps nothing. But he could tell the coroner had intended to write off Charles Duncan's death as a seizure, or perhaps a heart attack, and not investigate further. Now he would at least make a show of examining the body.

"I'm told," Ben said as he helped strip away Charlie's nightshirt, "that he was found around noon yesterday by his landlady."

The coroner grunted, busy examining Charlie's face. He studied a bit of spittle at the corner of the mouth and lifted an eyelid to peer at the pupils. "Said she was concerned that he hadn't shown his face since the previous night."

An hour later the two doctors shared heavy mugs filled with hot tea laced with whiskey.

"Poison," the coroner said. "But which one?"

Ben warmed his hands on the sides of the mug before he took another sip. He had no proof, but a possibility had suggested itself when he'd seen the state of Charlie's kidneys. It was readily available in certain circles, and capable of ending a man's life in a matter of hours. He told the coroner what he thought before returning to the hotel.

ഇൽ

Diana was waiting in Ben's suite, impatience writ large on every feature. "Don't tell me," she muttered in exasperation when she saw that he was alone. "Charlie's gone. Run off to avoid talking to us. Wen's unavailable too. I haven't been able to send a message to Ning."

"Charlie's gone, all right." Ben looked not at Diana but at Jane when he made his announcement. "He's dead. He was poisoned. It was meant to look like some kind of seizure, but given that Alan Kent, or should I say Lawrence Markham, had a forty-eight hour head start on us, I think he killed Charlie to keep him quiet. Charlie could link Markham to Evan Spaulding."

Jane's usual pasty color blanched further. Behind her spectacles, her eyes looked haunted. "That wasn't supposed to happen," she whispered. "He's not a murderer. He's a good man."

"Did you give him the Oil of Tansy, Jane?" Ben asked.

"No!"

"You had access to it. You spoke of it when Nellie mixed up her bottles. I imagine it's fairly common in places like the Elmira Hotel. Women have known for centuries that a high dose of tansy can abort a fetus. Of course, any dose high enough to kill an unborn child is also likely to kill the mother, but perhaps that's an acceptable risk in your business."

"Ben." Diana's hand on his arm brought him back to himself. He hadn't meant to launch into a lecture on the dangers of abortion, but it was a volatile issue with any physician.

"I didn't give him Oil of Tansy," Jane insisted. Her voice trembled and so did her hands. "I didn't. I wouldn't."

She was hiding something. Maybe she didn't know where Alan was, or how he'd gotten hold of poison, but neither was she telling them everything she knew.

"If you didn't get it for him, then he got it somewhere else. It isn't hard to come by."

"He killed Charlie Duncan?" Jane whispered.

"Who else would have had reason to?" Ben demanded.

Jane closed her eyes, as if she could not bear to contemplate the truth.

"What could Charlie have told us?" Diana wondered aloud. "We'll never know now, unless it's something Pearl knows too." Her voice rose to a squeak. "Oh, Ben! Do you think Alan Kent may try to kill Pearl?"

"I think we'd better warn her, just in case. And you're right, she's the only one left now who may have answers to our questions."

∞⌘⌘

Diana had not previously been inside Pearl's place of business, but she had little chance to compare the decor to the Elmira's before they were challenged by a young woman in a diaphanous gown.

"We're not open yet, sir. And we don't allow ladies to come in at any hour."

Another lightly clad female came out into the entry hall. "Why, it's the doctor who helped me," she said. "Never you mind, Priss. I'll take care of him."

"Hello, Gwen," Ben said.

Diana's hand tightened on his forearm. This *Gwen* person seemed entirely too pleased to see him, and he had never said exactly what it was he'd treated her for.

"I am Diana Spaulding, from the Elmira Hotel," she announced in lofty tones. "We need to speak to Pearl on a matter of some urgency."

Gwen stopped with her hand halfway to Ben's shoulder. With a shrug, she stepped back. "She's in her room. You know the way."

"Is she alone?" Ben asked.

"Except for the poodles. This is her day to do the accounts. She'll be at it till evening, if it goes the way it usually does. Counts every penny, she does." Gwen sent him a saucy grin as she disappeared into the back of the house.

"You go ahead, Jane," Diana said, tightening her grip on Ben's arm. "Tell Pearl about Charlie's death and our suspicions. I need a word with Ben before Pearl sees us together."

Neither of them spoke until Jane was out of sight. "Are you sure you trust Jane to explain?" Ben asked. "She's still got divided loyalties when it comes to Alan Kent."

"It's because I don't entirely trust her that I sent her on ahead. We need to talk to Pearl, but first we must take the underground passageway to Hop Alley. How do we get to this end of it?"

The urgency in Diana's voice had convinced Ben to comply without hesitation, though he had plenty of questions. At the foot of the narrow flight of stairs to the basement, Pearl's porter was at his usual post. If he was surprised by the sight of a strange woman on a gentleman's arm, he hid it well. It was not part of his job to ask questions.

"I assume it costs as much going one way as the other?" Ben inquired, handing over a generous tip along with the fee.

"Yes sir, but you pay on the other side." He handed most of the money back.

"Ten dollars," Diana complained in a low mutter as they stepped into the tunnel. "Outrageous."

"Five," Ben corrected her.

"What? Do you mean to say Gun Wa was going to charge me twice the going rate just because he thought I was desperate enough to pay it?"

Ben wavered between amusement and appalled dismay as she described the circumstances of that "desperate" situation. This was the first time he'd heard of it. Diana made it sound as if she now believed she'd never been in any danger, but Ben wasn't so sure.

"I'm glad Ning looked out for you," he said when she fell silent. He promised himself he'd reward the boy the next time he saw him.

He was less sanguine about the elderly gentleman in Chinese robes they encountered at the far end of the tunnel, but he made no objection when Diana insisted he pay Gun Wa an additional fee to direct them to the laundry belonging to Ning's aunt.

Ning himself met them at the door. He looked pleased to see them. His aunt's expression conveyed intense relief.

"You take her now?" the aunt asked.

"We will definitely take her now," Diana replied.

"Take who?" Ben asked.

"My mother."

Diana followed Ning's aunt through a room crowded with

washing tubs and hand-cranked wringers. The bulk of the business, Ben supposed, came from well-to-do housewives who put their laundry out to a laundress in order to placate the other servants. A maid might do the towels and dusters and her own clothes, but in the best households all the family's garments were professionally laundered.

"Well, Mother," Diana said as they entered the back room, "you've led us on a merry chase."

Ben was curious to get his first look at his future mother-in-law, but she was heavily veiled. He had to settle for a surface impression—a tall, stout woman holding herself stiff as the proverbial poker.

"You are the most annoying child," Elmira said. "Whyever did you go haring off to Torrence?"

"To find the truth. And I did. Alan Kent killed Father."

"What?" Astonishment had Elmira backing up a step.

"He's my late husband's brother. He found out, as I did, that Father had Evan killed. Motive enough for murder, don't you think?"

"Hmmm," Elmira said, unbending just a little. "I wouldn't have thought him the type."

"Anyone can kill, Mother."

"So, has he confessed? Am I free to leave here?"

"He hasn't been caught yet, and I doubt we can prove anything, but I think you've been in hiding long enough. Come away with us, Mother. We're going home."

She turned her attention to Ben. "With him?"

"This is Ben Northcote. Doctor Benjamin Northcote of Bangor, Maine. I'm going to marry him."

"You're welcome to live with us," Ben said. "My mother and brother already do."

"Why is she wincing at the thought?" Elmira asked, her veiled face turned in Diana's direction.

"I'm imagining your first encounter with Maggie Northcote,"

Diana said grimly.

"Well, I doubt I'll be making that trip. I have plans of my own."

"To stay here?" Diana challenged, waving a hand to encompass the laundry.

Elmira gave a bray of laughter that grated on Ben's nerves. "Ironic, isn't it? Here I am, once again surrounded by washtubs. Rub and boil and lots of elbow grease. Thought I'd left that all behind me." She made a tsking sound. "I wish I'd known years ago that there were so much easier ways for a woman to make money."

Without warning, the curtains that divided the back room from the rest of the laundry were swept aside. Jane rushed in, arms waving in agitation. "Hurry!" she cried. "Gun Wa called the police. They're on their way here to arrest Elmira."

"Damnation!" Ben swore.

"Follow me," Jane said. "I know a safe way out through the tenements."

Before Ben could object, Diana and Elmira had gone after her. Within moments they were deep inside a rabbit warren of buildings, out one door and through another until he'd lost all sense of direction.

Jane stopped when they reached a small, dark, upstairs room. "Stay here," she ordered. "I'll go ahead to scout for trouble."

Ben waited only a heartbeat before going after her. Jane should still be at Pearl's. She shouldn't have come in contact with Gun Wa, nor should she have known Diana had gone to the laundry.

Was Alan Kent lurking in the shadows up ahead? Ben entertained the nasty suspicion that he might be waiting for Jane to come and tell him she'd trapped Elmira, Diana, and Ben. If Alan *had* killed two people, he wouldn't quibble at three more.

Ben stopped and listened. He did not hear Jane's soft footfalls up ahead. He hesitated, wondering if he should go back and get Diana out of here, but before he could turn he was struck from behind. A heavy object came in sharp contact with his skull, rendering him unconscious before he hit the floor.

Diana crouched beside her mother, her breath coming in short uneven bursts, her sides aching from the effort of keeping up with the pace Jane had set. Elmira was in even worse shape, red-faced and panting. She'd torn off her veil to mop her face with it.

"Why would Gun Wa give us away?" Diana whispered.

"For money," Elmira gasped. "Why else does he do anything?"

"You know him, then?"

"I know plenty about that dishonest old reprobate," she muttered. "He's no more a Chinaman than you are. Name's W. H. Hale—an Irishman with a flair for the confidence game. Couple of years back he started wearing Chinese robes and selling aphrodisiacs to men about to take the underground passage to Holladay Street. He claims he's got rare herbs guaranteed to cure anything, but I know for a fact he just goes and picks mountain sage on the outskirts of Denver." She grinned. "Customers pay anywhere from ten dollars to a hundred for a treatment, depending on how much he thinks they're good for. Got to admire him. He takes in ten thousand dollars a month selling amber bottles full of *Gun Wa's Chinese Herbs and Vegetable Remedies.*"

"That doesn't sound like someone who's likely to send for the police."

"No." Elmira cursed softly. "Even if he were, he couldn't have known I was at the laundry. He'd think you went there looking for Ning."

"So Jane lied." Diana's stomach clenched. Ben had gone after the young woman and hadn't come back. "Do you trust her?" she asked her mother.

"I don't trust anyone."

"Did you ever talk to her about me?"

Elmira snorted. "She insisted on it. When she agreed to spy on

Will for me, she wanted to know all sorts of things about our happy little family, including details of your elopement."

So she'd lied about that too. How many other fabrications had there been? And why?

Had there been Oil of Tansy in Jane's room under the eaves? Diana tried to remember details from her one early morning visit. She recalled the photograph of Alan Kent. The books. The trunk. The cold water Jane had splashed onto her face to try and wake up.

Diana felt color leech from her cheeks as she recalled Jane's words. "As cold as Old Man's Whittud's heart," she whispered.

"What?" Elmira demanded.

"It was something Jane said. She pronounced it Whittud, but to anyone but a native of the town it would have been *Whitehead*. And Jane's eyes. Why didn't I see it before? She has *Evan's* eyes. Alan has the same hair, the same attitude, but Jane has his eyes. No. Not Jane. Julia. Julia Markham. That was the name in the telegram. She's not Alan Kent's sweetheart. She's his sister. She's Evan's sister."

"Very good, Diana." Jane stood in the doorway. She held a small, deadly-looking pistol in one hand.

"Where's Ben?" For a moment, Diana felt as if both heart and breath had stopped.

"Back there. Stay still!" The gun bobbled, then steadied. "He's alive, for the moment."

Diana exhaled a great gulp of air she hadn't been aware of holding.

"If you want to make sure he stays that way," Jane continued, "you'll do everything I say."

"All right, Jane. Or should I say Julia? We can work something out. There's no need to kill us."

"There's every need." The hand holding the gun trembled, but Jane brought the other one up to steady it and kept the weapon trained on Diana and her mother.

"I guess this means your brother did kill Father," Diana whispered.

"No!"

"Then you did?"

"Neither of us killed him."

Diana frowned. "If that's true, then why do you want to get rid of us? Oh! It's Charlie. You believe your brother murdered *him*. Jane, I think it's admirable that you're trying to protect him, but if he didn't stab Father, why would he poison Charlie?"

"Because Charlie would have helped you frame Lawrence for old man Torrence's murder. He had to protect himself. Protect me. So how can I do any less. I have to protect him."

Diana frowned. "If Lawrence didn't murder Father, and you didn't, and Miranda and Matt are innocent, then who did kill him?"

"She did!" Jane cried, jerking the gun at Elmira. "She's the one who killed your father. She took a knife and stabbed him. *She* did that. Not us. If she hadn't taken a knife to him, our plan would have worked."

Diana edged closer as Jane started to sob, hoping for a chance to grab the gun. *Keep her talking,* she thought, heartened by the fact that Jane didn't seem to know it had been a letter opener, not a knife, that had killed William Torrence. She hoped that meant neither she nor her brother were murderers.

"What plan, Jane?"

"To make Torrence pay. Pay with money. We didn't want him dead."

Elmira snorted. "Let me guess. Alan Kent embezzled from Torrence Mining Company, and you did the same at the hotel?"

Jane glared at her. "Yes. Why not?"

"I didn't have anything to do with Evan Spaulding's death."

"Mother, please," Diana interrupted. "Jane? Help me understand. I loved Evan, too, you know. I gave up my family, my home, to marry him. I know your mother died soon after Evan did. Was—?"

"You leave my mother out of this!" She swiped with one hand at the tears streaming down her cheeks but kept the gun pointed at Diana with the other.

"I don't think I can," Diana said. "Did she ever find out that Evan was dead? Did she care?"

"Of course she cared. She loved him! And when she was dying she made us promise we'd find out what had happened to our half brother. He kept in touch, you know, Evan. Wrote letters to Mother. And then they stopped."

"I'm sorry," Diana said. "If I'd known she existed, I'd have contacted her after he was killed. When I asked about his family, Evan always said he'd lost touch with them."

"He sent us presents when he was flush."

And ignored them the rest of the time, she'd wager, but Diana did not say that aloud. To Jane—Julia—he must have been the adored older brother.

"We came to Denver because we knew he'd been here, acting. It didn't take long to find out how he died, or that he'd been seen gambling in company with Charlie Duncan before he left for Leadville."

"Why didn't you use your own names? Did you suspect something all along?"

Jane shrugged. She seemed calmer now, but Diana wasn't sure that was a good thing. As long as Jane had the gun, she could use it.

"Lawrence said Evan wasn't the sort to die natural. He didn't want anyone making connections."

"So Charlie never knew who Alan Kent really was?"

"*Lawrence* scraped an acquaintance with Charlie because he had a connection to Evan. Then one night the two of them got drunk together, and Charlie ended up telling him a story about how he'd taken orders from his boss to a gunfighter and later an actor had ended up dead. That was enough to go on to figure out the rest."

"So your brother went to work for Torrence to get proof he'd hired a killer?"

"No, he went to work for him to rob him blind."

"And Miranda?"

"She was never part of the plan, until after Torrence got himself killed. Then Lawrence decided marrying her would be an even better scheme. He didn't take it well when she turned him down. Still, he got away with a lot of her money."

"Yes, he did. He's probably halfway across the continent by now. If he didn't stab my father," she said again, "then he had no reason to poison Charlie."

Jane blinked and looked confused.

"Little tart lied to me from the first," Elmira grumbled. "I should have known better than to trust her with my books."

"Hush, Mother!"

But Elmira's complaint jogged Diana's memory. She considered *all* the lies Jane had told and the pieces of the puzzle suddenly rearranged themselves in her mind.

"He didn't kill Charlie," she said. "Jane, think. Do you really believe your brother would be able to execute a murder as well as Charlie's death was managed? He made a hash of it when he attempted to kill Nellie."

"Not kill," Jane objected, confirming part of Diana's theory. "Just frighten."

"Because she knew when the two of you came in that night and it was going to play havoc with your alibi if she remembered."

Diana had her doubts about whether or not they'd meant to do Nellie serious harm, but she could easily picture Alan Kent planning to run her down in a dogcart and losing his nerve at the last second. Then he'd tried to shoot her and been too nervous to hit what he was aiming at. It had been *Jane's* effort to silence Nellie that had almost succeeded in killing her.

Diana regarded the gun. Whatever Jane had meant to do to

Nellie, she could not have poisoned Charlie. She'd been with Ben and Diana when he'd died. And if she could bring herself to shoot them, surely she'd have done so by now.

Diana reached out and took the gun away from her.

With an exclamation of distaste, she flung it away from her, into the darkest corner of the room. She looked up to find Ben propped up against the doorframe. A trickle of blood ran down the side of his face but his injuries did not appear to be life-threatening.

"Did she knock you out?" Her voice cracked, just a little, on the question.

"Yes. And tied me up."

"How did you get loose?"

Ning appeared behind him, carrying a length of rope. "I follow you from laundry," he said.

"Did she kill your father?" Ben's gaze moved to Jane, who had collapsed in a heap and was sobbing piteously again.

"No. Jane! Stop that noise. I think I know what happened, but you need to help me by answering a few more questions."

Jane sniffled, but managed to get control of herself.

"Why are you so sure Kent didn't kill my father?"

A bit of Jane's old spirit resurfaced. "*Lawrence* and I were together when we talked to him. When we left, he was expecting his mistress. I'd have thought she killed him, but when that glove turned up in Elmira's suite I realized she must have gone to his hotel room after we left." Jane glared at Elmira. "She *must* have killed him."

"She really believes it," Elmira said.

"Yes, but I think she's right that Alan—pardon me, Lawrence— is innocent. The real killer is impulsive but efficient . . . and not responsible for the actions of two clumsy, would-be murderers who never actually killed anyone, though they did apparently succeed in embezzling a great deal of money. Since we now know that Miranda was with Matt Hastings the night Father was murdered, that leaves only one suspect—Father's mysterious mistress."

"Pearl knows who she is," Ben said. "She said the woman left town, but if she's the one who murdered Charlie, it's obvious she didn't."

Diana turned to Jane, who was on her feet and listening in wide-eyed fascination. "Did you warn Pearl before you followed us here?"

Jane shook her head. "I knew you were up to something. I only went as far as the first bend in the stair and stayed there to listen to what you said to each other. Then I took the long way around to Hop Alley. I was just in time to catch sight of you leaving Gun Wa's shop. When I saw you go into the laundry, I guessed why. Elmira used to talk my ear off about the days when she took in washing."

In less than a quarter of an hour, they were back in Pearl's basement. "Has one of Pearl's girls left in the last month?" Diana asked the gaping porter.

Surprised by her direct question into answering before he thought better of it, he replied in the negative.

"So Pearl lied about that." Diana exchanged a grim look with Ben. "I wonder what other stories she invented."

"There's only one way to find out," Ben said, and led the way up two flights of stairs to Pearl's boudoir.

Diana let the others go ahead, drawing Ning aside to whisper instructions in his ear. She had no need to tell him to hurry. He was off like a shot as soon as he understood the importance of his assignment.

She arrived in Pearl's doorway in time to catch the madam's reaction to seeing Elmira in her house. "Well," Pearl said, rising from behind a small, paper-littered desk. "This is a surprise."

"I imagine it is," Diana said. "You must have thought planting that bloodstained glove in my mother's room would guarantee her arrest."

"I don't know what you're talking about."

"Oh, yes, you do. You lied about sending a girl to my father's suite that night. There was no girl, was there, Pearl?"

Pearl's eyes blazed with hatred, but still she did not speak.

"*You* were his mysterious mistress," Diana continued. "That's the only explanation that makes sense of everything. You kept your connection to my father a well-guarded secret. You only made one mistake. You decided to tell half-truths to Ben. This is Ben Northcote, by the way, the man I'm planning to marry."

Pearl's face was a perfect mask now, still beautiful but as lifeless as an ice sculpture. When one of the poodles nuzzled her hand she ignored it.

"You took a risk," Diana continued, "by mentioning spies, and you lost your gamble. I suppose you were worried by then. Was I too persistent? Did you fear that framing my mother wouldn't be enough to keep me from finding out the truth and decide to lay a false trail? Who did you think we'd suspect? Alan Kent? Jane?"

Pearl was made of sterner stuff than most. Merely making accusations was not going to startle her into a confession. Still, Diana soldiered on. She could see everything with startling clarity now.

"When we left for Torrence, you must have seen it as the perfect opportunity to eliminate Charlie. Poor fool. He was the only person who could link you to my father's murder. I wonder if he would have? He wasn't really very clever."

"He might have confided something damaging in one of her girls," Ben said. "He has a special favorite."

Ben had taken possession of Jane's gun back in Hop Alley and now he moved swiftly to Pearl's night stand to confiscate the revolver she kept there. Relieved of the fear that she might end up looking down the barrel of a pistol for a second time in one afternoon, Diana forged ahead with renewed self-confidence.

"You should have thought it through, Pearl. If none of the young women working for you was my father's secret mistress, that only leaves you. That means you killed him. Did something happen that night to make you lose control? I remember what my father was like. I imagine he said something that made you angry. The letter opener was handy. You picked it up and stabbed him and kept on stabbing him until he was dead."

Pearl's face was livid with fury. She had no visible weapons, but Diana backed a prudent step away from her, just in case. When her shoulder brushed against Ben, who had returned to her side, she inhaled sharply and was soothed by the comforting trace of Ivory soap that always clung to him.

"You're just like him," Pearl hissed. "So sure of yourself. So smug!"

"I rather think she takes after me," Elmira murmured. For the first time in Diana's memory, there was pride in her mother's voice when she spoke about her daughter.

Pearl ignored her, focusing all her venom on Diana. "Think you're smart, don't you? Got it all figured out!"

"Most of it. Do you want to clarify anything? Perhaps you had a good reason for killing my father. Self-defense?" She doubted it, and she was dead certain Pearl had murdered poor, stupid Charlie with malice aforethought.

"What do you want? A confession?"

"It would be nice to have no loose ends left."

Pearl's face twisted into a derisive sneer. "Why not? Sure. I'll tell you everything. Did you know your father wanted to run for governor? Can you believe that? Said he didn't want me around anymore because the holier-than-thou element might not like it if they found out he had a mistress. Hah! As if I was the only secret he was keeping!"

"I can see why you'd be upset."

When Pearl began to pace, Diana and the others gave her a wide berth. "He offered to pay me off if I'd leave Colorado, but it was a pittance. When I refused, he threatened me. Me! Said he could get rid of me permanently if I'd prefer. Bring in the same gunslinger who killed your husband. He laughed, and went to fix himself a drink. Ignored me, like I was nothing. That's when I lost my temper."

"You stabbed him in the back, then finished the job," Diana said, "but as soon as he was dead, you started worrying. What if someone suspected you? I'm sure you went in veiled. No one was supposed to know who you were. But, still, better safe than sorry. Is that the way it was, Pearl? Did you decide it would be best if there was an obvious suspect, right from the start, so no one would even think to look for anyone else? It must have been spectacularly easy for you to plant that glove the next day when you paid your condolence visit to my mother."

"I *am* clever at working things out." Pearl had maneuvered herself across the room until she was close to the door.

Before any of them realized what Pearl meant to do, she'd bolted. The door slammed shut behind her, and they heard the key turn in the lock.

"Damnation!" Ben threw himself against the wooden panels, but to no avail. The portal held. Rubbing his shoulder, he drew back to try a kick.

"She had an escape plan all worked out," Elmira said. "Good for her."

"She killed two men," Diana protested.

"No great loss, either of them."

A loud click distracted Diana before she could think of an adequate reply. Unlocked, the door slowly swung open.

"I do good, Mrs. Diana," Ning said, stepping into the room. "I bring Pinkerton men like you say."

In the hallway behind him, muffled curses confirmed that Pearl had been taken into custody.

◦)◦

Do you think we could leave tracking down murderers to the authorities once we're married?" Ben asked.

Diana looked up from the news story she was writing for Horatio Foxe and smiled. After dealing with a bevy of police officers and lawyers, they were back at the Elmira Hotel. Pearl was under arrest. So was Julia Markham. Her brother appeared to have vanished.

Ben turned his attention to Elmira. "I don't suppose you have any influence over her?"

"Never did." She went back to replacing jewelry and cash in various hiding places in her sitting room. "Besides, it's no concern of mine. I've changed my mind about abandoning a good, profitable business. In spite of Jane's pilfering, I've done well here. And I'm thinking about getting married again."

Diana dropped her pen and gawked at her mother.

Elmira brayed a laugh. "You should see your face. What's the matter? Don't you fancy Ed Leeves as a stepfather?"

Diana decided it would be the better part of valor not to answer that question. The look she sent Ben's way, however, spoke volumes. When Elmira left the room, Diana joined him at the window. She tucked herself under his arm to look out at Holladay Street.

"Does it bother you that my mother runs a brothel?"

"Does it bother you that mine claims to be a witch?"

They exchanged a smile of perfect understanding.

He kissed her forehead. "What have you decided to do about Ning?"

She wasn't surprised that he asked. He knew her well. "I've already given him money for a nest egg, but I'd like to do more. He's an intelligent boy. With a good education, he could be anything he liked."

"We could take him back East with us."

She considered it for a moment, then shook her head. "He has family here, and I don't want to take him away from them. But perhaps, when he's older, he might like to attend college in New England."

"Well, then, we have only one thing left to settle before we leave Denver."

"What's that?"

"A date for the wedding. It's May already. What do you say to sometime in June?"

"Wait another month?" she asked, fighting a grin. "Are you sure that's wise? Just look at all that's happened during each of the last two."